THE CALLING

Branwen went into an upland meadow carpeted with asters, tiny white stars, and pink bells. She stood in the middle of the open space, shook loose her hair, running her fingers through her tight braids, freeing them. And then she began to call—a calling not heard in centuries—a great, wild calling, to all the animals, to the field mice, badgers, to the shy ermine, the fox, even the wolves sleeping in the pale sun. She called through the skies to the raven first, and then the gulls, the plovers, the hawks, harriers.

Even the eagle heard her cry and came swooping down to see who had the power to call him.

DEATH OF THE RAVEN

DEE MORRISON MEANEY

ACE FANTASY BOOKS
NEW YORK

To Joe and the children,
who always kept my
priorities in order.

DEATH OF THE RAVEN

An Ace Fantasy Book/published by arrangement with
the author and her agent, Valerie Smith

PRINTING HISTORY
Ace Original/November 1983

ISBN: 0-441-14219-2

Ace Fantasy Books are published by The Berkley Publishing Group,
200 Madison Avenue, New York, New York 10016.
PRINTED IN THE UNITED STATES OF AMERICA

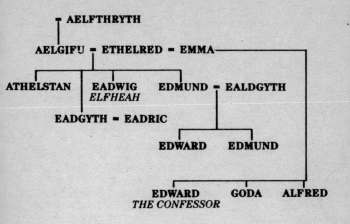

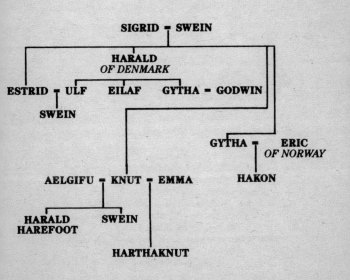

The story so far . . .

Volume I begins in 1011 as Branwen's mother dies, leaving her with her father, Wulfnoth, and her brother, Godwin, at their manor in Sherborne, Wessex. Soon after, a band of Vikings led by Thorkell the Tall arrives at Thornbury to speak to her father. While they are there Branwen treats Thorkell's wounded arm and discovers that there is an odd resonance of mind and heart between them. Thorkell leaves but sends an old wiseman, Ansgar, to Branwen as a thank you for the healing of his arm, for Ansgar knows much of healing and perhaps something of magic.

Ansgar teaches Branwen more of the herb lore she had begun to learn at the abbey school and from her grandmother. Ansgar helps her begin to discover her identity, an identity which sets her apart from other people but which she cannot fully understand. Under his tutelage she also learns the magical art of the shape-changer and that of bending other people to her will.

Thorkell returns and asks her to marry him but she refuses, unwilling to settle into a life she senses is not the one for her. She gives as her excuse that while she is yet a maid she wishes to seek a unicorn. Thorkell leaves, furious. He does not return for several years, during which time Wulfnoth dies and Branwen finds herself strongly attracted to the suave Saxon courtier, Eadric.

When Thorkell does return, it is as a hunted man facing death. He has lost his fleet and with them his identity and stands on the edge of madness, wanting only to take Branwen to find the unicorn. Together they set out for the Severn valley where Thorkell has heard there is a mysterious wood. Attacked by enemy longboats, Branwen, disguised as a raven, helps him escape, earning the title Lady of the Ravens.

They find the unicorn and Branwen meets the Great Earth Goddess for the first time. The Goddess tells her who her grandmother was and why her mother was so opposed to her learning any of the old lore, and something of the mythos which has been lost, the mythos of a time when women controlled the magic of life and death.

Having found the unicorn, she and Thorkell live as husband and wife, only to separate almost immediately as war divides them. Thorkell joins forces with Knut and Branwen goes to war with Edmund Ironside and her brother.

When Thorkell and the Danes are defeated, driven onto the Isle of Sheppey at the mouth of the Thames, Branwen weaves an illusion and saves them all from Edmund's forces. It was, however, too great an illusion, and tangled the web of fate that had to be put right at Ashington some weeks later.

Just before the battle, Branwen learns that it will be fought because of what she did on the Isle of Sheppey; she learns that unless she stands up and actively opposes it, the two armies will fight until everyone is dead. Refusing to believe that she wields such power, Branwen works among the wounded and dying all day while the battle rages around her. Not until the moon rises and Thorkell and Godwin face each other does Branwen act at last, forbidding the battle to go on. And then, as the men drop exhausted all over the field, she realizes that it was true: she could have prevented the battle that morning, all the dead could have been spared; that, in fact, they died because of her, because of what she had done at Sheppey and because of what she didn't do, until so late, at Ashington.

Chapter One

There was the unmistakable scrape of spades cutting into the rough gravel of the flood plain. Men who had slept only a few hours bent grimly over the work—digging the grave for those who had fallen in the battle.

There was one who stood and watched. He was a tall man. His hair was brown, cut short because in a fight a man's life can depend on such small things as cropped hair which will not blow suddenly across the eyes. Stiff leather armor encased the upper part of his body. It was not pretty to look at, undecorated, marked with random scratches and gouges, some darkened by years of careful oilings, others lighter, newer. One of his arms was bound neatly with a strip of white linen. He held it still against his chest. The man's name was Thorkell, called the Tall. He was a great chieftain in the army of Knut the Dane.

Knut, who would be king of this island his father had conquered once before; Knut, who had led his army against the army of Edmund Ironside in a battle which had raged from dawn until long after dark; a battle which might have raged until no man remained standing, for there had been an unnatural fury upon them; Knut, who stood now on the low hill overlooking the plain and watched, his helmet under his arm, his clear northern blue eyes, which missed little, coming back time after time to watch the small figure who worked beneath the trees among the wounded.

"I'll see her in hell for this, Harald," he said bitterly to the grey-haired warrior who stood beside him.

1

"For what, brother?" the man asked derisively. "If it is true that she somehow magically ended the battle last night—which I doubt—be grateful. Another hour, we would all have been dead." He spit.

"By Thor," Knut snapped. "Another hour and we would have wiped them out."

"Don't be a fool," Harald said.

Knut ignored him. "Eric saw her do it. He stood with me and we saw her, standing there, and we could not lift our arms."

"'And with the moonlight streaming over her, she forbade the battle to go on.' I know, I know. Everywhere the men are whispering of it. Exhausted men dream strange things, especially when they are standing hip deep on a bloody battlefield long after any sane commander would have made truce for the night."

"Truce," Knut hissed, "truce! We had them beaten, another hour and the island would have been mine."

"You're mad! We were all dropping in our tracks. We couldn't have fought another fifteen minutes and you know it. My arm aches today like it never did before," he added, rubbing his massive shoulder for emphasis.

"Believe what you will, brother," Knut said, "but I know what I saw and I won't rest until that witch is destroyed."

"Witch, is it?" the older man said, his eyes narrowing. "Have a care, brother. Don't go too far. We need him," he said, nodding toward the tall, brown-haired Dane crossing the field from the graveside to the trees. "You need him. Hemming's men pledged to him this morning."

"Aye, Thorkell," Knut said, frowning thoughtfully, "she has him mewling like an infant."

Branwen looked up as Thorkell came near and smiled at him, a small smile. Her face was grey with fatigue. Tear streaks had smudged the dirt on her cheeks. She was young, not yet hardened to the work she did though she had seen many battles during the past year.

"Come away with me," he said.

Her eyes were black, enormous in the light of the dawn. "I cannot, Thorkell," she said. "I need time to be alone." Her voice was low and there was a strangeness to it as if she were already speaking from a great distance.

"Where will you go?"

"Back with Ulfkytel," she said. "His men are leaving this morning. With Penardim perhaps I can . . ." Her voice trailed off.

"I'm afraid to let you go like this, Bran."

She smiled at his words. "Vikings know no fear, my love," she said.

"Come with me."

"I can't. Knut hates me now and I cannot fight him any longer. Let me go."

"You're my wife," he said hoarsely.

"Your wife?" She tried to laugh. "We have fought on different sides all summer. Oh, Thorkell, your brother is dead because of me."

"That's not true," he said.

She shrugged. Tears welled in her eyes. "It's true, Thorkell. It's true."

"You know I can't leave Knut now."

"I know, my love."

He put his hands on her shoulders, looking down at her. "I'll come back for you. I will not leave you for long," he said fiercely.

So it happened that the tall Dane rode westward with the tattered remnants of the Viking army while the dark-haired young woman, mounted on a stallion, rode slowly north along the coast road.

Two men, more severely wounded than the others, rode on the wagon with the body of Ulfkytel the Valiant. One had a belly cut Branwen feared would prove poisonous; the other had lost a leg, trampled under the hoofs of wheeling, charging war horses. There was no singing and little talk as they went home to the village they had left three days earlier; heads high then, eyes bright and eager. Seven who returned when twenty had set out. The September sky was clear. Only the creak of harness disturbed the warm afternoon stillness. Occasionally along the cartway a cottar, bending low to harvest his oats with a short sickle, would straighten up to watch them pass, his hand shading his eyes. The clean smell of freshly cut fields surrounded them, but her head was filled with the smell of blood and death and she did not notice.

Who would harvest the dead men's fields? she wondered,

riding at the end of the cortege, her head bowed. Elfheah rode beside her, his harp strapped to his back. His face was the face young girls dream of, framed in soft brown curls, finely featured, neatly bearded. His eyes were filled with sadness so that hearts softened at his stare, wanting to offer him comfort, though Branwen knew he would take none from any woman. There was no love between them.

"Why are you here?" she had asked him earlier. "Surely Edmund's brother has reason enough to ride elsewhere."

"I have no wish to be the brother of a king," he had said quietly.

"There is nothing I can give you, Elfheah. There is nothing left."

"And there is little enough I can give you, Branwen," he said, "but I owe you something, a debt to be paid, and I won't let you ride alone, without a friend."

"A friend," she echoed softly. "Hemming was my friend, great bear." She turned back in the saddle, looking south along the way they had come, remembering Thorkell's brother. There was a thick column of heavy smoke rising from the plain behind them. The bitterness of that smoke reached them although they had come many miles. "That's Hemming," she said, "charring upon the pyre with the other dead chieftains. Farewell, friend," she said, her voice hard. She turned back to Elfheah. "And now you would be my friend?"

He grinned at her suddenly. "A likely pair, eh, Branwen?"

But she did not return his smile and they rode on in silence.

When they reached the fields and cottages around Cynewithe the sun was just going down. Birds were chattering in the eaves as they went back to their nests for the night. The warm, friendly smell of the evening fires welcomed them. One by one the men left, their heads bowed, ashamed because they lived, though there was no just cause for their shame. Women came to help the wounded from the cart. Elfheah tied his horse behind and drove on through the twilight. A baby wailed, forgotten by his mother who stood unmoving in the doorway of a thick-thatched cottage watching them pass by, when none was left to return to her.

At last they reached a great house set on the sea edge. The old servants were gathered in the courtyard. Branwen dismounted. Elfheah sat on the cart, watching.

"Good evening, Wymer," she said, handing her reins to the old man. "Where is the Lady Penardim?"

"Gone these three days," he said. "She left ye this. Said I was to give it ye when ye brought the master home." He spoke without looking at her, his eyes staring at the body which lay beneath its shield in the back of the cart.

"Gone," she whispered. As if in a dream, she took the letter from the serving man's gnarled hand. She left them there and went into the hall.

The shutters were open along the sea wall. The sound of the surf was loud in the still room. No fire blazed on the hearth; no candle gleamed in the dusk; the room was cold and empty.

After a while, Elfheah came in and stood beside her, looking out. Only a few stars glowed in the grey sky. The night wind was already cold off the water. The moon had not yet risen. He reached out through the window frame and pulled the shutters closed.

A maid servant, her face deformed by a harelip, brought in a lantern and six long yellow tallow candles. She lit each one in turn from the flame in the lantern and placed them in their holders about the room.

In that smoky light, Branwen opened the letter from Penardim.

"My dear sister-child," she read. "It is with reluctance I leave you this day, though long have I waited to make this last journey to the land of our Mothers. I do not know why the unicorn has come now nor why you must bear the burden alone. I would I could comfort you but it is not to be.

"In the proper form are documents willing all Cynewithe to you. Stay as long as you need to. The people here are good and somewhat used to our ways. The household staff especially, though grown old in service to Ulfkytel and myself, are soft-spoken, gentle folk.

"If you are to find peace, you will find it more easily at Cynewithe than elsewhere, I think. Let the harper who rides with you sing in the night when you cannot sleep. There is magic in his song to soothe a soul's suffering.

"There is another who rode back with you. His name is Beorn. Rely on him. You will go far to find one better able to serve as steward. Put him in charge of the remaining harvest. It will ease his sorrow. His young son lies under the cairn at Ashington.

"The unicorn grows impatient. I pray peace and love will come to fill your cup once more, Branwen. You alone are left now of the mighty race which served the Goddess. We who have gone on ahead will wait for your coming. Penardim."

The letter lay in her lap. Despair welled up in her. She stared unseeing, her black eyes large in the candlelight. Elfheah took the letter from her and read it, his brow wrinkled at the riddles it contained.

After a while the serving girl came back carrying a heavy iron kettle in one hand and a basket of bread and cheese in the other. She set them down on the sideboard near the door and stood anxiously to one side.

"Well," Elfheah said impatiently, "what is it?"

"It's the salt, sir."

"The salt, girl?"

"Aye, my lord. It's locked up, you see, with the other spices and . . ."

"Ah yes, I see. Rabbit stew without any salt." He frowned. "Doesn't anyone have the household keys?"

"Oh no, sir, not to use. We was told to give them to the Lady Branwen when she should come."

"Well she is here now. Take the keys, unlock the cabinet, and fetch the salt." He spoke slowly, with exaggerated patience.

"Yes, my lord," the girl said backing toward the door.

"While you're at it, bring us something to drink. And none of your common ale either," he shouted after her as she ducked out the door. "God knows I've had enough of that these last weeks to last a lifetime," he muttered to himself, picking up the lid on the stew pot. He broke a chunk from the dark trencher and scooped up some of the thick stew. It needed salt but he was very hungry.

Branwen sat unmoving in a chair beside the shuttered window. He knew it was useless to urge her to eat but he hoped she would at least have something to drink. Where was that confounded wench?

The girl returned with a bowl of salt and a graceful silver pitcher filled with the dark potency of fermented honey. Elfheah poured two cups and took one to Branwen.

"Here," he said gently, bending over her, "drink this."

Obediently she took the cup from his hands and drank from it. She said nothing.

Just after moonrise, the door opened again and six men entered bearing the body of Ulfkytel, washed now, carefully dressed. They placed him gently upon the long table where he had sat at many a feast as the years went round at Cynewithe. Tall candles of fine beeswax were placed in heavy gold holders at his head and feet. More mead was brought in and more cups were filled.

Elfheah looked into the dark corner where his harp lay. It had been months since he had played the shining strings, not since Cobbe had died. He reached inside the soft elegance of his creamy shirt and pulled out the harp key, turning it thoughtfully in his fingers, feeling the weight of it, its warm smoothness. After a while he went over to the dark corner and picked up the small harp. Untying the cover, he ran his fingers over the strings, softly, listening to the discordances. He sat on the step of the dais at the dead man's feet, fitting the key onto the wrest pins, each in its turn, adjusting the strings slowly. The men stood in silence watching him, waiting. Branwen sat unmoving. She seemed almost asleep. He finished tuning the last strings and sat quietly, allowing the stillness to build before he began to play.

When the hush was very deep, he plucked out the full variation on a g-minor chord and began to sing. He transposed into the second mode, lowering the third, as he went along, pleased with himself that it came so easily. The ballad was an old familiar one, sung countless times in the hall before, although Ulfkytel had always muttered that it was a pack of lies. But tonight, the martial tones of the Ballad of Thetford keened as they had never done before, mourning now for Ulfkytel the Valiant, the great warrior who, years before, had fought the Danes on Wrentham Heath, giving orders to burn their fleet so that he and his men, although outnumbered, could fight to the death, no quarter asked or given. The king's brother sang of how the Danes drew back, defending their boats. And finally, Elfheah sang how the Danes, awed by the might and skill of Ulfkytel's deadly hand play, had withdrawn from the battle, not in defeat for their numbers were great, but in tribute to the valor of the enemy they faced.

The song was done and his cup was filled but he hardly noticed the men around him. He hardly noticed that the room

had filled with men, and women, too, coming in from the
outlying farms for the old hero's wake. He and the harp had
become as one. The magic Penardim wrote of was on him and
he began a song not sung before. He sang of how Ulfkytel, of
all the lords in the land, gave refuge to the old king's son,
Edmund Ironside, in his hour of despair. In his song he told
how here, at Cynewithe, Ulfkytel had called to Ethelred the
Unraed to come forth from his lair behind the thick walls of
London, a call that not even the king in his sickness and fear
could refuse. He sang of how Ethelred had met his son here
and been reconciled with him, bringing Edmund back to
London so that the prince might be there to take up the crown.
For death had laid its hand on the old king's shoulder and he
knew he had not long to live. So had Edmund, coming to
Ulfkytel in despair, ridden forth from Cynewithe to become
king of the land.

Then, at last, when the night was very late, Elfheah sang of
the battle of Ashington, the battle just fought, where many
brave men had fallen but the bravest of all had fallen first. He
sang of the reckless abandon of the Danish army who had
sallied forth singing that morning, when they thought there was
no hope. Then the harp sang in another key, like a wild thing.
The voice of the harper grew hard and every man felt the taste
of hatred in his own mouth, for Elfheah sang of the treachery
of Eadric Streona, the Grasper, who had turned away from the
battle just beginning. Three thousand men from Gloucester and
Wiltshire, from Hereford and Warwick followed the traitor's
command. And, turning away from the battle, they had begun
to march west toward the hills.

There was an angry murmur and a shuffling of feet, for
everyone in the room knew it was true.

Then the harp wept as it will when the hands that touch it
play truly, and Elfheah sang of the old warrior, Ulfkytel, who
drove his spurs into the sides of the war horse he rode and,
with a scream which rent the heavens, galloped across the
fields to cut off the betrayer's flight. No man of his company
sat horse for they had been held in reserve behind the lines. No
man could do anything but watch as Ulfkytel the Valiant forced
the retreating columns to halt. But only for a moment. No man
on the field that day could do anything but watch as arrows
pierced the old man's armor, toppling him slowly from the
saddle. Eadric's forces had given the body wide berth as they

marched past on their way to the hills, past the great war horse who stood unmoving beside his slain rider.

Elfheah strummed without a word for a few minutes while the mead pitcher was passed and cups were filled. When he went on to finish the Ballad of Ashington, his voice was steady. Now he sang how the army of Edmund and the army of Knut were evenly matched, how they fought man to man, how they fought and died while the sun rose higher and higher. And how there was no end to it while the sun sank, nor even as the twilight thickened. It was as if some strange power was upon the field, he sang, as men raised their arms against their enemies and seemed to know no weariness. Men who had slashed and thrust without food or drink throughout all the hours of the day showed no signs of slackening. By moonlight the blood still flowed from men new-killed. And then, weirdly, just at moonrise, the power was gone and the swords of men fell from hands too weary to hold them any longer. The battle was over. Hundreds remained alive where thousands had fought. Both sides were defeated, destroyed. His song was over.

When the soft tallow candles in their holders around the room had melted to guttering pools, Branwen took the pitcher which Wymer had kept filled all evening and poured mead into a large two-handled bowl. Jewel-crusted and gold-banded, it had been a gift to Ulfkytel once, long ago, from a king. Quietly she moved among the men and women, passing the mead bowl from one to the other, as was the custom when the feasting was done.

Still sitting on the corner of the dais, Elfheah watched her and, as the guests prepared to leave, some picking up their sleeping children, he began to sing the prayer of a dying hero, a prayer known to many in the room, for it was from the Ballad of Maldon, Ulfkytel's favorite, one which he had often called for when there was someone to sing for him. As they filed past the candlelit bier, grim-faced men joined their voices with Elfheah's praying.

> Great thanks to Thee, I give, Ruler of Nations,
> For all the earthly joys which I have known.
> Yet now, Maker Mild, great need have I
> That Thou to my soul Thy blessing grant,
> So my spirit freed may fly to Thee this day.
> I pray the fiends of hell may not it snare;

In Thy power, Prince of Angels,
May my soul find peace.

Branwen woke at first light. Taking up a woolen wrap which
hung on a peg against the wall, she pulled it closely around her
and went out into the courtyard. Already there was smoke
rising from the cookhouse roof where new bread would be
rising in great wooden tubs. The buildings were greyer here,
weathered by the salt-laden sea wind. Odd flowers she did not
recognize grew in the thatch. She crossed over to the kitchen
door and went in. The room smelled of the yeast in the rising
bread.

"There is so much to do," Branwen said softly. Her eyes
were dull, her face drawn. "Where is Wymer?"

"Run and fetch your father, girl," Elsey said to the maid
servant.

"Are there others here?"

"There's only four of us here, m'lady. The old biddy, here;
she's been poorly of late, mostly she keeps warm in here by the
fire. But she's no trouble and she don't eat much," she added
quickly, defensively. "Say 'good morning' to the Lady Branwen, mother," Elsey said, but the old woman just rocked back
and forth on the low stool and didn't look up.

"There's no need to worry, Elsey," Branwen said wearily.
"I won't turn her out."

"Budda's the only one of the children left here," Elsey went
on, relieved. "We have four others but they have married and
gone off. Budda stays but it frets her that she is too ugly to get
a man of her own—and she nearing twenty—too old to wed
now. But she's a good girl and a help around the place."

The door opened behind her and Wymer came in. Like his
wife, he was thin and the cords of his muscles roped and
knotted under his coarse work clothes. Their teeth were bad,
those they still had, dark and crooked. They had been slaves
once when they were young and it had left a mark on them
which years of freedom could not remove. That their children
were free farmers, owning their own land, was their greatest
pride. They had stayed on at Cynewithe once out of loyalty to
the man who had freed them; now they were old and set in their
ways. Their place had been here for too long; they would not
leave.

"The girl said ye needed me, my lady," he said.

"Cynewithe is mine now," she said staring into the fire.

"Then the Lady Penardim ain't comin' back?" Elsey asked.

"She said as much, wife, when she left," Wymer snapped.

"But where's she gone? Who'll look after her?"

"There was family she hadn't seen in a long time," Branwen said. "She is with them now. There is no need to worry."

"Oh, my lady, what are we to do?" Elsey moaned.

"What needs to be done," Branwen sighed. "Today we must build the pyre. Will you see to it, Wymer?"

"Aye, lady. 'Twill be an easy thing. Everyone will want to do his share."

"I need to speak with Beorn," she said, sinking down onto a stool which stood beside the worn kitchen table, running her hands over her eyes.

When Beorn rode into the courtyard a little later that morning, Elfheah had wakened and stood leaning idly against the wall in the chill morning light. The sky was overcast as it often is along the coast. Gulls were wheeling and screaming overhead, diving to feed along the littoral exposed by the receding tide. Beorn stood beside his horse, absently fingering the reins, watching Branwen cross the courtyard toward him.

"Many men lie beneath the cairn at Ashington," Branwen said to the short, broad-shouldered man, "but I wish there were one less."

"He died well, lady. I am a fool to grieve. Only that it should have been me. My life is full; his was only just beginning."

"I am sorry," she said, turning away. Looking off between the outbuildings, toward the beach, she said, "Will you be steward? It was Penardim's wish."

"Nae, lady, I canna," he said slowly, taking off his broad-brimmed haying hat and rubbing his hand over his balding head. "There are tales the soldiers tell which I would know are false before I serve you."

"And if they are true?" she whispered.

He shrugged.

"I want to distribute the treasure of Ulfkytel among the families of those who followed him into battle. At least see to the handing out for me. It is not for a stranger to do."

Beorn looked at her gravely. "Why do you do this?" he asked.

"Men call me many things," she said wearily, "but not

thief. The treasure rightly belongs to those who followed him to Ashington. I will not keep it.''

"And so you hope to buy our love," he said shrewdly.

"Not your love," she said, turning to look at him; "only the freedom to live among you without fear as Penardim did. Our way, hers and mine, is the same."

"So be it then," he said. "That much I'll do for you—as to the other, we will see."

She left Beorn in the treasure room among the cups and bowls, the rings and torcs, and went out to the line of dunes. Throughout the morning she sat with her arms wrapped around her knees, watching the waves and the birds while the men built a pyre of pine and oak, rowan and birch on the beach just above the high water mark. By noon the sun had burned through the haze. The breeze fell so that the coarse sea grass growing in clumps around her stopped whispering. The sand fleas began to bite, but Branwen did not notice.

Budda came out to get her. "My father says it's time," she said timidly. "Will you come now?"

"No," Branwen said and then, when the girl seemed uncertain, she added, "tell Wymer to go ahead. I will watch from here."

She stood alone near the top of the dune when the body of Ulfkytel was borne out of his hall and laid on top of the brands. His shield was laid over him; his sword broken and laid at his side. Branwen stood silently while his war horse was led out. She saw Beorn swing his axe, bringing it down heavily on the horse's forehead, killing him, that the great horse might go into the warrior's hall with the chief he had served so well. There were many voices raised as the torches were set to the pyre.

"It is right and just, Ulfkytel Snellinger," she said, thinking no one would hear her. "For you alone Ashington was right and just. The blood of hundreds stains my hands and I'll never wash them clean, but not your blood, old man, not your blood.''

"So much guilt is a hard load to carry. Why take it on yourself, Branwen?" a voice asked behind her.

"Elfheah," she said.

He stood beside her and neither of them spoke for a while, watching the heavy smoke rising from the pyre. The cracking and snapping of the burning wood was loud in the still air. After a while, Elfheah said, "When I first saw you laughing with my brother at Holcombe you were so beautiful; young, pleased with yourself, yet innocent. How I hated you, whom all men desired except me."

Branwen said nothing.

"I loved Cobbe, Branwen. Waking or sleeping I still see him lying there."

"Don't, Elfheah," she groaned.

But he went on as if he had not heard her. "He died so easily—while still there was a smile on his bloodied mouth," Elfheah said incredulously. "You touched him and he died so easily." He turned and looked at her. "I owe you for what you spared me." He shuddered.

"You know what I am, Elfheah."

He did not answer her.

"A shape-changer. My shape or yours I can change at will. You've seen me do it. But it's not just a magic trick, it's a power which is mine because I am of the race who serve the Great Earth Mother, the last of my people."

She could see on his face that he did not believe her. Uncaring, she went on, "When we were outside of Otford, Edmund's army drove the Viking, defeated, onto the Isle of Sheppey. There he might have destroyed them, but I . . ." she hesitated. "I did not want them killed." Her voice was only a whisper and she stared at him unseeing. "Not killed, not Thorkell, not Hemming. So," she said, taking a deep breath, "I wove an illusion. You have seen me do it, remember?"

He nodded.

"Well, this was no ordinary magic. Greater than any illusion woven on this island in the memory of man was the spell I wove that day. The power flowed from an ancient wellspring, long forgotten."

"We would not have killed the Danes. We could have made peace."

"Perhaps you are right, Elfheah, but then I was caught up in a madness and. . . . The illusion spread out, covering the shore, reaching out across the tidal race along the dunes on the other side."

"The fleet," he said. "We never understood how Knut's fleet arrived that dawning."

"The fleet did not come until sunset. You saw what I willed."

"But we walked on the isle that day and there was no trace left of the Vikings."

She smiled grimly. "I was very proud of my handiwork. It was hard not to laugh at the despair among the remnants of Knut's army who waited on the island that day. I wanted to dance, to shout out that I had saved them—me, alone. Only later I learned what I had done, tangling the threads on the loom of fate for my will alone. I had disturbed the great pattern and Ashington had to be fought to put it right. I saved them from defeat to send them to their death—even the great bear, even Hemming, dead now."

She looked at the face of Elfheah, grown ashen as he listened.

"That's not all," she said bitterly. "You want to be my friend; then listen. I came to Cynewithe then. I met Penardim who, like me, served the Great Goddess. She told me that I could still halt the coming battle. The power of the Goddess would flow through me if I raised my hands against the armies. There could be no battle if I opposed it. But I didn't believe her."

Just then the pyre groaned and settled monstrously down on itself, becoming an inferno of flame which reached high into the sky. All up and down the beach, sea birds rose screaming into the air, all except the little sandpipers who chased the waves with single-minded unconcern.

After a while Branwen went on, her voice dull. "All through the day I worked among the dying, refusing to listen to the voice which spoke in my heart. Not until the moon rose did I at last end what I had started; did I at last stand against the evil I had loosed. All those dead. All that blood and pain."

"Now will you comfort me?" she asked angrily. "Will you tell me, 'never mind, it will not seem so bad in time'?"

"I will not leave you here alone," Elfheah said simply.

That night, while the sea wind scattered the cold grey ash, Branwen had a dream, a strange fantasy unlike any she had ever had before. In the dream two women hid among the bracken of tall ferns while one labored to give birth. Heavy-browed, their long, matted hair hung around them. Their bodies were naked though the air was cold. There were two small children nearby, laughing as they played along the edge of the trees. Their mouths were stained with the berries their awkward fingers clutched from laden branches. Each was

surely no more than two years old. Their brows lacked the
heavy bones which shadowed the women's eyes. The woman
in labor cried out as the pain came stronger. The other woman
turned then and seemed to look right at Branwen, asking for
her help. Her eyes were bright, defensive but unafraid. In her
dream Branwen went toward the women, speaking to them in
the ancient tongue of the animals and the birds; and they were
glad, for her skill at childbirth was great. When the child was
delivered, a beautiful, lusty infant who cried loudly until she
was given suck, Branwen asked the women, "Who are you?
Where are your people?"

She woke with a start, hearing her own words ringing in her
ears. She sat up and looked around the dark room, confused.
The dream had been so vivid. Unlike the shadowy, flickering
world of ordinary dreams, this one had been real, down to the
rows of tiny black spores on the underside of the fern fronds.
She was puzzled, too, because she remembered it so clearly; it
didn't seem to be slipping away from her like other dreams.
She lay back, pulling the down-filled coverlet close against the
chill, and fell asleep again, wondering who the women were
and why had she dreamed of them. But the dream did not
return, as she half hoped, not that night. But on other nights it
did. The same women. And she began to know the way there
and she began to wait for night to come.

She could not bear to see the people around Cynewithe, for
everyone had lost a brother or a husband, father or lover, at
Ashington.

Her days were filled with trivia, meaningless conversations,
empty actions, and always the awful guilt behind her, driving
her along uncharted roadways, deeper and deeper into herself,
seeking a sanctuary, a refuge. Until even in the day she would
seek out the land of her dream where she was free from guilt.
For hours she would sit staring, silent, as if she were asleep but
Elfheah knew, watching her, that she was not, and it worried
him. Where did she go, he wondered? What if one day she
didn't come back?

Finally, one day in early October, she found the drying racks
of the herbalist where Penardim had worked, and in the small
room at the back of the cookhouse she came upon the rows of
small drawers, each neatly labeled with an exquisite drawing
of the cure-all within. With only the faint memory of the
pleasure she used to feel, she began to go into the autumn

fields and woods to gather the roots and berries which must be brought in during those months. Elfheah sighed with relief. At last, he thought, her healing is beginning. But she went out automatically, without thinking. It was just something which had to be done, like getting dressed in the morning. The drawers were empty, the herbs which were left were dried and old. She did not go because she wanted to, she went because she had been taught to go, had been taught that the work must be done, done in its season. She went because something deep inside her clung to this small routine when there was nothing else left.

But by November, it had begun to rain steadily, day after day, a cold, soaking rain and neither Branwen nor Elfheah went out much, staying in close by the fire. One afternoon, while Elfheah paced back and forth restlessly in the great hall, Branwen sat quietly in the big chair by the fire, carding wool. They did not speak to each other, lost in their own thoughts. The sea was quiet, the shutters closed against the rain which dripped in through the smoke hole in the thatch. There had been no word from Thorkell or Godwin. They had no way of confirming or denying the rumors which persisted that the country had been divided—that Cynewithe lands were to be ruled by the Dane. Branwen wondered if the rumors were true. How would Edmund accept such a settlement? Probably not easily, she thought, suddenly missing them, Edmund and her brother, wishing she were with them where she could help. But then the black cloud, as dark and cold as any November storm, descended around her again and she smiled grimly, remembering how she had helped before—helped so many men to their deaths.

Unconsciously, she rubbed her hands along the rough wool of her skirt, wiping at the sticky wetness of fresh blood long ago washed off. She stared at the fire, unseeing, her mind fleeing a world she could not bear, fleeing along a path she had worn to another time and place, a refuge she had found, a place of peace. The room around her began to fade, dissolving into greyness. When she looked up, she was in a small cave. A familiar stillness was all around her. She cried out with joy, feeling the guilt fall from her, not caring why or how she had come to be here; to be here again was enough.

A fire had been laid in the opening of the cave. Beyond and below she could see the ocean. Dried sweet bracken had been heaped at the back; the floor was littered with broken clam shells and fish bones. Against one wall a mound of beechnuts had been piled. There was a not unpleasant complication of odors in the air. The fire itself was a curious affair, for one end of a dead tree had been fed into the coals while the other end stuck out along the edge of the cliff. Branwen laughed. Standing in the cave mouth, she could see the path which ran down onto the beach. Hearing their voices, she started down toward them.

They were gathering mussels from the bank of the stream where it emptied into the sea. They were old friends, for she had found refuge here many times. The baby she had helped deliver was tied on a carrying board and propped against a tree, where she wailed angrily. The two small children, seeing Branwen coming toward them, ran to meet her, hugging her knees. She bent down and hugged them and then went over to quiet the baby. Suddenly a voice called to her as if from a great distance. She looked up. The voice called again. The women were bent over their work, intent on filling their baskets before the tide turned. The voice called again.

The scene was fading, shifting; the voice kept calling her name, "Branwen," it called, insistently, "Branwen." She felt as if she were struggling up from a great depth. Suddenly there was a man bending over her. She stared at him for long moments, trying to remember. She looked across the shadows of the warm rich room, with its carved oak chairs, its intricately woven wall hanging. Her hands felt sticky, and she began to rub them on the rough wool of her skirt.

The man frowned and put his own graceful hands over hers, stilling them. She heard his voice say, "Let's walk for a while, Bran. The rain has stopped."

She stared at him, trying to understand his words.

"Come on, the air will do you good."

Woodenly, she got up and allowed him to wrap her cloak around her and lead her onto the sea cliff.

But the light along the edge of the sea was very strange. There was no sound but the unhurried crashing of the breakers. Everything that lived had disappeared. Even the tiny sandpipers had vanished. The sky was windswept and empty and the late afternoon sun burned on the cold sea.

She wanted to turn and run but the man held her hand and she could not pull free. An aura of fear, like an incarnadine mist, lay on the land. Terror rose up in her. Her breath came in ragged gasps as if she were choking on it.

The man went on, walking along the sand. He did not hear her; he did not seem even to be aware of her hand tugging at his.

Beneath her booted foot, Branwen felt the world grown thin, like a bird's egg, only a thin shell of reality spanning an abyss below. She whimpered.

Unmindful, Elfheah stomped along beside her. "Don't you ever wonder what's been happening in the world these last two months?" he asked.

But she could not answer him. Evil was on the land. Terror gripped her.

Then they saw the men, dark-cloaked, upon the cartway. Time came out of joint. The shell was cracking beneath them. She saw the bows bent, heard the arrows hissing through the still air, their awful thud. Beside her Elfheah slumped to the ground, pierced through and through. She crouched beside him, cradling his head against her breast, her dark hair falling around them.

"Poor Bran," Elfheah whispered. His eyes caught hers, wild now, and then his head fell back.

As he died the shell beneath her shattered and she fell, with a small cry of hopelessness, into the abyss.

Chapter Two

In another part of the island, rain fell steadily on the thick thatch of an inn. Hissing, it dripped through the roof hole onto the fire in the center of the room. Long tables stood along the walls and a company of Danes spread around them in small groups, some loud and filled with the laughter which comes in a jug of ale; others quieter, watching or just staring into the fire, thinking the thoughts men think when they are far from home. The air was thick with smoke and redolent with the smell of roasting pork spitted over the fire.

Thorkell the Tall, his hair longer now, sat with his lieutenant off to one side of the crowded room at a thick oaken table spread with maps. He rubbed his arm absently where an angry red scar pulled tightly across an older one now faded white. A candle on the table guttered in the draft which blew under the door and through the cracks in the shutters.

One hundred miles separated the inn at Oxford from the dunes at Cynewithe, but there was an uncanny bond between the tall Danish commander and the shape-changer men called Branwen, and Thorkell heard her scream as Elfheah died.

"Branwen," he said aloud.

"Branwen?" the man said sitting beside him.

Thorkell shook his head, trying to clear it; but the scream hung there and would not leave him. "Take over, Orm," he said. "I'll meet you in Maldon. Something's wrong. I've got to go."

"Now, chief? It's pouring out there. The night will be as black as pitch."

But Thorkell did not hear him. The Dane was already striding toward the door, his great leather cape swirling around his legs.

It was a miserable night. The rain penetrated his cloak before he had gone five miles. His rain-soaked legs, gripping the flanks of his war horse, froze as the night grew cold. But still the scream rang in his ears and he kept on. Hour after hour he rode, picking his way through the dark, grateful that the road was a main one and well kept. At last, pity for his horse brought him into the familiar warmth and shelter of the monastery of St. Albans where he had stayed often in the past few years. He had gone fifteen miles and the hour was late. No one stirred as he tended the horse in the well-kept stable, wiping him down and filling his bucket with grain. When the man had finished he turned toward the small hospice which stood nearby. It was empty, as he had expected, for no one traveled the roads in such a season. A fire was laid but unlit in the center of the small room. Benches with thick blankets folded on them ran around the walls. An intricately worked clothes tree stood empty against one wall. Thorkell smiled at the good monks' foresight. He lit the dry tinder under the logs, striking the spark with the flint and steel he carried. He stripped off his wet clothes and hung them over the tree pulled nearer the fire. Wrapped in the luxury of two blankets he stretched out on a bench and was instantly asleep.

While the tall Viking lord rode through the storm that night, frightened servants had carried an unconscious girl in from the rainswept sea cliff. Anxiously the women had washed the blood from her hands, stripped off her wet, stained clothes, laid her in Penardim's bed, and covered her warmly with thick quilts. She seemed unharmed. The murderers must have fled as soon as they saw Elfheah fall. Perhaps they had heard rumors about the woman with him, rumors they would not wait to have confirmed. In the dark night at Cynewithe, the servants built up the fire in that small back room. There was nothing else to be done for her. She did not regain consciousness. Men came, Beorn among them, to tend to the slain harper. Arrangements were made to give him burial the next day in the small churchyard at the crossroads. There was no way for them to know he was the brother of a king. He had not told them.

In the early morning darkness, far from the sea, when the chapel bell at St. Albans tolled the hour of prime, calling the monks to prayer, Thorkell sat up. He had slept deeply for six hours and woke quickly, instantly alert, his hand on the handle of the heavy battle axe leaning against the bench. He smiled then, seeing where he was, and lay back. There was no need to hurry. There wouldn't be any food until the monks were finished with their prayers, and food was what he needed if he was going to make Cynewithe today—rich stew, thick and smelling of rabbits and parsnips, dark crusty bread with sweet yellow butter spread in chunks, even warm mulled wine from the monks' own cellars. . . . Suddenly ravenous, he got up and dressed quickly; the fire had gone out and the room was cold but his clothes were dry. He left the hospice as the silent monks streamed out of the chapel toward the refectory, their hands tucked into the long thick woolen sleeves of their dark robes.

"Welcome, my son," the abbot said as Thorkell came into the room. "Brother Geoffrey told me you came in late last night," he went on, leading Thorkell to a place at table where they could sit together.

"Aye, Father, and very glad for the fire which was laid and waiting for me," Thorkell answered, sitting down and helping himself to a heaping pile of fresh bread and honey and a bowl of thick stew, not rabbit by the smell of it, some kind of fish. It must be a holy day, Thorkell thought ruefully.

"You eat like a man who has far to go," the abbot said with a smile. He himself had taken only a piece of bread which he ate dry without butter or honey.

He was a thin man, the skin of his face deeply furrowed, his brown eyes sparkling with the pleasure of having a familiar guest to talk with. In the early eleventh century monasteries like St. Albans were holy places where believing men dedicated their lives to serving God, taking their triple vows of poverty, chastity and obedience seriously. Frequent fasting kept them lean. The stew kettle was dipped into only by those whose assignment that day would involve heavy manual labor in the fields or barns. The others—scribes and students, the gatekeepers, the cooks, beekeeper, cellerer—all had only a slice of whole grain bread to hold them until dinner at midday.

In answer to the abbot's question, Thorkell swallowed what he had in his mouth and said, "If the rain holds off and I can find a fresh mount along the road I will make fifty miles today, Father."

"All the way to the coast, is it?"

"Aye, all the way to the coast."

"Have you word of the king, my son? We are isolated here and would welcome what news you have."

"Which king, Father?" Thorkell asked, his mouth full.

"Edmund, who is called Ironside, is rightful king of the land, my son."

"Edmund is dead," Thorkell said without looking up.

"Dead?" the abbot echoed, crossing himself.

"Aye, dead two weeks now. There is but one man to rule here now."

"Knut, the Dane," the abbot said, his voice filled with despair.

"Come, come, Father," Thorkell said, looking at him. "As Edmund was different from his father, so Knut is different from Swein Forkbeard. There was a man you were right to dread, but not so his son. You will see, mark my words. But I've got to be going," he said, pushing himself away from the table. "Orm is following with my men. They will be here tonight at the latest. Make them welcome," he added with a broad grin, "and you will have news enough to last you through all the long winter nights ahead."

"Then, my son, we will keep watch for them. God speed you on your journey."

He found a fresh mount shortly after noon at Chipping Onger, staying only long enough to melt the ice out of his bones and fill his stomach with goat's-milk cheese and dark bread at a filthy inn at the crossroads there. The rain held off and a cold sun shone down on the frozen ruts of the roadway. A stiff wind blew from the west, pushing him on.

Late in the day he drew near the city of Maldon, a low hill fortified by the Romans a thousand years earlier. Its motley walls, repaired countless times over the centuries, rose out of the flood plain at a bend in the Blackwater. He stopped at an alehouse to ask the way for he had never been to Cynewithe before.

"There must be a goodly crowd gathering there by now," the fat man said, handing him a mug of hot cider.

"How so?" Thorkell asked, leaning casually against the wall near the door.

"Two nights ago, or be it three, Grum," the man called

across the room, "them others was in asking the way to Cynewithe?"

"Three," the other growled without looking up.

"'Three,' you say," Thorkell asked, his voice carefully unconcerned, friendly. He finished the mug and flipped a coin in the innkeeper's direction.

"Ayę, and mean-looking bastards they was, too, wasn't they, Grum?"

The other man, hunched over his mug, growled something unintelligible.

"Thanks," Thorkell said and then he was gone, not to find lodging for the night as he had planned, but a fresh mount instead. The news he had heard in the tavern goaded him on. "Mean-looking bastards they was, too." He heard the words over and over again. Ignoring the complaints of his sore and tired body, he rode east out of Maldon, hurrying down the last twenty miles as the sun disappeared behind him.

"Where is she?" he asked, pushing past Wymer who stood gaping in the courtyard.

Elsey came to the door. "Oh sir, do ye know what ails the young miss?" she asked, wringing her hands.

"Where is the Lady Branwen?" he demanded, striding ahead into the hall.

"This way, sir, only it won't do no good. She just lies there. She ain't moved, not since night afore last. They killed the young man, sir, but what they've done to her . . . oh sir, what're we to do?"

He stood beside the bed, looking down at the still figure of the small dark-haired woman whose heart had cried out to his, calling him here. Now there was only stillness and silence. "Oh God, Bran," he groaned, "where have you gone this time?" Without turning he said to the old woman standing behind him, "Leave us."

"You won't harm her?" the old woman cried, suddenly frightened.

But he didn't answer, sinking down to his knees beside the bed. "Branwen, Branwen," he called softly, gathering her up into his arms.

The old woman left. The night grew darker. The candle burned lower. Still he knelt beside the bed. There was no one to see or know how his heart searched the void for her. Long and far he sought her, until at last he found her, in a time before time was even counted, on a beach where she was playing with small children.

She heard him and looked around. "Thorkell," she said happily. Her shape shimmered in that time and place and was gone as her soul, hearing his call, flew back to where he waited.

"I was afraid you had gone too far, Branwen," he said.

"You shouldn't have worried. I would have come back, my love," she said. She smiled then, reaching up to touch his face, still travel-soiled. "But I am glad you are here. Your hair has grown longer," she said. Touching his arm, she added, "Your wound is healing nicely."

"What happened here?" he asked roughly.

"They killed Elfheah," she said.

"No, not that. What happened to you? If they . . ."

"They did not touch me, my love," she said quietly.

"Then what?"

"I could not bear it here," she said simply. "When he died . . . there is a place," she said, "where the first of the race of the Goddess live. I have gone there many times. I teach them what I can—weaving, herbs. It is a place of great"—she paused, looking for the words—"innocence. There are no men when I have been there; they say men pass through along the game trails sometimes. And sometimes they stay for a while. They do not think as we do. They do not know anything," she said and smiled, "not even that a child has a father."

"Branwen, Branwen," he moaned.

"Poor Thorkell." She laughed. "He was there, too, you know, the unicorn, and the Great Goddess," she added softly.

But he wasn't listening. "I was afraid when you left me at Ashington," he said, his voice hoarse with emotion. "I should never have let you go off like that."

"I'm all right now, Thorkell," she said quietly, sensing at last how shaken he had been.

He held her gently in his arms, for there was a fragility to her and he feared he might crush her. But she needed no arcane skill to know the depth of his need. She turned her face up to him. He would have kissed her chastely, his own longing held in tight rein, but her tongue flicked over his lips and her hands slid under his tunic. His hunger swept over him, like the waves crashing onto the shore beyond the windows.

Much later that night, when they lay quietly in the warmth of each other's arms, he said, "You're sure you're all right, Bran?"

"I'm all right, Thorkell. Guilt for the dead at Ashington was not mine. Evil exists until someone stops it, not because no one stops it. Evil rises out of man's greed for power and can be stopped by love, but that there is no one who loves does not cause the evil. I was not damned, only human."

He yawned and she smiled, tracing with the tip of her finger the lines graven around his mouth. "I was so afraid of you once. Do you remember?"

"That was a long time ago, Bran," he said, his eyes closing, "a long time ago."

In the morning, when they had eaten, Thorkell looked at her and said gravely, "Edmund's dead, Branwen."

She put down her spoon. "Is Godwin safe?" she asked.

"Aye," Thorkell said, "he is safe. It was an accident, Bran."

"I still have his crown. I never gave it back to him," she said, her eyes brimming. After a while she said thoughtfully, "That's why Elfheah was killed. He would have been the king."

Thorkell was silent.

"Tell me," she said, "from the beginning, from when I left, tell me what happened."

"Well," he said, leaning back against the rough plaster wall, "I saw your brother before we left Ashington. He confirmed what we all knew was true. Edmund no longer had the strength or the will to fight. I told him the same thing was true with our forces although Knut still held out hope of raising fresh troops in Denmark."

"It is not possible," she said incredulously.

"No, it isn't, but Knut is young and needed time to accept the inevitable. I told your brother to allow a couple of weeks before suggesting a meeting. I knew he would be ready then. Both Harald and Eric had told him that neither Norway nor Denmark could send more men."

"We have heard that Olaf is king in Norway now. Is it true?"

"Aye, it's true. Olaf left the Norman court and returned to Norway as soon as Eric was committed to Knut here. He defeated Eric's brother, Swein, in the Oslo fjord last summer and has set himself up as king. Eric cannot go back.''

"I am sorry for Norway and for Eric," she said. "What happened after you talked to my brother?"

"What was left of the two armies moved west, avoiding each other but never far apart. Then, one day, a messenger arrived from Eadric Streona." He stopped, waiting for her reaction.

"Eadric," she hissed, "how did he dare?"

"Oh, quite easily, my love. I doubt that even if Edmund and Knut had combined forces they could have defeated Eadric in battle. His resources are great and his men unscathed. He dares much, you may be sure of that."

"What did the messenger say?"

Thorkell smiled. "Eadric summoned Knut and Edmund to an island in the Severn near Deerhurst."

"Summoned? Oh, my God, Thorkell!"

"Aye." Thorkell laughed. "It was a fatal mistake although Eadric doesn't know it yet. Knut can forgive a man many things, but he will never forgive that insult."

"Did you go?"

"Yes," he said, "it was time to end it anyway. Godwin and I had already agreed to arrange a meeting. Actually, Eadric provided an element of common ground, an enemy we both despised."

"So you met and divided the country between you."

"You knew?" he asked, ignoring the bitterness in her voice.

"We had heard it was so. Elfheah was surprised that Edmund would agree."

"He had no choice. It was no longer possible to fight," Thorkell said. "There was no blood lust left."

"No," she said, "and it will never return to the men who stood upon the field at Ashington."

"What do you mean?" he asked, his eyes narrow.

"Just that. The men who stood on the battlefield at Ashington when the moon rose that night will never fight again."

"So." Thorkell laughed with no trace of gaiety in his voice, "You have unmanned us."

"No, my love, not unmanned," she said; "only there will be no more fighting and killing. It is over." After a while she said quietly, "They were Eadric's men who came here and

killed Elfheah. Eadric's men who had left the field.'' Her voice
was very soft.

Thorkell got up and walked over to the door. He stood
looking out for a long time. At last he shook his head. She
frowned, sensing that he had decided what she said simply
could not be true.

"Edmund didn't take the division of his kingdom well,'' he
went on. "You see Knut gained half a kingdom and so was
satisfied, at least for a while; but Edmund lost half of his
inheritance.''

"Tell me how it ended,'' she said sadly.

"There is no better way to turn enemies into allies than a full
cup and so a great feasting was begun. Each night there was a
party in one camp or another. Soon, what with drunks sleeping
it off wherever they fell, it was difficult to tell which was Dane
and which island-born. But Edmund,'' he said, frowning,
"Edmund was more violent in his drink than any other. He
was rarely sober. It was as if he could not face his shame.
Godwin sent word to Ealdgyth and she came with the children
to see if she could put an end to his despair.''

"His sons,'' Branwen said, "I had forgotten them. And
were they murdered, too?''

"The order was given too late. When Edmund died . . .''

"How did he die?'' she interrupted.

"He was very drunk. I was there at table with him. Your
brother was there, too. Edmund choked to death, Branwen.
There was nothing we could do. The meat he tried to swallow
would have choked a horse and we could not dislodge it.''

"Ealdgyth, was she there?''

"She was there. She had been nursing the baby when it
happened, sitting in the shadows. But she stood there, turned
to stone, her clothes in disarray.'' He paused before going on.
"She left that night with her sons, sailing down the Severn
under cover of darkness, on her way to Normandy and
beyond.''

"Under whose flag did she sail, my love?''

"Would you have me murder infants?''

"No, not you. Tales are told of Viking raiders tossing infants on spear points and laughing, but I never believed it of
you.''

Thorkell was silent.

After a moment, Branwen said, "Poor Elfheah, there was none to save him."

"Had I been able, I would not have saved him, Branwen."

"Why not?" she asked angrily.

He came back from the doorway and sat down opposite her at the table. "While Elfheah lived, Knut's kingship could not be secure; he would not share it with Elfheah."

"Elfheah didn't want to be a king."

"Would you have me think well of him?"

"Can't you?"

"If I thought well of him, I wouldn't have let him leave Ashington with you. Only that I knew him for the unman he was, was he free to go with you."

Her eyes flashed across the worn wooden kitchen table. "I will have whatever man I choose," she said, "not you, not any man, shall tell me otherwise. If I had wanted Elfheah, he would have wanted me as well."

"That may be true," he said, thin-lipped, "but I will share you with no man. Choose another and you will do without me."

"When my need was great, Elfheah was there. If we did not couple like animals, how is it that I should love him less?"

"Did you love him, Branwen?" Thorkell asked quietly.

"No," she said with tears in her eyes, "not as I love you. But I would not have had him killed. He, too, was trying to find reason for his existence."

"It was for that reason he had to be killed, Branwen," Thorkell said gently. "Knut and Edmund were of the same cut. Together they might have reigned. But Elfheah was no match for Knut. He was not of the stuff of kings."

"No, my love, he was not the stuff of kings," she said. After a moment she asked, "And what of Godwin? How is my brother now?"

"I am not sure. I did not stay for the funeral. Knut has made me Jarl of East Anglia. I thought it time I saw the land which I am to rule in the name of the king."

"All of East Anglia?" she asked, her voice hushed, for it was indeed a royal holding.

"Aye. Eric will oversee Northumbria and Yorkshire while Eadric will at last have control of all Mercia."

"And who controls Wessex and the south coast?"

"Knut hasn't yet assigned jarls for Wessex. He is worried

about the threat from Normandy and has assigned all the men he can afford to garrison the coast. Even my own fleet winters at Wight.''

"What threat from Normandy can be so great," she scoffed, "that you are deprived of your men and must travel the countryside alone, like any commoner?''

"I traveled alone because I travel faster that way. It seemed important to find you.''

"Why?''

"I heard you scream.''

"I don't remember screaming.''

"Nevertheless," he said, "at an inn in Oxford I heard you scream.''

"So you leapt on your horse and galloped to rescue me.'' She laughed.

"It didn't seem funny at the time," he said, an edge to his voice.

"No, I suppose not," she said, reaching out to touch his strong hand which lay on the table.

Elsey came over and stood beside them, refilling their jeweled goblets with warm spiced wine. "You are sure you are all right, my lady?'' she asked as she had several times before.

"Quite sure, Elsey," Branwen responded with a warm smile. "I'm sorry to have worried you so, but I am quite all right now, really.''

Elsey appeared doubtful but went back to punching down the dough which had risen in the wooden trough.

"What of the threat from across the Channel?'' Branwen asked. "Why is Knut so worried? You've been in Normandy with Duke Robert. Do you think he can mount an invasion?''

"It's not just Robert. Emma is with him and so are Ethelred's two young sons. They have valid claim to the throne. It is quite possible Robert will back them.''

"I thought Emma hated those boys.''

"That may be, but they are not just boys any longer. They are princes of the royal blood. They can mean a return to power for her. She's still young, Bran, not yet thirty. She's not the type to retire gracefully to a convent somewhere.''

"Well, what happens now? Will you stay the winter here at Cynewithe, with me?''

Thorkell got up from the table again and walked back to the door. He stood there looking out over the mud of the courtyard. The mire had not yet frozen hard although there was ice rimming the puddles.

"Thirty men-at-arms bear my standard eastward from Oxford. They should be in Maldon tomorrow. Shall I billet them here?"

"I think not." She laughed. "But whose men are these if your fleet holds the south coast this winter?"

"Hemming's," he said without looking at her. "He died without issue. His wealth, treasure, and lands come to me. His men, too, have chosen to follow me—those who are left."

She crossed the kitchen to his side. There was no need for her to put into words her own sorrow at Hemming's death. Thorkell knew she grieved for his brother even as he did himself. She slipped her hand into his and together they walked out into the sunlight. Picking their way carefully between the puddles, they came out onto the edge of the sea cliff.

There, sheltered from the west wind by the buildings behind them, the sun warm on their faces, Thorkell said, "I will go to Maldon. There is work which must be done there. The Thing has been summoned; I must sit in judgment. And then, in a few weeks, I will go on to London for the midwinter feast. Knut will expect me to attend."

"So," she said brightly, turning away so that he couldn't see her face.

He took her by the shoulders and turned her around, holding her away from him, looking down at her. Tears spilled unheeded down her cheeks. "Come with me, Branwen," he said. "I need you."

"I cannot," she whispered.

"Why? There is nothing here for you."

"I can't come with you. Not as I am. Don't you see?"

"Of course," he said, "it comes down to that again. You will not be my wife. The Lady of the Ravens—you like that, don't you? The Angel of Death." His voice was hard and his eyes snapped angrily. "You could be my wife, couldn't you? You could act like a normal woman, but you won't. That's it, isn't it?" he said, shaking her roughly.

"Oh, Thorkell, is that what you really think?" She broke away from him and ran down to the hard wet sand at the edge of the waves. He did not follow her. She walked and walked until the chaos of her thoughts settled down and the voices in her head spoke more calmly to each other.

He'll never understand.

He never really believes any of it, does he? Not even when he sees it with his own eyes.

You won't be able to explain what it means to give up an identity he thinks is unreal to start with.

But I've struggled so hard to find it.

So the magic of the earth is yours. Is it worth it?

But how can I give it up? How can I stand by and watch people suffer when I could heal them?

Ha, that's a two-edged blade, isn't it? Don't lie to yourself. Healer/killer. You've been both.

Maybe I could just be his wife as I am. I could try.

You've been warned not to try that. You know how there are always some people who hate you, whether it's envy or fear or both. It doesn't matter. And hatred will grow. . . . Oh, not among those who are close to you, you can always handle them, but all those people who hear about you, hear stories, bits and pieces, rumors. They'll hate you.

I'll deal with that. I don't care if they hate me.

And when they hate Thorkell because of you? What if they try to hurt you through him?

No, they can't. I won't let them.

You can't be everywhere.

But what am I to do? Give it up? The power of the healer, the magic of the shape-changer, the freedom to fly?

You can't do it, can you?

No, no, I can't. It's too much.

How will you watch him leave you? He needs a wife. How will you feel when another woman stands beside him?

Oh God!

Your mother denied it all. She gave it up for Wulfnoth. Can't you do the same? Don't you love him enough?

Oh, Mother of Mothers, help me. I have to try. I have to try. I love him too much to let him go.

But Branwen forgot, that day, as she went to find Thorkell, that her mother had married Wulfnoth when she was still very young. Her mother had rejected the heritage which was hers without ever having used it, without ever having known its power, and without anyone else ever knowing her for what she was, ever hating her for what she was. It would be harder for Branwen.

Later in the day when dinner was over and the hall was, for a few hours at least, a place of quiet, Branwen left Thorkell deep in conversation with Beorn. She walked alone along the cartway toward the crossroads at Clacton, smiling to herself, thinking of poor Beorn, who would now have to agree to remain on as steward. She knew he would have come to that decision sooner or later, but now there was no time for them to wait. Either he would accept the stewardship or Thorkell would send one of his carles to Cynewithe to see the work done. Hardly a choice Beorn would wish for his friends and neighbors. Still, the work would not be easy, knowing as he would that he was answerable to the Jarl of East Anglia.

At the crossroads there was a Saxon chapel made of wood and thatch. It was a small unimportant chapel and there was no priest to serve it regularly. Beside it, shadowed by the bare branches of ancient rowans, was the graveyard. Elfheah's grave was a raw cut in the dark ground. A plain wooden cross bore his name, a humble marker for a king's son. She leaned down and strung over the cross the heavy gold chain on which hung his harper's key. Wymer had saved it for her. The key banged against the wood loudly in the stillness. She made a simple sign and the chain and key vanished, hidden by magic to spend eternity marking a harper's grave. She stood for a long time beside the grave before turning back to Cynewithe and the world which lay beyond.

When she returned to the kitchen Elsey was dozing, her head laid on the kitchen table. Branwen went over and woke her gently.

"Aye, my lady. Sommat wrong?" the cook asked, sleepily.

"No, Elsey, everything is all right. Only I needed to speak with you."

"If it's about tomorrow, Lady Branwen, the panniers will be packed and ready when you ride out."

"Would you let me have Budda to take with me as my maid servant, Elsey? I shall need a woman and she is a quiet girl, which suits me well."

"Oh, my lady, we would miss her sore."

"You said yourself that she is not happy here."

"But who would do her work?"

"Cynewithe will be closed for months. I don't know when we'll be back, probably not before summer. There will be little enough for you and Wymer to do until then."

"She would be glad to go," the woman said, blowing her nose on the corner of her soiled apron.

"Go to the barn and speak with your husband. I will send Budda out to you. In the end she must be the one to decide. I don't want her weeping and miserable."

But Budda's misshapen mouth was twisted into a broad smile when she returned from the barn to the sleeping room where Branwen stood at the window, watching the crashing surf.

"My lady?" Budda said, waiting in the doorway.

"Ah, Budda, you'll come then?" Branwen said.

"Yes, my lady, though it's little enough I know of being a lady's maid."

"Then we are even," Branwen said with a smile, "for it's little enough I know about being a lady. Go now and say your goodbyes. Pack what you need. It will be many months before we return."

Chapter Three

The winter marsh was brown and grey, beaten down by the wind and rain. There was a barren flatness to the flood plain now where, in the spring, the moorhen would nest hidden by tall, gently waving reeds. Only the clear song of the thrush remained hanging, wraithlike, in the empty air. The sun shone thin and cold; the horses' hoofs rang sharply on the frozen cartway.

Riding across the wasteland, they saw the city from a great distance. On a low hill where the Chelmer emptied into the Blackwater, the Romans had erected the walls of a city. Part of the great stonework remained; crudely patched, it had nonetheless withstood the Viking attacks of the last century. Maldon had grown into a strong center of trade with the continent. The great gate stood open as they rode up, for the jarl was expected. A column of armed men rode out to meet them. The stiff December wind whipped at the raven banner held aloft at the column's head. Branwen felt a moment of dread, for now at last she must become, in the eyes of all men, Thorkell's wife.

"You tremble like a hawk new brought to hand, Branwen." He did not smile for he knew she was afraid and it irritated him.

"Oh, my love," she said softly, "it all begins now. I will try to be a good wife, I really will, but what if I can't?"

"Will it be so hard," he asked, "being my wife?"

"No," she said smiling at him gently, "not so hard." Too late now to explain her fear. Too late now.

34

He reached out to touch her hand and then turned his attention to the men who were approaching.

A red-faced Viking rode at the head of the column. He wore a conical helmet, formed of stiff, boiled leather, but instead of the hard breastplate which Thorkell wore, this man wore a coat of iron mail. What dead man yielded up his mail to you, Branwen wondered, watching him rein up in front of them.

"Well met, Thorkell," the man said.

"How goes it, Orm?" Thorkell answered. "Any trouble along the road?"

"No trouble," the man said, breaking into a grin. "We suffered only from an excess of hospitality at the monastery of St. Albans. It seems we were expected. Every head was aching the next morning when it was time to ride out."

Thorkell laughed. "They were anxious for news. They must have decided to take no chances with close-mouthed Vikings. What of the city? Any trouble here?"

"None, chief. The sokemen await your pleasure. The Thing will gather tomorrow. There's a lot waiting for you, I'm afraid."

"You've found a house?"

"Aye," Orm said slowly, "but ye must know we have been here only a day ourselves. I am afraid it is . . ."

"What's the matter?" Thorkell asked, his voice hard. "Surely you've been able to find something suitable."

"Oh, yes, it's a fine house, no doubt of that. Very large and directly across the square from the Church of All Saints. Newly built by a Norman friend of Emma who was queen, even has Norman fire pits built into stone walls at the ends of the hall."

"Well then, man, what's the matter with it? Come on. I don't have all day."

"It was stripped, Thorkell, when they went back to Normandy. There is nothing in it, and it seems the villagers have been using it as a barn for their animals."

"Well, get it cleaned out. The Lady Branwen can see that the proper furnishing is obtained. Detail some men to give her a hand."

Thorkell turned back to Branwen who sat silently astride Beornwig, the chestnut stallion she rode. "You don't mind, do you? What you can't find among the tradesmen here we can order in London."

"As you wish, my lord," she said respectfully, for Orm's benefit. Thorkell's laughter welled up in her heart although his face remained stern.

A little while later, she pushed open the heavy iron-bound front door of the great hall. She wrapped her cloak more closely around her for inside was the damp cold of a room which had not been heated for many months. It certainly does smell like a barn, she thought, frowning.

Then, turning toward the men who had been detailed to help her, she asked the youngest, "What's your name?"

"Trygg, my lady," he said unhappily. Cleaning house all day was going to cause a lot of laughter at his expense in the camp that evening.

"Well, Trygg, you can get the fires started. See if there is any wood in the courtyard. Then find a woodman and tell him the Lord Thorkell will have two weeks' supply of wood neatly stacked by sundown. Head up, boy, you have orders from the Jarl of East Anglia. He will be quick to anger if these people cross him."

"Yes, my lady," the boy said with a grin. He bowed awkwardly and ducked around the side of the building where an alley led to the courtyard behind the hall.

She turned to the two men who stood waiting. "They call you Aki, don't they?" she asked with a warm smile.

The man nodded.

"You and your friend . . ."

"Grim, Lady Branwen."

"You and Grim make the round of the inns. Tell anyone who is looking for work to come and see me. I will have need of every guild in town if the hall is as bare as they say it is. And mind you come back sober." She laughed. Turning back to the chill dark doorway open in front of her she said, "Come on, Budda, let's see what we can do."

A richly paneled hallway ran through the house from front to back, dark and narrowed toward the rear by a staircase descending from the upper floor. Just to the right of the patch of sunlight which shone through the open front door, there was another heavily banded oak door. Branwen pushed it open. Inside was a small square room with a fireplace along the outer wall. Branwen smiled, remembering the only other fireplace she had ever seen, at Winfrith's manor along the Severn. Why, she wondered, were there so few island-born who could work with stone? Surely these Norman fireplaces were better than the smoky central hearths which were found in every timber and thatch hall, whether great or small.

Dimly, for the room was windowless, she saw that heavy cabinet doors lined one wall. This was the treasure room where the household valuables could be locked.

She went back out into the hallway where Budda was waiting for her. Together they picked their way carefully through piles of refuse and animal droppings. In the great hall, glassed windows let in the light high overhead, shining between oaken timber supports and cross beams. Lower, along the street, the windows were still shuttered and dark. A second fireplace gaped blackly from the other end of the room but here a central fire pit had been set into the stone floor as well, for the room was very large. It will hold two hundred men, she thought and, in her mind's eye, the room was filled with the sight and sound of men at table devouring hind and hog, their hairy chins running with grease; overturned goblets were dripping sticky mead onto the floor where the dogs snarled and growled over the bones. She sighed and then, squaring her shoulders resolutely, turned to Budda and said, "What we need is a broom. We can sweep all these broken reeds into the fire pit and get some good out of them while we wait for Trygg. Go and see what you can find."

"Oh no, my lady, I can't."

"Don't be silly, girl. There is no one here to harm you. Go on now." Branwen put her hands on her hips and looked at the frightened woman who had never been beyond the fields of her small village. "Go on," she repeated.

"Yes, my lady," Budda said reluctantly.

Branwen stood in the room, looking at the dirty walls, sadly in need of whitewash, the empty tapestry hooks, the broken, dried and filthy reeds which littered the floor. There were no benches along the walls. There were no tables, no sideboards for serving. And what of the cookhouse, she wondered? Probably not even a pot. She knew that Thorkell would want the hall filled with his men of an evening, eating and drinking. She wondered if he would settle for one night in a tavern anyway. Perhaps by tomorrow if . . . and she began to plan how the work must be done.

Just then Budda returned, her lip trembling. "There's wagons in the courtyard, lady, and Vikings, too," she said.

"Where? Show me."

"This way, my lady," Budda said, leading her through a cloister which ran along the edge of the courtyard.

There were indeed six Vikings in full armor leaning against two heavily loaded wagons. Their battle axes gleamed in the sunlight. Branwen stepped into the courtyard and the men were instantly on their feet, watching her as she walked across to them.

"What's this?" she asked.

"Lord Thorkell's treasure wagons, Lady Branwen," one of the men answered.

She regarded him closely but could not remember his face. "You know me?" she asked.

"Aye, my lady. We've seen you many times. We were Hemming's house carles before he was killed. We serve his brother now."

"Do you know what's in these wagons?" she asked, for they were covered.

"Aye, some. There's locked chests we've not seen opened, but the rest we know."

"I don't suppose there is a broom?" she said.

"A broom?" The thegn exploded with laughter. "No, my lady, I'm afraid not."

"Very well then, a candle or two?"

"A candle or two, perhaps. Shall we go through the wagons now?"

"Look," she said, "there is a treasure room near the front door. It is dark inside. I want the room lit with candles. I want the floor swept out and a fire blazing in the fireplace. Then I want these wagons unpacked, and Lord Thorkell's treasure stowed safely away in that room. Will you and your men see to it?"

"Yes, my lady. But there's precious little firewood."

"With luck there will be more soon. In the meantime there is enough litter on the floor to burn for a while. I would like that one room habitable so that, when my lord arrives, he can at least warm himself."

"Yes, my lady."

"Oh, and tell me. The kitchen, is it bad?"

"Yes, my lady," he said, trying to be grave. He pointed at the sturdy thatched building on one side of the courtyard.

She walked slowly across the frozen cobbles and went into the cookhouse.

"Oh," she groaned as her eyes swept the empty room. "Not even a pot hook left. There will be only simple meals served from this room for weeks. I hope the smithy is well stocked. We'll need pots and cauldrons, ladles and skimmers, and God knows what else."

Only a light patch remained on the wall to show where the spice cabinet had once hung. A new one would have to be built. A mortar and pestle would have to be found to prepare spices for cooking. The water barrel which had held live fish was split and useless and probably could not even be replaced until the sap began to flow in the spring. But the ovens were thickly walled, and their doors still hung squarely on their heavy hinges.

Turning back into the yard, she met Trygg, who had returned with a wagonload of logs. A woodman had begun to stack them neatly against one end of the cloister. "Good work, Trygg," she said. Picking up two logs she balanced them on her outstretched arms while the young Viking stacked three more small ones on top, laughter playing around the corners of his mouth, for they both knew it was not fitting for her to carry wood.

"I found one, Lady Branwen," Budda called excitedly as she reappeared out of the darkness of the stables. "'Tis not a very proper broom but 'twill work well enough, I warrant."

So among them the treasury was swept clean. A brightly enameled candle rack, wheel-shaped, was unpacked from the treasure wagons and hung on a chain from a dark beam spanning the ceiling overhead. Gleaming white beeswax candles were wedged into its cups and lit. The warmth from the fire had begun to drive back the damp chill when a small, richly carved oak table and two chairs, like gracefully curved x's, cushioned with crimson velvet, were brought in from the wagons and set against one wall. In the midst of confusion, a small glow of order began to grow.

Trygg brought dinner for them all early in the afternoon, hurrying across the wide square from a nearby alehouse, carrying a basket covered with a linen napkin. There was pork pie, seasoned with saffron and cinnamon and smelling of currants and finely crushed cubebs; there were trencher loaves to scoop up the juicy goodness of the pie; and a heavy jug of ale to wash it all down.

Tradesmen began to arrive, pushing and shoving, eager to supply what needs and wants the Jarl of East Anglia could be expected to have when faced with an empty house. In a neat hand, her letters small and close, Branwen kept an account of the flours ordered from the miller, wheat and rye, whole grain as well as the fine white flours for the wastrel loaves; she wrote down on a sheet of parchment long lists of herbs and spices ordered from the apothecary as well as the pepper from the pepper trader. There were carpenters who went to work building benches and trestle tables for the great hall. There were butchers and an alewife anxious to fill her orders. And in among the tradespeople were women looking for work in the household. The first half dozen she took on for the remainder of the day, giving them directions to see that all was swept and dusted and fires lit to drive out the cold.

It was not until much later, when the winter sun was setting and her head was swimming with the sea of new faces, that she looked up into eyes folded closely between the wrinkles of a round face. A pressed apron spanned the wide comfortable girth of an ageless woman who stood in front of her.

"Praise to the Mothers, you've come at last," Branwen said.

"Beg pardon, lady?"

"I thought no one would ever come to take charge in the cookhouse. But, you've come after the job, haven't you?"

"Yes, my lady, if you'll have me."

"It's bare, you know. They've taken everything away. You'll have to make do with what you can bring with you, until we can get new from the tradesmen."

"Supper will take a bit of doing then, my lady. I will need time to get my things together."

"Supper." Branwen laughed. "I had little hope for dinner tomorrow."

"Ach, dinner will be no trouble, my lady. I'll see the ovens fired tonight so they'll be good and hot in the morning when the dough has risen. And then, if you've no mind for anything fancy, we can make do, no doubt. There's a woman I know, snares rabbits, and very nice ones, too; perhaps a pot of stew would be best," she said thoughtfully, "with some turnips.

They're right sweet now, having been touched with frost, you know."

"That would be fine. Can you fix enough for twenty? There will be more, I know, when we've got things properly set up, but tomorrow I'll ask my husband to keep it simple."

My husband, she thought, tasting the newness of the word in her mouth: If I am his wife then he must be my husband. What has changed that I am no longer Branwen, but Thorkell's wife, and he not Thorkell but my husband?

"When we've found more help and stocked the kitchen then he can fill his hall," Branwen said, hardly hearing her own words, thinking about the strangeness of things which changed even when they seemed to stay the same.

"I'll ask about the kitchen help, myself, if ye've no mind," the woman said, bringing Branwen back to the problems at hand.

"Good." Branwen nodded. "There are so many things to do," she said, suddenly tired. "I don't even know your name."

"I'm called Bridey, my lady," the woman said. After a moment she added hesitantly, "My husband, Jack, he'll be needed here, too, I think."

"Yes, there will be more than enough for Jack, too," Branwen said.

Why was this woman here, looking for work? she wondered. She wasn't like ordinary serving women. She seemed strong and capable, as if she could easily take charge of a household, knowing what must be done without needing to be told.

Not until several days later, when they had grown more comfortable with each other, did Branwen ask her about herself.

And then Bridey explained, "We had a bit of land, Lady Branwen," she said, looking down at her hands buried in the dough she was mixing. "It was a right good piece, rich bottom land, you know, and we done well at it; but then just this last year we had to borrow against it, seeing's how we had two sons who would go off after Edmund Ironside when he came through here on his way to war. We had to borrow to see the boys horsed and armed. Didn't do no good though. Might as well have sent them off on foot."

"Both killed?" Branwen asked, her voice hushed.

"Aye, my lady," she said.

"At Ashington?" she asked, feeling her heart sink.

"Oh no, they were killed long before that. Not much for fighting, I guess," she said, wiping her eyes with the corner of her white apron. "They was killed taking a bridge outside of London, they was, both together."

"Brentwood," Branwen whispered, seeing the channels under the bridge clogged with bodies.

"Aye, Brentwood, that were it. Do you know the place?"

"I was with Edmund at Brentwood," Branwen said. "He had just learned he had a second son. Edward, they had named him. Leofric told us." She paused, remembering. After a while she said, "The Danes fought hard that day. There were many who fought bravely to take that bridge. There were many who died on both sides before Edmund forced the crossing."

Bridey finished mixing the dough, turning it out to rest before kneading it. After a while she said, "There was no way to pay back the money we borrowed and so the farm was taken. But it ain't no concern of yours," she added brightly, "and we'll work hard. You won't be sorry."

"No, Bridey, I daresay we won't," Branwen replied.

But on the first day in Maldon she did not ask. Instead, she showed the woman the way to the cookhouse through the hallway which was bare and clean now, still cold but lit by candles in silver sconces along the wall.

Beyond the hall was the cloister itself. Running the whole length of the south side of the house, it was separated from the cobbles of the courtyard by a ribbon of garden broken up into tiny patches which could only mean that herbs would spring up there with the coming of warmer weather. The thorny canes of last year's roses still clung to the slender arches. The round shape of a chaffinch nest, once hidden by leaves, was bared and empty now. Underfoot, blue and white tiles lay half buried in windblown leaves. Here, in this place, women could sit to sew and weave, protected from the wind and weather. This was where an infant might take his first steps, chasing the butterflies which would come to the roses.

Leaving Bridey in the cookhouse, Branwen went back into the main hall and climbed the stairs to the second floor. At the top, in a room over the treasury, three women were gossiping, perched like hens on low carved chests which stood in the middle of the debris. Branwen stood in the doorway watching, as the women started guiltily, and began to sweep the broken reeds into the fireplace. The dark oak chests, with deeply cut ribbons incised in tight curvilinear patterns over every surface, were locked with heavy brass padlocks. She wondered what was in them. The treasure was to have been put away behind the heavy doors downstairs. Why had these chests been left here?

"You," she said sharply to one of the women, "go down and see that a load of logs is brought up here straight away." She and Thorkell would sleep here tonight if they could drive the chill from the room in time. There was no bed but there was plenty of straw in the stable, she knew that. She would have it piled in the corner; the great lord and his wife would sleep on the straw like any peasant this night; better than enduring the fleas which infested every inn. Finally, impatient with the work the women were doing even as she watched, Branwen said, "Here, give me the broom. You two, go down to the barns and bring up some clean straw so that we can make a bed here in the corner."

"Oh no, my lady," they started to say, but Branwen turned the intensity of her black eyes upon them and the power of her will blazed forth angrily. The women did as they were bidden.

Not until after they were gone did she realize what she had done. The power to bend another's will was one she had thought to deny, like the others which rose up in her from the old magic. I will deny it, she vowed silently. I won't use it again. It's just that I was tired. It's been a long day. She picked up the broom and began to sweep the wide oak boards. She was lighting the dried reeds with a spark from her tinderbox when Trygg arrived with a towering armload of firewood. He set the logs down with a great clattering and started to stack them alongside the hearth. Branwen swept up the woodchips which had fallen from his arms.

"Beg pardon, my lady, but it won't do for you to be sweeping like that."

"Beg pardon, Trygg," she said, mocking him gently, "but it won't do for the fleas in this litter to wake up hungry in the warmth of the firelight. I don't want to lie awake all night being bitten."

"You're not going to sleep here?"

"And why not?"

"There's no bed. Are you going to sleep on the bare floor?"

"I've sent two women to the barn to fetch clean straw."

"There's feather ticking in the bottom of the wagons, and down coverlets besides," he said sheepishly. "Shall I bring them up?"

Branwen stopped sweeping and looked at him. "Of course," she said. "Were you going to leave them out in the yard all night? And suppose you tell me why these chests are up here and not down in the armory where they belong?"

"Those are the chests Lord Thorkell ordered packed for you," he said respectfully. "Shall I take them downstairs?"

"No, Trygg, leave them here," she said wearily. There would be food tomorrow. There was a place to sleep tonight. A certain amount of order was being wrung out of the chaos of a few hours ago. She sat down heavily on one of the chests while Trygg laid three logs on the kindling which was burning hotly. He left the room. She was hardly aware that thegns helped two frightened women pile straw in one corner of the room, topping it luxuriously with feather ticking and warm down coverlets sewn in fine, closely woven blue linen. The fire grew bright and spread its warmth and light into the corners of the room. She roused herself with an effort and went out, shutting the door behind her to keep in the heat.

Thorkell had just come in downstairs and with him were the men-at-arms who would serve as his house carles. And among them this first night Branwen saw two Viking chieftains she knew well, Ulf who was married to Knut's younger sister Estrid, and his brother Eilaf.

"My lord," she said courteously, "I didn't know you were in Maldon."

"We're on our way to Thetford," Ulf said. "We hoped to catch Thorkell here first."

"I hope we are not intruding this evening, Lady Branwen," Eilaf said with a small bow.

"Not at all." She smiled. "Come in, come in. Where is the Lady Estrid and your little boy, Lord Ulf? Are they in Maldon, too?"

"No," Ulf answered, "Estrid is staying with Knut until spring when a house will be ready for her at Thetford."

The empty hallway rang with the clank of armor until the men spilled into the great barren hall beyond. There were pegs

Branwen had not noticed along the wall between the window shutters. On these pegs the Vikings hung their shields and helmets, their battle axes and swords. The room was still too cold to hang up their softly hued woolen capes. The men stood around the fires, rubbing their hands and laughing over some incident which had occurred on their way in.

"Have you unpacked the carts in the yard yet, Branwen?" Thorkell asked.

She looked up at him, annoyed, for he might have found a warmer greeting. "Yes, my lord," she said. "The chests have been put in the treasury behind you."

"Good," he said, "come with me. We have to get out some cups."

But he stopped when he went into the small room for it was warm and already bore the mark of a woman's caring hand. She knew in her heart that he was glad. He took a ring of keys from under his long cloak and knelt to open the chests which stood against the wall. Branwen watched. In one were silver goblets and bowls crusted with amber and amethyst, banded with intricately worked gold ribbons in patterns similar to the carvings on the outside of the chests.

"Here, this one will do," he said. He closed the lid and effortlessly picked up the box which she had seen two men bend under earlier in the day.

"Come along, Bran. You will pass around the mead cups in my hall this night."

"Yes, my lord," she said, dropping a curtsy behind his back.

They had brought a barrel of mead back with them, and she dipped from it, filling the graceful silver pitcher Budda had polished earlier with warm, new wood ash. Passing among the men, she filled their cups, greeting each in turn. Some returned her smile with a word but many looked at her with eyes that were cold and wary. Those were the men who had been at Ashington. Last of all, she filled a small goblet for herself with the heady drink, and took her place beside her lord. There was a quiet in the conversation as if suddenly everyone realized that the hall was bare. There was no food, not even a bench to sit on.

"A toast, Thorkell," Ulf said then, his voice ringing clearly through the room. "To the new Jarl of East Anglia and the brave and loyal men who follow him. May tonight mark the

beginning,'' he said with a grin, "but tomorrow bring us
benches and the pleasures of a bustling cookhouse.''

"Hear, hear,'' Thorkell shouted amidst the laughter and the
clank of cups.

"Will you sing for us, Branwen?'' Eilaf said quietly. "I
remember hearing you sing once when we were all your guests
in Wessex.''

"That was a long time ago, my lord,'' she said, "and
tonight I have no instrument to play to keep the tune.''

"Well then, perhaps we can repair your lack, lady,'' Thorkell said. Turning to Trygg, who stood unremarked in the
background, he handed him a small ring of keys and the boy
disappeared.

One of the carles brought in the small backless seat from the
treasury and Branwen sat down. Thorkell grinned; folding his
long legs under him, he sat at her feet. The others, too, settled
down upon the floor, sitting cross-legged around the central
hearth as if it were a campfire. Branwen looked around from
face to face, suddenly realizing how they missed Hemming this
evening. The awkwardness among them would never have
withstood the great booming good nature of Thorkell's dead
brother.

When Trygg returned with a lovely dark dulcimer, inlaid
with tiny bits of white ivory, she tuned the strings softly, her
eyes downcast. The room was very quiet and she began to
sing. Her voice was low and the key was minor as she sang
first for those who were no longer with them. After a little
while the threnody changed; the key rose a half step becoming
major, martial, the song of fighting men who still lived. The
mead worked through them, warming them. One by one the
men began to sing with her; only the chorus at first but soon
the verse as well. Then they were asking her to play others,
and some she knew and some she did not.

Thorkell himself passed the pitcher among them so that the
magic of her singing might not be broken. And it was magic,
although those present that night would not have believed that
it was more than just the mead and the joy of good friends
singing around a fire together. But Branwen knew, and Thorkell knew as well, the men who had come in fearing the Angel
of Death, the Lady of the Ravens, would leave fearing her no
longer. But it was only their fear she took from them that night;
though she might have done more, she would not. Only what

was fair would she impose on them. They feared her because of her magic; and so, through that magic, she would take away that fear. That and no more. Whatever else they might feel toward her, she would allow to happen as with any woman. And it did not seem to her that she was breaking any vow and perhaps she was not, although the line was very thinly drawn.

Late in the night, after Branwen had passed around the mead cup to each of the men who had been their guests, Eilaf turned in the doorway and said, "Will this be our only taste of battle now, Thorkell? Singing old songs?"

"Are you afraid your sword will grow rusty?"

"Aye, and my belly fat and my arm soft."

"So plow the land! That will keep you hard."

"That's what Ulf tells me," Eilaf said shaking his head, "but it isn't for me. I miss the song of the sword."

Laughing, Thorkell clapped him on the back. "It's only three months since Ashington. Even you can't hope to fight all the time."

"Perhaps not," Eilaf said. "Still . . ."

"Ulf's asleep on his feet," Thorkell said gently. "Take him across to the inn; put him to bed. We'll talk more of this in the morning."

Branwen and Thorkell stood in the doorway watching them make their way unsteadily across the square to the inn where they would sleep until such time as Thorkell's hall offered more than bare floors. When the square was empty again, Thorkell shut the heavy door, sliding the bolt across with a thud.

"Now, wife," he said. Picking her up in his arms like a child, he carried her up the stairs to the great mound of hay and down where the fire had been built up by some unknown hand.

"Where is your serving girl?" he asked.

"I have sent her off to help the woman I hired to cook for us, my lord."

"Then perhaps it were well that I help you with those pins," he said. "It isn't right that you should have to do them for yourself."

But her clothes were simple and easily undone. Long they loved and well that night, for there is a flame which brightens when a commitment has been made. Here, in the shell of a great house, in a town where they were strangers, they felt they were truly wed and would not part again. Like a warm day in

February when it seems impossible the snow can fall again, so did they think of all the nights ahead when each would be there to warm the other.

She woke early in the morning, but Thorkell was up before her. Dressed in his narrow court trousers, he seemed even taller and harder than he did in his loose-fitting riding clothes. The muscles of his legs were corded through the tight fabric and the knots of his shoulders strained against the fine blue wool of his tunic. She lay quietly, watching him as he looked out the window, deep in thought. After a while she called softly to him, "Good morrow, my love."

He turned to her and said, "So you're finally awake."

She laughed. "If I'm too tired to rise eagerly from my bed this morning, it is only you yourself who must take the blame."

And the fierce Viking laughed too, real laughter that sprang from a well of happiness deep within him. "Not all the blame, my little one," he said, "not all the blame. But here, perhaps this will make it worth getting up." He reached into one of the chests which had stood locked the day before. "Every time I see you," he said, "you are in rags. This last time was not so bad, but only I think because Penardim left things for you. But now that you're the wife of the Jarl of East Anglia, you must have rich clothes like other men's wives. Here, try this, and this, and this, too." Reaching into the chests, he tossed garments at her.

"Oh, Thorkell," she said, delighted, for there were soft white woolen stockings and fine-woven creamy petticoats. There was a beautiful, silky, wide-sleeved undertunic made of the softest rose, embroidered around the collar; and an over-dress of deep, dark burgundy, full-pleated front and back, so that the warmth of its heavy folds would keep away the chill winter drafts.

"But no cap, my love," he said tenderly, reaching out to run his callused hands gently over her long dark hair, tangled with sleep and loving. "No cap."

She took his hand in her own and kissed the rough palm. "Thank you, Thorkell," she said.

"There is more," he said, dropping the keys into her lap. "And what is lacking you must have made. Whatever you desire."

"And when we get to London I will really be the great Lord Thorkell's wife. I won't shame you," she added.

He frowned. "You have never shamed me; even in rags you are beautiful. Even in the black wool you begged from Father Anselm one Christmas, do you remember, when you came to Salisbury, you were wonderful."

"You sound like a boy with his first love," she said, smiling at him.

He might have answered her but there was a knock at the door. Pulling the blankets around her shoulders she said, "Come in."

Budda pushed open the door. "I have hot water and a basin, my lady, so you can wash."

"Hot water? How wonderful. Wherever did you find a kettle, Budda?"

"'Twas Bridey, my lady. She and Jack was up all night moving their things into the cookhouse. They even had some flour sacks and there's dough risin' now in proper wooden tubs set near the fire. She's gone to market already to see the pots filled for dinner."

"Will you be back for dinner, Thorkell?"

"Aye, if you can manage a table and some benches by then."

"I think we can," she said, "but I told Bridey only twenty, for we have found no one to help her yet. On the Feast of the Virgin," she added suddenly, "then we shall have the sokemen and whomever you like. Then we shall have a feast worthy of their new jarl."

"Good," he said, "for then we must leave for London."

Chapter Four

The picked fighting men of Thorkell's flagship, the *Raven's Wing,* delivered the widow of Edmund Ironside and her infant sons safely on the continent, and turned back toward the island to rejoin their commander. The Channel, roughened by winter storms, was a crossing not normally attempted; the heavy seas were capable of breaking apart the trading vessels of the eleventh century, which were descendants of the Roman trireme, and stiff and unyielding. But the *Raven's Wing* was different. The keel, made from a single piece of wood, was a supple backbone which, when tied into the solid blocks of stem and stern posts, was capable of resisting the pressure of a pounding sea. The hull of the *Raven's Wing* was sheathed with eighteen rows of planking, overlapping and caulked with tarred rope. The planks, nailed together, were lashed to the ribs with ropes, giving the craft great flexibility, and allowing it to move through the rough sea without fear of cracking. This elasticity had made the first crossing very difficult for Edmund's widow, unused to the sea; but it gave Ragnar quiet, real pleasure as he stood in the bow, his feet wide spread, feeling the ship alive under him, watching the estuary of the Thames open up on the horizon ahead of him.

He was young to have command of the flagship, not yet twenty; and he knew that it was not his skill which had won the honor for him. Service on a Viking flagship was an honor which was given for bravery or sometimes birth, if it seemed the breeding had run true—hero begetting hero. Well-born of a brave Viking carle, Ragnar had been a strong boy who learned quickly and fought well whenever challenged. He had come young to the *Raven's Wing* as an oarsman—one of thirty-six free men who rowed freely when the wind was too light or coming from the wrong quarter. Short and powerfully built, he was fair and bearded—to hide his youth, and make him look more the way a commander of a flagship should look.

He had fought bravely at Ashington. When the fighting there ended, he had been so exhausted he had not cared how much of the blood which soaked his clothing was his own. Not until the next day when he had a chance to bathe in the sluggish river which ran through the plain did he learn to his amazement that he was unmarked—sore and bone weary, but unmarked. Of the thirty-six oarsmen who went into that battle, only four survived and two were grievously wounded. The third was an old man, the ship's bone-setter, who had worked behind the lines among the dead and dying. So that December, when Ragnar stood steady on the living deck of the *Raven's Wing,* his pale eyes were clear and there was no pride in him—just grim determination that Thorkell the Tall would never regret having given the command to him.

On their return from Normandy, they moored their ship in the Thames, among the winter-still quays of London, and rode overland to Maldon.

If he was surprised to see Branwen playing lady to Thorkell's lord, Ragnar said nothing. Of all the Vikings in Maldon that year, he was the only one left who had been with Thorkell six years earlier when they had first met Branwen at Thornbury. Only he and Thorkell knew how she had come to be called the Lady of the Ravens. Where other men had heard rumors to be believed or not as they pleased, Ragnar knew the truth. She was not like other women. Watching her, on those cold winter evenings, pouring the mead in Thorkell's great hall, he felt a chill of foreboding—as if something evil rejoiced in her foolish pretense.

He was glad when they rode out from the city at last and turned toward London. He watched the raven banner catch in the winter wind and unfurl above her head as she rode at the head of the column beside the Jarl.

Her dark hair blew as the wind teased it out from under the deep, fur-lined hood of her winter cloak. Once she turned and looked back at the city she was leaving, her gaze lingering fondly on the gentle hill which rose above the river.

Four heavily laden treasure wagons banged and creaked along the frozen ruts. Budda sat in the first, bundled up against the cold, her harelip hidden under a scarf. She had changed in the last weeks—not as shy now, still not worldly, not bold, like city-bred serving girls, but not as frightened as she had been. Her eyes sparkled with excitement and her cheeks and nose were rosy with the cold.

They rode west out of Maldon. Avoiding the south road which ran through the plain of Ashington, they climbed into the hills before turning south toward London. Early in the day they came to Chelmsford where they stopped at an inn for dinner. Branwen sat quietly by the fireside in the common room of the inn, watching hungry men cut their meal from the side of a spitted deer turning over the fire. There was mulled wine to keep them warm as they rode through the December chill that afternoon. Young Trygg, who had grown accustomed to looking after her needs, kept her cup filled and saw to it that the best cuts were given to her. The men who rode in the company treated her with a new warmth and respect which was not altogether due to her position. They were beginning to doubt the stories they had heard told about her, allowing themselves to be reassured by the warmth and hospitality she had lavished upon them.

Several hours beyond Chelmsford they came to a walled and moated manor called Noak Hill. Here Byrtric, Ealdorman of Essex, held a great estate. For many years he had been a powerful nobleman in the court of Ethelred, and only grudgingly had given his support to Edmund Ironside after the Un-raed died. Thorkell made for Noak Hill to accept the thegn's obeisance, but whether it would be easily given remained to be seen. Sixty men-at-arms were a force to be reckoned with, but the storming of a well-fortified hill position would not be easy. They drew rein out of bowshot of the manor walls late in the afternoon. The gates were closed.

"Ragnar," Thorkell called, turning in the saddle, "take the standard bearer and tell them the Jarl of East Anglia desires the hospitality of Noak Hill for the night."

"Aye, Thorkell," Ragnar said, waving the standard bearer forward.

They were not gone long.

"The ealdorman has not yet returned from war, although he is expected any day," he reported. "The lady will admit no one while he is away."

Thorkell laughed. "No one? Orm, move the column up."

When the men were deployed in obvious readiness to storm the walls, Thorkell said, "Ragnar, ride up and tell them again that the Jarl of East Anglia desires the hospitality of Noak Hill this night."

Branwen, feeling the ice of battle readiness closing around her as Thorkell prepared to fight, moved back, away from his side and as she did a sinking feeling began in the pit of her stomach. What will they do, she wondered, when they realize they cannot fight? Every man here was at Ashington. They have all come under the interdict of the Goddess and none of them will lift a weapon in war again. She watched anxiously as Ragnar returned once more from the manor walls.

There was an audible creaking and the gates began to swing open.

Suddenly, she thought, what if it's a trap? Once inside the walls they'll be defenseless. They can be cut down like so many sheep.

She spoke softly to Beornwig and the small stallion she rode moved quietly along the column toward the now gaping gate. She went in just ahead of Thorkell and, if no one noticed, it was because she saw to it that they did not.

The courtyard was empty, but more than empty. There was no sign of anyone, save for the thin wisp of smoke rising from the manor hall roof. The outbuildings, though thick thatched and apparently well cared for, were cold and dark and very still. Dead leaves blew in eddies over the cobblestones.

"Where is everyone?" she asked.

"It looks deserted right enough," Orm said.

The column had filled up the courtyard and no one noticed that Branwen was suddenly there among them.

"There's smoke coming from the hall though. There must be someone there," Trygg said nervously. He was young and liked his enemies out in the open.

"Ragnar, take your men, search all the buildings. I want no surprises behind me," Thorkell said. "Orm, let's go."

Branwen followed them up the low steps to the door of the manor hall. Thorkell turned to say something to her but, seeing the determination flash in her eyes, he laughed and pushed open the heavy oak doors.

Inside they were struck with the smell of decay. Great pools of tallow lay under candleholders uncleaned for weeks. There was a sour stench of vomit and the thin wail of children. A dark, heavy-browed man cowered in the corner as they came in. There was a rasp of drawn steel as Orm moved quickly, stepping past Thorkell. Terror filled the man's eyes and a dark stain spread over the front of his trousers.

"On your knees, cur," Orm growled in disgust. "Where is your mistress?"

"There, sirs," he whimpered, pointing toward the arched opening to the main room where shadows flickered against the wall.

"Get him out of here," Thorkell said, going past into the firelight.

A young woman stood alone near the fire. She was pale, her cheeks were sunken, her light hair hung in filthy strands from under her cap. Her stained apron bulged over her stomach for she was with child. She looked at them, her eyes darting from one to the other while her fingers, thin bones covered with almost translucent flesh, fluttered nervously about her face. She did not speak.

"Are you mistress here?" Thorkell asked. His voice boomed in the cavernous room and the strange woman looked around wildly at the sound.

Branwen laid a hand on his arm. "She's starving, Thorkell," she said. "I wonder how long since she has eaten. Let me talk to her."

Thorkell nodded, relieved.

Branwen went closer to the woman. She held out her hands, palms up. "I am Branwen," she said.

Then, like a wind rattling the thatch, the woman muttered, "My name is Godgifu." After a pause, she added, "Welcome to Noak Hill." She began to laugh.

"Hush," Branwen said, touching her. "There is sickness here. I am a healer. Will you let me help?"

"The children," Godgifu said, avoiding Branwen's eyes, "the children are crying."

Branwen and Budda went through a curtain and the sound of a child wailing grew louder. In the sleeping room the stench was overpowering. Branwen staggered as from a blow.

"Where are the servants?" she asked no one.

"Not here," Budda said, shaking her head.

"Who has cared for you and the children?" Branwen asked Godgifu who had followed them into the room. "The man who met us in the hall?"

Godgifu looked around wildly, her bony fingers raised up over her head as if to ward off a blow.

"How long have the children been sick?" Budda asked, standing beside the bed. The sheet was stained, filthy.

"Sick?" Godgifu asked vacantly.

"Budda, we'll need the kettle filled. Ask Trygg to bring in the small chest of herbs from the wagon. Thorkell?" Branwen called.

"I am here."

"These people need food. Will you send one of the men to find some? How has this happened?"

"Branwen," Thorkell said steadily, "we are leaving in the morning."

"We cannot leave them like this, Thorkell. They will die."

"The world is full of people dying. You can't save them all."

"Because I cannot help them all, shall I help none?" she asked gently.

He stared down at her without speaking for a moment and then he said, "I will see what I can find."

When he returned there was an old woman with him. She was carrying a large iron kettle which was covered with a lid. She was crying.

Branwen looked at the old woman's tears and said, "What has happened here?"

"Oh, my poor baby," the old woman wailed, "and her so young to be having bairns of her own."

"What has happened?" Branwen repeated. "Why didn't you help her?"

"'Twas him, the steward, my lady. Killed little Dyka, he did. Just cut her down as she went to the well. Laughing, too, he was. We couldn't stay then, could we? Oh, my poor babies. Will they die?"

"No," Branwen said wearily, "they will be all right, I think, but you must not leave her again. She cannot do for herself."

"But when you leave, he will return and kill us all, my

lady,'' the old woman said, and the fear in her voice was unfeigned.

"How do you know the steward killed this 'Dyka' as you say?" Thorkell's voice was hard as he spoke from the door.

"Oh, we saw him, my lord. We all saw him; just cut her, he did, as she was going to the well. Used the butchering knife, he did."

Thorkell turned and was gone. Outside the curtain, Branwen heard him say to the men who waited in the hall, "Find him. Bring him to me."

They did what could be done that night. The soup in the iron pot was thick and rich. Branwen warned that the children and their mother should receive only a little each time they woke. She went out into the cold hall to find Thorkell. He was not there. She started to the door, but was stopped by a long scream from the courtyard. They had found the steward. She turned back toward the fire for she had no wish to witness Viking justice meted out in the frozen courtyard. Someone had heaped the logs high in the fire pit. Perhaps it would drive out the cold in the room after all. Idly she went to the sideboard, hoping there might be wine to offer Thorkell when he came in. There was none.

They slept that night on the benches in the great hall at Noak Hill. It was not the hospitality they had looked for when they drew up outside the walls that afternoon.

Dawn had just begun to lighten the eastern sky when she woke. The children were crying softly. She got up, wincing as her feet touched the cold floor. Slipping on her boots, she drew the folds of her thick woolen tunic over her head. She stood a moment looking down at where the man still slept. His soft brown hair had fallen across his face, his head was cradled on one arm. I will miss you, my love, she thought. You should have wed a better wife. She slipped silently past him into the dim light of the other room.

Both of the children were crying, hardly awake, burning with fever. Godgifu lay in the other bed, her eyes open, staring, her hands twisting around each other. There was a hopelessness about her that rocked Branwen. The fever which gripped the two small children was an illness she could deal with. There were strong brews which could be made from the soft, pungent leaves of meadowsweet purchased one afternoon in Maldon, and wormwood from Cynewithe, dried on the old racks she had found there. But the madness which seemed to eat at the frail woman's heart was beyond her reach; yet if it were not healed, it would be more dangerous than any fever.

"Get up, Godgifu," Branwen said gently, "the children need you."

Obediently the other sat up. While Branwen helped her dress, pulling long woolen stockings over her fleshless legs, Godgifu's busy fingers were turning in her hair as if she would arrange the filthy strands into curls.

Branwen poured boiling water from the copper kettle on the fire over the crushed herbs, stirring them around, watching the infusion darken.

"You must give this to the child," Branwen said, handing one wooden bowl to Godgifu, "a spoonful at a time."

While Godgifu spooned the bitter brew into one son's tiny mouth, Branwen sat across the bed tending the older boy. Between spoonfuls, she looked across at Godgifu, dismayed, for she saw no flicker of emotion, no sign of tenderness or concern on her face.

"They will get better," Branwen said. "They are young and the fever will go out of them."

As if she had not heard, Godgifu began to hum softly to herself.

When Thorkell woke, he saw that Branwen was gone. Finding her with the children, he said quietly, "Come, Branwen, it's time to go."

"I will stay," she said, looking up at him, knowing how she hurt him.

He looked down at her and felt the sad hardness of her heart. He saw that she did what she must do but his anger welled in him, unbidden and unreasoned. She waited for a sign, anything; but he said nothing. After a moment he turned and went out of the room.

A cold grey rain fell steadily all morning. Budda found fresh linen, and together she and Branwen saw the room clean and the children washed and put back in bed. While they worked Godgifu seemed hardly aware of their presence, humming to herself. Her hands seemed to have a life of their own, never still, always moving over her face and hair, or twisting together as if talking to themselves.

Towards noon Branwen heard men's voices in the hall. Curious, she went out. There were Vikings standing around the fire, their cloaks dripping as they warmed themselves.

"Ragnar," she said, "I thought you had gone."

"No, Branwen," he said gravely. "Thorkell told us to stay and see that no harm came to you." It was better this way, he thought. Look at her. She even looks different, whole again! Not that I begrudge Thorkell's right to sleep with her; not that, but he has no right to ask her to be less than she is. Oh yes, it's better like this. "We brought a hind," he said out loud. "There's a joint hanging in the cookhouse. And thick coney stew by the smell of it."

"Now tell me that you've found a cellar stocked with Norman wines and we shall be well fed indeed," Branwen said with a lightness she didn't feel.

"Like this, my lady?" Trygg asked with a grin, holding up a carafe of thick glass glowing dull red in the firelight.

"Oh, Trygg," she said, turning away so that he could not see the tears stinging her eyes. "Poor Thorkell, he left too soon," she said. "If he had stayed he might have enjoyed the hospitality of Noak Hill at last."

But what merriment there was at dinner that afternoon had a forced quality to it, for no one could help but be affected by the strange behavior of Godgifu. Silently she sat at table with them, mechanically eating the food which was set in front of her, neither seeming to taste it nor to desire it, although the ravages of starvation were painfully evident. Even the wine which Branwen poured for her, full and strong as it came from the carafe, had no effect. When they had finished eating, Godgifu looked up from the bits of trencher her fingers were picking and said to Branwen, "Where is the steward?"

Branwen looked at Ragnar.

"He is dead, lady. You have nothing to fear from him now," the thegn said.

"Oh," Godgifu breathed, her voice only a whisper, like the breath of a shadow, "dead."

A cold hand gripped Branwen's heart. She knew no magic to release a soul from the torment of its own making.

Three days passed and the fever left the children. Before the week was over, they had grown strong enough to run laughing, on short, little-boy legs through the hall. The old woman who had come to cook for them smiled and caught them up to her warm breast. Even Godgifu smiled. Perhaps it was knowing that the children would not die, perhaps it was just the simple nourishment of good food, but she, too, seemed to be healing. Although she seldom spoke, when she moved among them or sat at table, she seemed less strange, more relaxed. Now there were times when her hands were quiet and unmoving. Once when they were at table she had looked at Branwen, quietly, sanely, and said, "It is very kind of you to stay with us at Noak Hill, Lady Branwen."

Oh, Godgifu, Branwen thought hopelessly, if only you weren't pregnant. Aloud, she said, "When your baby is safely born, then I must be going. It won't be long now, I think."

But several days and nights passed, and the moon grew old waiting for the child to be born. Branwen watched anxiously for she knew that the waning moon meant that the dark side of the Goddess walked the land. Although the full moon brings fertility and the promise of new life to the land, that promise of growth wanes with the waning of the moon; and, for those few days each month when the moon is dark, barren death holds sway over the land. So that life may not smother under the weight of its own unchecked growth, death exists. So are there two aspects of the Great Goddess, not good and evil, for the Deity is beyond good and evil, but life and death.

There had been no moon in the sky that night, no moon to flee the sunrise on the morning when Godgifu's labor began. The children were sent out to the cookhouse to play while Branwen remained to wait with Godgifu.

"Tell me about yourself," Branwen said as she settled herself into a chair beside the fire, taking up the soft, washed wool she had found in a great mound under the eaves, starting to card it between two curved, sharp-toothed paddles, making the even rolags which would be spun into thread. Godgifu walked back and forth across the room. The contractions, although strong and closely spaced, did not seem to trouble her as she waited easily for each one to pass. In the quiet space between, as she walked, she said, "What is there to tell? My father, Raedwig, holds land at Walthamstow. I was betrothed to the ealdorman when I was a child. We were wed five years ago when I was thirteen. I have lived here since."

"Are you happy here?" Branwen asked without looking up.

"Sometimes . . . when he is away . . . when it is warm and I can go out . . ." Her voice stopped as another contraction tightened and she waited for it to pass.

"And the ealdorman," Branwen prompted, "what of him? What is he like?"

Godgifu shook her head and wouldn't answer. For a while she paced in silence and then she said, "Tell me about the ocean. They say you live on the edge of the sea. What's it like, the sea? I wanted to go to the sea. It isn't far, you know. I wanted so to go to the sea." Her voice drifted off.

Branwen looked up, watching Godgifu pace up and down—from the doorway, around the fire pit in the middle of the room, across to the door on the other side which led out to the gardens beside the courtyard. Her long pale hair hung in loose braids; she looked like a child, still too thin, the swelling of the unborn child strangely out of place among the angles and planes of her body, unsoftened by any of the curves common to women. And then, watching the woman, she felt her heart sink. Godgifu's hands had come alive again, fluttering over her face; as if, possessed by a stranger, they were exploring this body they found themselves chained to. When a fresh birth pang, stronger now, gripped her, her hands, like claws, began to tear at her loose robe, struggling as if they wanted to get at that part of their prison which caused them such pain.

"Oh Mother," Branwen groaned. Quickly she set down the wool and crossed the room to where Godgifu labored in earnest now. Branwen held out her hands, hoping Godgifu would take them in her own. But the other woman's hands fled away and Branwen had to reach out and capture them, holding them firmly, steadily in her own. "Come, Godgifu," she said, "come closer to the fire where there are clean rushes."

Godgifu looked at her wildly, uncomprehending. But it was that brief interval between contractions and Branwen was able to lead her closer to the fire. "Budda," she called loudly, "Budda, where are you?"

"Right here, my lady. Is it time? So soon?"

"I think so but she is . . ." Branwen looked across at the serving girl, unwilling to finish, to say the word aloud.

"Oh my lady, you were afraid of this. Remember, just the other day you said . . ."

Godgifu's scream cut her short.

"Here, hold her robe back," Branwen said, pulling Godgifu's hands down and down until the two of them were squatting over the clean rushes beside the hearth. And there the baby was born easily, too easily, a tiny girl slipping wetly onto the soft weeds. Branwen dared not let go of Godgifu's struggling hands and it was Budda who reached between them and lifted the baby, gently wiping her face and clearing her mouth of the birthing fluids, until she began to cry weakly. When the after-birth was delivered Branwen led Godgifu, docile now, toward the clean warm bed which had been readied for her. Branwen packed strips of linen rags between Godgifu's legs and covered her with the down blankets so she could sleep. Budda, who had wrapped the infant in soft swaddling bands, laid her now in her mother's arms. She and Branwen stood quietly beside the bed and waited.

Godgifu smiled at the child like a madonna, and gently lifted the tiny infant to her breast. Branwen held her breath, watching. But the infant would not suck. With a groan Branwen bent down and, while Godgifu watched, still smiling, squeezed the first drops of thin new milk onto the lips of the baby. But the child had gone hungry for too long. The milk ran down her cheek unheeded.

"We'll have to find a wet nurse," Branwen said, "and quickly. One who can coax the baby . . . teach her to suck," she added lamely, refusing to give up, yet knowing how futile it was to hope to teach a newborn what should have been natural.

"I'll go," Budda said eagerly, not understanding the hope-lessness of it all.

"No, you stay here," Branwen said, desperate to get out, to get away. "I will go." Then, seeing that Budda was afraid to stay alone with Godgifu, she added, "It will be all right. She won't hurt you." They looked at the woman lying on the bed and Branwen's heart sank. While her pale thin fingers fluttered over the baby unceasingly, Godgifu's eyes stared vacantly into the shadows. "Call if you need help. Someone will be in the hall outside."

Her shoulders sagged and she felt very tired as she turned and went out of the room.

In the great hall beyond, Ragnar sat rubbing his sword with wood ash, cleaning off the invisible rust. It was a common sight to see a thegn working over his sword blade, sharpening or polishing. How like Ragnar his sword is, she thought with a small smile. It was unjeweled and the hilt, once deeply incised with a pattern of gripping beasts, was softened with wear. The blade, forged in layers for strength and flexibility, shone with the striping of fine Rhenish steel.

He looked up from his work when she came in, waiting for her to speak.

"I've got to go down to the village," she said. "We'll have to find a wet nurse."

He dipped his hands in the bucket of water beside his stool and then stood up, rubbing them dry on the grey polishing rag which had lain across his lap. "You look tired, Branwen," he said. "I'll send Trygg. The old woman can tell him where to go. She was here just a little while ago asking if there was any news yet. I'll go and find them. Sit here," he said, and added a thick log to the fire which was trying valiantly to drive back the winter chill.

"Oh Ragnar," Branwen cried, her eyes brimming with tears, "she is quite mad. What are we to do? The baby is so small."

Ragnar turned away. After a moment he said, his voice stony, "I'll speak to the old woman, my lady. Wait here."

When the wet nurse arrived Branwen was asleep in a tall-backed chair drawn near the fire. Someone had covered her with a thick fur robe.

"It's the woman from the village," Ragnar said, seeing her eyes open. "Trygg's back."

"They said ye needed a wet nurse, my lady," the young woman said, rubbing her hands to warm them over the fire. She was a round, ruddy-faced woman. Though she was still young, there were laugh lines around her eyes which were squeezed narrow by the roundness of her cheeks.

"What's your name?" Branwen asked looking up at her.

"Trude, my lady."

"Well, Trude, you've milk to spare?"

"Oh aye, my lady." The other laughed. "The good Lord's seen fit to bless me with more milk than my wee one can drink. When he wants to suck for comfort sake suddenly there's rivers of white that he can't possibly drink, just makes him angry, that does. Oh, he'll be glad of an empty tit to suck, you may be sure of that."

"Well, wait here. Warm yourself. We'll get the infant and bring her out to you."

She looked at Ragnar and said, "Will you help?"

"Aye," he said.

Budda looked up from her handwork as they came in. "Sh," she motioned, her fingers to her lips, and they could see that Godgifu was asleep, one arm resting protectively around the tiny infant who lay beside her.

Branwen leaned over the bed and gently began to lift Godgifu's arm from around the baby, loosening her hold upon the infant. Suddenly the woman woke with a fierce snarl, like an animal's. Branwen stepped back, trembling. She looked at Budda, who stood clutching her shawl tightly around her shoulders, and then at Ragnar still standing awkwardly in the doorway. He stepped forward to help her. She made a small gesture with her hand. "Too late," she said. "It doesn't matter. The baby is dead. Already cold."

"Oh, Branwen, what are we to do?" Budda cried.

Branwen shrugged. It doesn't matter what we do, she thought. It is in the hands of the Mother now. Madness and death—both beyond anything we can do here. "I'll sit for a while, Budda," she said aloud. Then, turning to Ragnar she added, "There is no need for either of you to stay. I will wait until she is asleep again and then. . . . Give the woman a coin for her trouble, will you, Ragnar?"

"Aye," he said, frowning.

"You're sure, my lady?" Budda said, gathering up her things.

"If I need you, I'll call," Branwen said.

The curtain swung back behind them and was still once more. She was alone with Godgifu and her dead child. Only the crackling of the fire disturbed the stillness of the room around her. It was a simple room, filled with the clutter of every day. Godgifu's sewing basket, overflowing with the shirt she had been mending, sat forgotten on the top of a chest. There was a stick horse lying where it had slipped down from the wall where one of the children had propped it yesterday. The pieces of a broken toy lay in a pile under the window waiting for someone to come along and pick them up. Idly Branwen wondered if they could be mended again. A ship, she thought, they look like the pieces of a sailing ship. Tired and dusty branches hung forgotten from the rafters. Rowan. Godgifu must have planned to dye some length of cloth grey. A dress, perhaps, or some pants for the boys. Rowan. One of the sacred trees of the Goddess. Birch, rowan, ash, alder, willow, hawthorn, oak, holly, hazel. And others, too, not really trees but sacred since the beginning of time. Ivy, elder, heather, yew. Yew, the tree of the dead. Branwen shuddered.

Godgifu's eyes glittered in the firelight. She lay unmoving, the dead infant in her arms.

It was mid-December and night came early. The silence was profound. The fire died down to glowing coals. Even the small noises were stilled. Branwen pushed a chair under the hanging rowan and climbed up on it. Reaching over her head, she took the branches down and placed them carefully, reverently, on the fire. The flames leaped up, crackling noisily, for the wood was very dry. Branwen looked across the room to where Godgifu lay on the bed. Her eyes watched warily. A thin grey smoke rose from the hearth, spreading through the room like a mist. The fire burned up around the rowan, which blackened, and then turned to ash in the center. Branwen leaned down and pushed the unburned ends of the branches toward the center of the fire. When she looked up, the Goddess was there.

Like an old crone, She was bent over a staff. Her nose was long and whiskers sprouted from Her chin. "Greetings, Daughter of the Moon," She said.

"Greetings, Mother of All," Branwen replied, not surprised at Her presence, knowing that she had been waiting for Her.

"To know death and yet go on living is to accept the unacceptable. It is this, My Branwen, which sets the children of women apart from all creation." Her voice creaked when She spoke.

"And if Godgifu won't accept it?" Branwen asked. "If she chooses madness instead?"

"Then she will be lost to you." The Goddess, leaning heavily on the gnarled cane She carried, hobbled closer to the bed where Godgifu lay, watching them, sheltering the dead infant in the curve of her arm, crooning to it. Standing there, the Ancient One called her name.

The crooning stopped and the mad woman looked around— like a wild thing feeling the snare tighten around it.

"Godgifu," the Crone repeated.

Godgifu looked at Her and saw in Her eyes the reflection of her own innermost soul.

"Give Me the child," the Hag commanded.

An eternity passed while Godgifu stared into Her eyes, struggling with the birth pangs of her own womanhood, which rent her soul more fiercely than any mortal labor.

Branwen waited, hardly daring to breathe, knowing that if Godgifu could give the child to the Goddess of her own will, could accept the baby's death, she would be able to go on. From the beginning of time dead infants had been laid at the feet of the Goddess, knowing that She alone was the source of life, that all life belonged to Her. The life of the dead child had never been Godgifu's to lose—it had always belonged to Her from Whom it came. Now Godgifu must give the infant back to Her.

Suddenly Godgifu uttered a long, keening wail, clutching the cold, tiny corpse close against her breast. She stood up, barefoot on the rush-strewn floor. Like a priestess, she raised the infant in her hands, an offering to Death Herself. And gently, Death received Her gift. When it was done, Godgifu stood there, alone, wide stains of spilled milk darkening the front of her tunic.

Looking up at the Goddess, Branwen groaned. "Why must it be so hard?"

"It is not always so, My daughter. Only those who reach for the fullness of their humanity meet Death face to face. Godgifu thought to wall herself off from Death, but she walled out Life as well. Now her prison is crumbled. It is well you stayed with her, you who know what it is like to behold the face of Death alone."

And Branwen knew She spoke of the rainswept afternoon on the sea cliffs at Cynewithe, the hour when Elfheah died. Immense sorrow washed over her, taking her by surprise. Instinctively she reached out and took Godgifu in her arms so that, clinging together, they might somehow survive. "Elfheah knew too," she whispered at last. "Elfheah knew the face of Death."

"He knew," She said, "and in the end his curse became his blessing as well."

"His blessing," Branwen repeated, doubtfully.

"To love another without thought of self is the greatest good, Daughter of the Moon. It is the gift of womanhood. Few men ever share its blessing. In the end, through you, Elfheah did."

"I thought I loved Thorkell like that. I thought I could love him—that loving him was all I needed," Branwen said, her eyes full of tears, "yet I hurt him so."

"Love is not a simple gift."

"Why must there be such pain?"

"If you continue along the path you have chosen, My child, pain will surround you and engulf those who love you. You cannot live in both worlds."

"I know, Mother," Branwen groaned, "I have tried. It is so hard."

"You cannot live in both worlds. Others have tried and failed."

"I promised him. I have to try."

"You knew it would not be easy," Her voice said, hanging in the air. Then She was gone. Of the infant there was no trace.

The two women stood silently in the small room, unwilling to shatter the stillness, the peace, the aura of the Goddess which remained after She had gone.

After a long time, Godgifu sighed and, gathering herself, withdrew from Branwen's embrace. "Where are my children?" she asked. "Are they all right?"

"They are fine," Branwen said blinking back her tears. "I'll go get them."

Neither child woke as Branwen carried each one across from the little cottage where they had been put to bed that night. Godgifu took her sons and laid them gently in their own bed, covering them carefully against the night chill.

"Sleep, my little men," she whispered, lingering over them. "The night mare has gone back to her nest. We are safe now." Then, turning to Branwen, she said haltingly, "I owe you a lot, don't I? I hope that some day I can repay the debt."

"I hope we can be friends," Branwen said, holding out her hands, as she had before, palms up.

This time Godgifu reached out shyly and took them in her own. "I hope so, too," she said.

"I must leave in the morning."

"I know. I have held you here too long already. But I will be sorry to see you go. . . . Oh, Branwen, I'm so tired." Her eyes were closing even as she spoke and she sank down onto her bed. "Will you come back?" she asked softly as Branwen pulled the down quilt up over her. "Will you come back and tell me who She is? . . . Odd, She wasn't frightening at all," she said and then she was asleep.

"I'll come back," Branwen whispered. "I'll come back, Godgifu."

It was two days before Christmas. When the sun rose, Branwen dressed in her warmest tunic and fur-lined cape. She gave orders that the horses were to be saddled and the wagon packed. The distant bells had not yet rung sext and the sun was still climbing when they left Noak Hall, flags flying, and turned at last toward London.

Chapter Five

London spilled out over its walls like forgotten bread dough out of a bowl. Like ragged pieces of dough fallen onto the hearth, lumps of houses rose amid empty fields and bare winter woods.

Once before she had ridden up to these walls. Once before, when Edmund had delivered the city from the Danes. Was it only last summer? she wondered. Can the world have changed so much? And in her mind's eye she saw again the summer sky dark with smoke; she smelled the acrid burning in the air which drifted up from the fields south of the city where the Vikings had set fire to the land. Vikings who now held court in a city which had never yielded to them. Vikings who were not faceless warriors but were Thorkell and Knut, Eric and Harald, Ragnar and Orm. Then she had been a Wessex thegn, daughter of a Saxon lord; today she rode toward the great north gate, the wife of a Viking jarl. And Edmund was dead and everything they had fought for, lost.

Inside the city gate they were caught up in the crowds moving through the streets, buffeted by the stench and the noise. Beornwig danced nervously. She spoke gently to the stallion, quieting him. She turned in the saddle to look for Budda but the cart was not in sight. Behind her the rank of Vikings rode tall and proud, their eyes sweeping the crowd, challenging anyone who would make trouble for the woman they escorted. Ragnar rode up ahead, letting his heavy war horse make his own way through the crowd, opening the road for her.

Everywhere she looked she was assaulted by color. The grey-green and brown of the winter countryside had vanished. Here men and women wore brightly dyed woolens—yellows and red, blues and vivid greens. Even the timbers which cut across the plaster walls of the houses were no longer dark brown but gaily colored, pine green or deep crimson. Like a country girl, she gaped wide-eyed at a woman standing in a doorway; her hair was a bright unnatural red. The woman returned her stare with an obscene gesture. Branwen laughed and waved back, excitement mounting in her.

"How much farther, Ragnar?" she called.

He turned around to answer and the sight of her made the words stick in his mouth. Her dark hair curled around her head like an anadem. Her eyes were wide and filled with light. Her cheeks glowed from the winter ride. Her smile was childlike, open and unaffected. Innocently she radiated her exuberance and it fired the full bloom of her womanhood.

"How much farther, Ragnar?" she asked again.

Taking a deep breath, he said, "Not far, my lady. See, the river gleams there ahead of us as it passes under the bridge."

The Thames, great open mouth of the land, lay before them. As they rode down the gentle slope toward the water, the houses grew taller, grander, as if nourished by roots which drank from the strength of the river. They turned aside before they reached the bridge. Along the river, the road ran between the piers and docks on their left and the great merchant houses on their right. New houses built of stone had insinuated their way between the older, half-timbered Saxon halls. As they rode upriver the houses began to spread apart, allowing room for the barns and stables of great nobles who came into town with all their household for high holidays. It was to one of these that Ragnar pointed.

"There, my lady," he said. But even as he spoke his brow furrowed and he drew rein abruptly in the street.

Branwen stopped beside him and asked, "What's wrong?"

"The landing, my lady. The *Raven's Wing* is gone. Wait here."

He spoke to the heavy-set Viking who waited behind them. The escort moved up, taking positions all around her, freeing their weapons as they readied themselves for whatever the absence of their flagship meant. Ragnar rode up to the door of Thorkell's great Saxon hall. He stood in the stirrups and banged on the iron-bound oak with the haft of his spear, each crash reverberating down the street.

After a moment the door opened and a man stepped out, holding a jeweled cup in his hand. "Good God, man, are you trying to break down the door?" he said, leaning back casually against the jam. His eyes swept the street unhurriedly. Seeing her, surrounded with her Viking guard, their weapons drawn, he grinned and said, "Well, look who's here at last." Turning back toward the darkness behind him, he said, "Leofric, Branwen has arrived. Come and see for yourself with what style my sister travels now."

"Godwin," Branwen called, urging Beornwig through the guard. "Godwin! What are you doing here? Where's Thorkell?" She slid out of the saddle and embraced her brother. "And Leofric, too," she said with a warm smile. "What are you doing here? Oh, it's good to see you both. Ragnar," she said to the frowning Viking who waited behind her, "you remember my brother, Godwin, and my father's fosterling, Leofric."

"Aye, my lady," Ragnar said slowly, still wary.

"Well come in then, out of this bloody cold," Godwin said, leading the way into the hall where a log of ancient lineage burned brightly in the central hearth.

A Norseman stood in the flickering light. He was young, his hips still narrow in the tight court trousers he wore beneath his fur-trimmed tunic of fine wool. His beard and hair, cut short, curled loosely over his head.

"This is Hakon Ericsson," Godwin said.

"My lord," Branwen said warmly, "I know your father. I am sorry that we meet in such bitter times."

"We have both been defeated by men who learned their skill from Thorkell the Tall," Hakon said with a bow, "you and your countrymen at the hands of Knut Sweinsson, and my father and I defeated by Olaf Haraldsson."

"He came to Thornbury once," Leofric said. "Do you remember, Bran?"

"I remember Olaf," she said, seeing in her mind the crude, outspoken man.

Suddenly there was a rush of black feathers as an enormous raven, his wings spread wider than a man's arms could reach, flew down to the chair back beside them.

"Blaec," Branwen cried delighted to see him. *"Tu ebethe*

meletior?'' Unthinkingly she had spoken in the ancient language, and the room grew suddenly silent. Her voice, those uncanny words, hung in the air. She stopped, embarrassed by what she had done. She hardly heard the raven's reply.

"Well, men, I give you the Lady of the Ravens," Godwin said. He held up his goblet, saluting her.

"Lady Branwen," Hakon said formally, his eyes veiled, unreadable.

"Branwen," Leofric said quietly, raising his cup to her.

"The Lady of the Ravens," Ragnar said. Catching her eye, he grinned reassuringly. The Lady of the Ravens, that's who she was, by Odin, and it was all right with him.

The men drank deeply from their cups. She stood stroking the inky iridescence of Blaec's feathers. When they had done, she said, "Now, tell me, where is Thorkell?"

"Gone to Normandy," Godwin said with a wicked grin. "Gone to find a more docile wife."

"A wife?" Branwen said archly, refusing to be baited by her brother, whom she knew too well.

"Aye." Godwin laughed. "A wife for the king. Knut wants to marry Emma."

"Emma? Ethelred's widow?" Branwen asked, sinking down into the soft cushions of the chair beside her. "What about Aelgifu of Northampton?"

"Conveniently, it seems Knut has never officially wed Aelgifu. He is quite free, so the church says, to marry Emma."

"And Aelgifu will bear this shame?"

"There is no shame, Lady Branwen. She will do what must be done for the good of the land," Hakon said. "Others have sacrificed more."

"If Emma accepts Knut's offer, Aelgifu will be given great honor, lands and wealth, and sent back to Northampton. There Eric and Hakon can keep an eye on her," Godwin said.

"And on their son, young Harald Harefoot," Leofric said, adding, "Does this make him a bastard, I wonder?"

"She has his love, such as it is, and his son. She knows he cannot care for this other woman, a woman he doesn't even know," Godwin argued.

"But Thorkell knows Emma, doesn't he?" Branwen said. "He spent a winter in Ethelred's court once. He must have come to know her well."

"Aye, he knows her. That's why Knut sent him," Leofric said.

"The marriage is a good one," Godwin said, "for both sides of the Channel."

"So he'll be gone for a long time," she said, "even if the Channel crossing goes well."

"It will go well, my lady," Ragnar said. "No one sails with the spirit of the sea and the wind as he does."

"I am sorry you were not here to sail with him, Ragnar," she said, sensing his disappointment and chagrin at being left behind. He had not held rank on board the *Raven's Wing* long enough to let it sail willingly without him.

Turning to the others she said, "Why were you here today? Is Ragnar mistaken? Isn't this Thorkell's house?"

"Oh, it's his house, there's no mistake," Godwin said. "But the great lord asked us to keep an eye out for you, that's all. He seemed a bit vague about when you would be coming. It seemed unwise to press him too closely about it. He was quite tight-lipped, you know, when the subject came up. So we have waited for you each day. The food is good. We found the waiting not too tedious."

"Isn't your father in town, Leofric?" Branwen asked.

"Yes," he said slowly, "my father's here."

"Surely you won't ask us to move in with him!" Godwin exclaimed.

"No." She laughed. "I couldn't do that to you. You are more than welcome to stay here."

There was a general shuffling as the men who had ridden with her from Noak Hill came in after stabling the horses.

"The wagon has arrived, Lady Branwen," Trygg said, drawing near the fire's warmth. "But Budda's afraid to come in."

"Very well," she said. Turning to her brother she said, "I hope we can talk more later."

"Whenever you like," Godwin said, bowing elaborately. "I am at your service."

She smiled at him and went out through the back of the hall into the courtyard. Budda was huddled miserably on the wagon. There were tears in her eyes.

"What ever is the matter?" Branwen asked, holding out her hand to help the girl down.

"Oh, my lady, I was so frightened something awful had happened to you."

"Don't be silly," Branwen snapped. "Now wipe your nose. There's work to do. We must see if the cook here can be persuaded to feed us all. Come along."

She turned and started across the frozen yard toward the cookhouse, feeling not nearly as sure of herself as she pretended. I am mistress of Thorkell's house, she told herself sternly. I shall simply tell the cook we will have dinner.

She pushed open the kitchen door and stalked in. A red-faced woman looked up startled from the kettle she was stirring. Another turned around to stare at her from the ovens where she was putting in a deep pastry.

"Lady Branwen?" the red-faced woman asked.

"I am Branwen," she answered.

"I be cook, my lady. I thought ye would all be wanting dinner. Shut the oven door, Wigga. If ye can wait for the pasty, the chickens will be done then, too; and if the foolish lad will stop gawking and keep turning, we'll have a joint as well. Not more'n an hour, my lady."

"That will be fine," Branwen said, deflated. "Is there anyone to give my maid a hand with the unpacking?"

"Aye, my lady. Gwen can help." Turning to the girl Branwen had seen serving in the hall, she said, "Gwen, show the Lady Branwen to the room we have readied for her. 'Tis a long ride, they say, from Noak Hill. Ye must be tired."

"Thank you," Branwen said lamely.

As they followed the girl across the yard Branwen couldn't help wondering what she was to do here, waiting for Thorkell's return. I'll have to content myself with needlework—a tapestry, perhaps, like other men's wives. And what am I going to do about Blaec? He can't stay here, not now. And where is he? Asleep on the warm rafters somewhere, no doubt.

But Blaec was not asleep. She found him waiting for her in the bright, warm room Gwen showed them to. Sending the two women down to unpack the wagon, she went over and stood by the fire, waiting for the bird to speak.

I am glad you have not forgotten me, he said at last.

"You did me no favor picking that moment to drop by. Leofric and Hakon were . . ."

Leofric and Hakon are of no consequence, the raven inter-

rupted. *It is well known you are unlike other women. There are
many who know you can speak the ancient language.*

"Still," she said with a shrug, "not Hakon."

Hakon already knew. He was not surprised.

"How did Hakon know? I've never spoken with him before."

They talked of you some weeks ago.

"Who talked of me?"

*The king of men grew angry with him whom you have chosen
to mate. He would have him set you aside, send you away. The
king was most unhappy to hear you were coming to London.*

"And Hakon?" Branwen asked wearily, knowing that what
the bird said was only too true.

*He was there, with his father and the others. Hakon thought
the king spoke nonsense. Eric told his son that it was not.*

"And then what?"

*The king only laughed. Then your mate said you were no
enemy and wanted only to be left in peace to live as other
women. He is a fool, Branwen. The streets are full of men who
know you are more than mortal women. They call you the
Angel of Death. They will not forget.*

"They will forget. I will be too ordinary to even notice, but
not if the king of ravens keeps me company. Go back to Knut.
There is more glory for you there."

*He hates me. I remind him of you. I am not eager for death.
I will not return to him.*

"But, Blaec, you can't stay here."

Will you never fly again?

"Is it too great a price to pay?"

*Once you refused to be my mate, to live in the skies. You told
me you had to be free to be yourself.*

"That was a long time ago. I am older now. A lot has
changed."

Has it? he asked. *Has it?*

Later in the day, after they had eaten, Leofric and Hakon
went off to pay their respects to old Leofwine. The Vikings
disappeared, glad to be back in London, seeking friends and
news around the city. Budda was busy upstairs, pressing
wrinkles out of Branwen's rich new court clothes which had
been unpacked. Only Godwin and Branwen were left, sitting in
the high-backed chairs, drawn up to the fire.

Godwin stared at the flames in silence for a long time.

Finally, without looking up, he said bitterly, "Did he tell you? Edmund killed himself. We could only stand by and watch. All those hopes and dreams faded and turned to dust. I would have been a great noble."

"You sound so hard, Godwin," she said gently. "I remember when you loved him."

"I loved him. We both loved him—you and I."

"And now we have a new king."

"He is much more complex, Bran, deeper, a difficult man to know." The dark Saxon paused. Then he turned to her and said with a wicked grin, "He is easy to amuse, though. I've never known anyone who loved being told how great he is as much as that Dane." After a while he added, more seriously, "Knowing Thorkell has meant a lot. Knut depends on him more than you know, Bran."

"Eadric Streona told me once that you were hedging your bets by allowing me to"—she paused—"'entertain Thorkell,' I believe was the way he put it."

"Ah, Eadric. There is a man who would be better off dead."

"Is he in London now?"

"No. It is said he holds court at Warwick, and all the Midlands have been summoned to the Christmas feast to pledge their fealty to him. He must be happy now."

"Eadric will never be happy, Godwin."

"What's that supposed to mean?"

"Eadric cares only for himself and there is nothing within him that can satisfy his need."

"Pah, Eadric! May he roast in hell!"

They sat in silence watching the fire burn low. Godwin added another log and then he said, "What did you answer Eadric when he said I used you?"

"I told him it was not true," she said simply.

"And what if it were true, Branwen?"

"Oh Godwin," she said shortly. "I knew it was true, at least a little, but you see, it doesn't matter. You will pay many times over for whatever good you took from me."

"Have you learned to see into the future, too? Have you added that to your other little tricks?"

"Does Knut know you are my brother?"

"Yes," he said, eyeing her narrowly.

Branwen looked up, surprised. "How far will you get, Godwin, with a sister he hates so much?"

"He's not sure he hates you, Bran. Not anymore, not now that Edmund's dead."

It was quiet for a time with only the snapping of the fire between them. Then Godwin stood up and went across the room to the serving table where he poured wine into two cups. Offering one to her, he said, "Why are you here in London?"

"Thorkell wanted me to come. He wants me to be his wife, to behave like other men's wives. He thinks that if I do Knut will forget Ashington."

"He will, Bran, he will, if you give him a chance. And what about the power you have over men's minds? Can't you make him stop hating you?"

"The power over men's minds," she echoed distantly. "Do you remember how long my power lasted when I used it as Edmund commanded at Coventry?"

"When you bent the will of Eadric?" he answered quietly. "He gave us his word that he would fight with us against the Dane. He gave us his solemn oath."

"He betrayed us," she said. "So much for solemn oaths. No, it's a two-edged sword, Godwin, this power over men's minds. If I touched Knut's mind, he'd know it. He'd never forgive that. I don't dare use it. Still," she said with forced brightness, "there are other ways, ways any woman knows."

Godwin laughed aloud. "God help him."

Leofric returned alone after dark. Branwen looked up as he came into the hall and her fingers fell silent across the strings of the dark dulcimer. Ragnar, Trygg, and the others who sat around the fire turned toward the door, watching him shrug off his heavy cloak. He unbuckled his sword and hung it on the peg as well. Looking over at Branwen, he grinned wickedly and said, "My father was pleased to learn that you are in London, Branwen. He bids you attend Christmas Mass with him and return to his hall for the feast. And you, too, of course, Godwin."

"Oh hell," Godwin said.

Leofric's leer widened. "It will be worth coming, my friends. The king will honor us with his presence."

Branwen paled.

"Well, we must go then," Godwin said. "Your father must be flattered."

"The old fool is bursting with it. He does not see that the king only panders to the old guard," Leofric said, warming his hands over the fire. "Where is the serving girl with the wine?"

Branwen set the dulcimer down beside her chair and crossed to the sideboard. Her hands trembled as she poured wine into a goblet for him.

Godwin came over and stood beside her. "You must go, Bran," he said fiercely.

"How can I? Thorkell is not here. How can I face him alone?"

"Don't be a fool!" her brother snapped, his voice low. "Don't you see it's better this way? If you are going to succeed you've got to do it on your own. Thorkell can't help you. Not with this. And," he hesitated a moment before adding, "if you fail, you are better off without him. He'd destroy himself defending you, you know. You've got to go tomorrow, Bran. You can do it. It's no different from—how many hundreds of feasts have we been to together? And you've always been absolutely charming. Why should this be any different?"

"I don't know what you are worried about, you two," Leofric said, holding out his hand for the goblet, "but I know this. For many months now I have heard soldiers whisper strange stories of the Lady of the Ravens who some dare to call the Angel of Death. Even in the dark of night such stories made me laugh, for I remember the little girl who grew up while I lived at her father's house." He paused and drank deeply from the goblet. Then he said, "What happened to that dark-haired child, Branwen? I'm afraid I've lost her."

"I am no longer a child, Leofric, but I am still Branwen. For a while, perhaps, the stories you heard may have been true; but not anymore."

"That's what Thorkell says," Leofric said thoughtfully. "I'd like to believe him. I think even Knut would. Can you do it, Bran?"

"I'll try."

Christmas day, 1016, dawned dark and stormy. The wind blew wet snowflakes through the streets of London. The sky was leaden.

Budda woke Branwen early to help her wash and dress. Branwen moved slowly, deliberately. Everything had to be perfect. She chose a soft green undergarment, woven of the

finest thread on a foreign loom. Its long sleeves fell in gentle
folds around her wrists. The cuffs were stitched with pink
eglantine and dark green leaves. The tiny thorns on the twining
vines were picked in gold. The neck was plain, rounded with
the smallest stitches so that it would lie flat. The Saxon tunic
which Budda dropped carefully over her head was stiff
damask, intricately woven, and dyed with alderbark to a dark
pink, matching the roses around the cuffs.

While Budda brushed out her hair, Branwen sat at the jewel
chest Thorkell had given her, turning each piece of gold and
each jewel over carefully in her hands. From among the riches
of Viking plunder she selected a heavy chain of square gold
links to hang low over her hips. Around her neck Budda
clasped a flat gold torc, beautifully incised with tiny ribbons of
gripping beasts.

The clothes she wore were traditional Saxon. She wasn't
ready yet to put on the ornateness of Viking women's dress
with its straps and buckles of heavy gold and precious jewels.
Today she needed the gold torc, she needed its tradition, she
needed the strength and pride of her own people, the Celtic
roots of her Saxon heritage. If Thorkell were here, she thought
to herself, I might have chosen differently, content to be his
Viking wife. But since I am going to have to stand alone, I will
stand as I always have, a Saxon woman—equal of any man,
able to hold land, make contracts, inherit property and
power—my father's daughter, if not my mother's, she thought
ruefully.

Closing the jewel chest, she showed Budda how to braid
dark burgundy ribbons through her hair. She would wear no
matron's cap. When they were done, Budda wrapped the dark
wealth of northern sealskin around her. It swirled around her
warmly booted feet.

"Thank you, Budda," Branwen said.

She turned and went down the stairs to meet her brother who
was waiting to take her to the cathedral. He grinned foolishly
when he saw her. Her face was very pale. Her eyes were dark,
the lambent light which usually flickered extinguished by the
ice in her heart.

"Knut doesn't stand a chance, my dear," Godwin said,
leaning over to kiss her carefully on the cheek. "Fear suits you
well. It makes your eyes bigger."

Riding out of the courtyard, Branwen was startled by a

weird sound overhead. She looked up into the bare branches of an old rowan which stood beside the gate. The great raven sat there, perched on the stub of a broken limb, laughing at her—a strange, unnatural act, for laughter and tears were given to the children of women alone when the world was new. She wondered what he found so funny but she was afraid to ask.

Leofwine, waiting with his son, met them just inside the cathedral doors. "Branwen, my child, it is good to see you once more."

Branwen curtsied deeply to the Ealdorman of Hwicce and said, "Thank you, my lord. It was very kind of you to invite me."

"Not at all, my dear, not at all. Have you met Father Stigand?"

Branwen looked up at a young priest standing beside the ealdorman. "No, Lord Leofwine, I do not believe I have."

"Lady Branwen," the cleric said with a bow.

"Are you celebrating Mass for us this morning, Father?" she asked politely.

"Oh no." He laughed. "It's too rich for me on the altar this morning. A veritable synod of bishops will concelebrate the Holy Sacrifice of the Mass today. The king is coming, you see."

Branwen shivered.

"Come then, my dear. You are cold. We will go in and take our places," Leofwine said.

"Another time, Lady Branwen," the priest said, "I'd enjoy talking with you further."

St. Paul's had been built when Aethelberht was king of Kent and Augustine was converting the pagan tribes to Christianity. Inside the ornately carved round arches of the main doorway, the profound quiet, the ancient peace of the Romanesque cathedral engulfed her. Five hundred years had passed since foreign artisans, working with the creamy rose of Roman brick, had built thick walls to support the barrel vault spanning the dark interior. The curve of the ceiling was repeated in the narrow arched windows set deeply into the thick walls. Between the windows, in shadowy niches, were tombs of forgotten men who had been important once, their effigies now covered with dust seldom disturbed through the long centuries. But it was to the chancel, and the main altar, that all eyes were drawn. As they waited for the king, Branwen watched an acolyte, robed in fine white lace over a long red alb, lighting great banks of white candles set about the circular apse. Illuminated by the candlelight, the rich colors of a triptych, hung above the tabernacle, told of Christ's passion and death in a language all men could understand. The air was heavy with the tolling of great bells.

Branwen stood beside a pillar, deeply moved. She had forgotten the ancient power which had chosen this channel to reach the hearts of men. She had been away from Mass too long. Perhaps she had too jealously resented the Son Who had been born to remind mankind of the message they had forgotten. She remembered suddenly an old noblewoman in a rose garden who had spoken of a Deity Who was not contradicted by Goddess and Son, a Deity Who surpassed human understanding. Aelfthryth, Edmund's grandmother. Is she still alive? she wondered. How far away all that seems now. Will I ever go back to Thornbury?

The ancient peace of the sanctuary was broken by the loud entry of a great crowd of Norse nobility, laughing and talking with each other. Hidden in the shadows, Branwen turned to watch the king's men come in. Eric of Norway, grey-haired, his beard grizzled, walked beside his son Hakon. With them was Knut's older brother, Harald, wearing the crown of Denmark. They were magnificent in deep furs, grey wolf and squirrel, bear and seal. Jeweled ceremonial swords hung from heavy gold chains linked around their hips. With them were tall women dressed in Danish finery, still strange to her eyes, with a king's ransom of gold and jewels draped across each ample chest. Their gowns, richly dyed, reds and blues, yellows and greens, were heavily embroidered, trimmed in fur. Their yellow hair was braided and bound up on their heads, confined under lace-trimmed caps, glowing white in the shadowy cathedral.

She only recognized a few of the women. There was no place in this crowd for most of the women she had known, those who had followed the army of the conqueror from camp to camp even as she had done at the end. But she remembered Estrid, Knut's half-sister who was married to Ulf, so proud beside her. With them, carrying his nephew, Swein Ulfsson, was Eilaf, laughing with the boy, apparently unimpressed with the atmosphere of triumph these friends of the conqueror displayed as they made their way down the middle of this Saxon cathedral in the town which had been forced to yield to them after all. Walking with Estrid was a pretty child with the promise of womanhood already playing in her eyes.

"Who is she?" Branwen asked.

"That's Gytha, their young sister," Godwin whispered.

Suddenly the king was there, just inside the portal, greeting the delegation of black-robed clerics who had waited for him, their hands tucked into the sleeves of their cassocks. While the heads of obscure saints stared down emptily from the massive columns supporting the entry arch, he stood facing the nave and his eyes slowly swept the assembled crowd. Long before his gaze reached the far side of the cathedral where she stood between her brother and the Ealdorman of Hwicce, Branwen bowed her head so that the deep hood of her cloak covered her face. She did not look up again until Knut had moved past the place where she stood and mounted the communion step.

As he took his place within the chancel, the choir began to chant the antiphon. The half pagan crowd quieted a little. Bishops robed in cloth of gold, their miters tall on their heads, entered the sanctuary. Mass began.

When it was over Leofwine took them quickly out the side door of the transept. They hurried through the thickening snow, anxious to reach their destination ahead of the king. At one point, Godwin laughed and she turned her head to ask him why.

"We've lost your Viking escort, Bran," he said with a grin. "They will be frantic when they realize you have only Saxons to protect you."

"They may be Vikings," she said, frowning, "but they are my friends and I'm sorry if I'm worrying them."

The hall they entered had been in Leofwine's family for centuries. Thick walled and heavily thatched, it rambled along the street like a wealthy dowager who, although sagging a bit here and there, maintains an elegance only a long lifetime of the finest care could have achieved.

Leaving the others to wait for the king by the front door, Leofwine led Branwen into the great hall where the tables had been set out for feasting.

"Will you wait here, my dear?" he asked, obviously anxious to see that all was in readiness for the king's arrival. "I'll send in a maid servant with warm wine for you."

"Of course, my lord," she said with a smile.

Left alone she walked slowly across the room and stood by the window on the far side watching the snow fall. Over her head the great hall was open to the vaulting roof blackened with the smoke of centuries, supported by thick beams, richly carved. The walls were hung with fine tapestries whose soft colors had been muted by years of wear. Even the dark oak furniture shone with a patina of generations of polishing.

In a few minutes a maid appeared and took her cloak, offering her warm spiced yppocras. Branwen accepted the jeweled goblet gratefully, warming her hands on the bowl, offering a silent prayer that the spiced wine would warm the ice in her heart as well. There was a soft sound among the rafters as a great black raven flew in through the windows open under the eaves. He called once to her and then settled out of sight high overhead.

She had barely tasted the wine when the king arrived. She heard him in the entryway laughing with Leofric and Godwin. As they came into the hall she turned slowly to face him across the emptiness.

He stood there, looking as she remembered him. Only the heavy gold crown of the island kingdom was different, four lily spikes rising from the band, Edgar's crown. The cold intensity of his blue eyes glowed like stars in the winter sky. He did not smile, nor did she.

"Branwen," Knut said, "I'd heard you were in London."

"My liege," she said, curtsying deeply to him.

Across the room he laughed, his hands on his hips. "Does it stick in your throat, lady, to call me that?"

"No, my lord," she said softly. "I pray you can forgive me my loyalty to a dead man." Her eyes were wide and the light from the window behind her glowed through her dark hair.

"Such loyalty needs no forgiveness, Branwen," Eric said, coming into the room.

"Thank you, Jarl Eric," she said to the man who had given up a Norwegian kingdom to fight against Edmund's army.

"It wasn't your loyalty that needed forgiving," Knut said, so quietly that she was not sure she had heard him. Then he turned away from her to join the richly dressed guests who began to fill Leofwine's hall. Pipers began to play.

She was looking for her brother and Leofric when a voice beside her said, "You must be disappointed to find Thorkell gone this winter, Branwen."

"Yes, I am," she answered, turning to see Knut's brother, Harald, smiling kindly at her. "We had looked forward to spending the midwinter feastings together this year."

"There will be many such feastings for you both in the years ahead," the king of Denmark said, adding, "Since Sigvaldi's death, and, of course, even more so now that Hemming, too, is dead, Thorkell has had to stand alone. I am glad you have found each other."

"Thank you, my lord," she said with a warm smile, "but it seems we are both still alone."

"Never mind, my dear, he'll be back soon, and you have your whole lives ahead of you."

Something in the way his words slurred, as if he had already been drinking, caught her attention and, at the same time, she noticed the fetid odor of disease not altogether masked by the scent he wore. It was the same sickly smell her father had had before he died. Not wine, she realized sadly, but some strong drug he needs for the pain.

Just then Leofwine came up to them and said, "You must sit beside the king at table, my dear, for you are the loveliest woman here."

"Oh no, I cannot."

"Of course, you can, my dear," he insisted.

"Oh, but you must," Harald said, "and I shall demand the prerogative of rank and sit on your left. By the time the afternoon is half over I'll have made you forget the tall Dane altogether," he said with a smile only a little forced.

Poor Harald, she thought, I wonder if anyone knows he's dying. She smiled at Leofwine, thanking him for the honor and, taking Harald's arm, they went up to their places on the dais.

As she stood beside him, Knut turned to her and said, "I should have realized you were known to the old man."

"My father was his friend."

"And his son grew up in your house, didn't he?"

"Yes," she replied cautiously. "Leofric was our fosterling."

They were prevented from saying more when the bishop began to intone the blessing.

When the prayer was done, great steaming tarts were brought in by liveried servants and placed among the tables. Aelfric of Hampshire, a thegn whose father's lands had been confiscated by Ethelred some years before, acted as steward, pouring wine from an elaborate jeweled carafe into the goblets set out on the head table.

After the spicy pork and currant tarts, there were platters of roast goose, stuffed with garlic, fruit and herbs; there were long skewers of venison chunks, and mounds of tiny songbirds to dip in bowls of vinegar sauce spiced with galingale and walnuts. There were rastons, loaves of bread scooped out, tossed with melted butter and fennel seeds and replaced beneath the unbroken top crusts.

Between each course Aelfric and two serving maids passed among them with bowls of warm water scented with aromatic spices so that each of the guests might wash the grease from his fingers.

During it all, wine flowed freely; no one's goblet was allowed to remain empty. Dogs snarled over the bones cast down among them. Laughter and shouting competed with the shrill piper's music, filling the room.

Knut ignored her—laughing and shouting to his friends seated around the room. Harald ate little, seeming to doze as the drug held him. Branwen smiled to herself. I never expected to be bored this afternoon, she thought.

When the last of the food was cleared away, the trestle tables were folded back against the walls. A small boy worked his way around the edges of the room, lighting beeswax tapers. A drummer and harper joined the two particolored pipers and the dancing began.

"You must have been disappointed to have missed Thorkell," Knut said, leading her out into the space which had been cleared for dancing.

"I was," she said.

"He is in Normandy on my orders," the king said.

"So I've heard. You honor him with such an important task."

"He was the obvious choice to send, you know. He's such an old friend of hers," he said.

She smiled at him radiantly over her shoulder as the pattern of the dance carried them apart. She had turned on her brother's arm when the music stopped. They stood together in the crowd for a moment catching their breath.

"Have you met Byrtric yet, Bran?" Godwin asked, nodding

toward the lord of Noak Hill who stood a little way off, leaning against a pillar holding a goblet in one hand.

"No, Godwin," she said sharply, "nor have I any wish to."

Godwin smiled too widely for he was as drunk as any other. "How is it you go about the countryside making enemies?" he asked.

Angry color rose in her cheeks. "Perhaps it's because I don't place a premium on other men's opinions as you do," she said, her words, too, slightly slurred, her temper exaggerated by the wine.

But her brother threw back his head and laughed. "So I'm to feel the venom of your words, too? Don't you know I'm immune, having grown up in the same nest? Come on, Bran. If I can't introduce you to Byrtric you must meet Gytha. Eilaf's sister, you remember; you asked about her this morning."

What words she spoke to the pale young girl that evening she could not remember, for as she stood beside her brother she caught Knut's eyes watching her and there was such a look of triumphant amusement in them that fear rose up in her once more and she trembled. "I want to leave now, Godwin," she said suddenly.

"But that's impossible, Bran," he said, scowling at her. "No one can leave before the king, least of all you. Besides, you've obviously charmed him. He hasn't taken his eyes off you all evening."

"He's not charmed, Godwin. He's very drunk. There's going to be trouble if I stay."

Just then the music began again and as the dancers moved out into the figure, a page came up to her and said, "Beg pardon, m'lady, but King Harald would speak with you, if you've a moment."

"Of course," she said, following him toward the dais where Harald sat, leaning back against the wall behind him. As she came near she saw that he had grown pale and beads of sweat stood out on his forehead. The drug wore off more quickly than he expected, she thought. Worrying how she was going to help him, she was startled to hear the loud voice of Knut beside her.

"You and Branwen are old friends," he was saying to Leofric.

"Aye, my lord, we grew up together."

Branwen stood still, looking only at Harald, her hands clenched, hidden in the long green sleeves of her silken under-tunic, as if she were waiting to be hit.

"Then you must know all about the wonderful tricks she can do?"

"My lord?" Leofric asked in the sudden silence.

"Come now. Do you mean to say you've never seen her commanding the birds and the animals?"

Leofric was silent.

Knut continued, his voice thick, "Well, she will show you then, won't you, Branwen? Show us all. Though perhaps nothing difficult. You must be tired, the hour grows late. But see, there, by the table leg, a mouse. Call it to us. It's a clever trick she does," he explained to the crowd who watched.

"No, my king," Branwen said, turning slowly to face him. "You are mistaken."

"Call it," he commanded.

"Not now, Knut," Harald said wearily.

"Call it," he repeated, not taking his eyes off her.

Fool, she thought, how dare you command me? Am I some juggler to do tricks to amuse your courtiers? Have you forgotten so soon what power is mine?

Filled suddenly with disdain beyond anger, she gathered her fine clothes under her and crouched down to speak to the fat mouse who foraged under the table. The words she used were strange but the mouse hesitated only briefly before running to her outstretched hand. She lifted her up and set her among the gleaming silver goblets on the table.

"*Cy ragga tuy e skul,*" she said. "Be still and do not fear. No one will hurt you, you have my word."

The mouse sat up, her whiskers twitching.

Knut clapped loudly and the others who were watching began to clap as well. Branwen waited, knowing the drama was not played out. In a sudden move Knut drew his dagger. The gleaming blade flashed to impale the tiny mouse, but stopped suddenly in midair. As if another, stronger than he, had grabbed his wrist, Knut's hand was held, stopped by the force of her will which would not let it fall. Slowly, deliberately, Branwen reached under the blade and took the mouse. She placed her back among the crusts and bones under the table and dismissed her. Then Branwen stood up and faced the king. Releasing her hold over him, the dagger fell, stabbing deep into the thick oak. Defiantly she met the hatred in the king's eyes.

"Get out," he hissed. "Get out. I never want to see you again."

"As you wish," she said scornfully, and vanished from the sight of all those in the room.

High among the smoke-blackened rafters a raven flew across the room and out an open window.

It was very late when Godwin came into the room where she lay in bed watching the flames. The abbey bells of St. Paul's had already tolled for compline.

"Well, Bran, that was quite a performance," he said gently. She said nothing.

"What are you going to do now?"

"Leave London, I guess."

"Where will you go?"

"I'll stay at Noak Hill for a while."

"Noak Hill will be closed to you."

"It won't!"

"Don't be a fool. You frightened many people today. Byrtric won't let you stay at Noak Hill." He chuckled. "The fools thought you had transformed yourself into a raven."

"Blaec never has done much for my image," she said, trying to laugh. "Oh Godwin, I'll go back to Maldon. I'll wait for Thorkell there."

"You could give it up, you know. Go back to Thornbury."

"Not yet," she said with tears in her eyes. "He's going to be awfully angry with me when he gets back."

"What about Ragnar and his men? Will you ask them to go with you?"

"I tried to persuade him to stay here but he won't. He has his orders from Thorkell."

"Pity," Godwin said. "He seems a competent soldier. This will finish him, you know."

"Maybe not. Someone close to the king may remind him gently that any ruler needs loyal men who will follow orders regardless of personal cost."

"I'll remind him," Godwin said thoughtfully.

After a while she said, "You'll be a good advisor for Knut. You know the land and the people. Knut will come to rely on you as he never can on the old ealdormen like Leofwine."

"I'm going to marry Gytha," Godwin said quietly.

"Gytha?"

He nodded.

"Do you love her?"

He looked away. "Does it matter? She is young. I am kind to her and so she loves me. She won't let them arrange a marriage with anyone else."

"And so you will use her and become a great noble."

"There I can look after the interests of our people, Bran. Someone must," he said, looking at her.

She smiled. "It is cleverly said, Godwin, but don't let yourself be fooled as well."

"Do you think I'm wrong to do this?"

"I can't judge you, God knows. Many men have taken the path you choose. For some it has led to the mountain top; for the rest, into the black mire. I think that if you give others a place in your heart and do not think only of yourself you will reach the mountain top. Care for Gytha. If you will pay that price, then perhaps you may use her without fault. But it is a price you must go on paying always or the bargain will fail and the penalty will be exacted."

"By God, Bran, you sound like an oracle when you do that! Do you practice in front of a mirror?"

She laughed halfheartedly.

Bending down he kissed her forehead. "I'm sorry we won't have more time together," he said, as he walked toward the door.

"Don't let Thorkell quarrel with Knut over me, Godwin," she said.

"I'll do what I can," he promised.

Chapter Six

The early April rains had turned the roads around Maldon to mud. Behind the jarl's hall, sheltered by the cloister, the rose canes were red with new growth. In the courtyard the fallen leaves had long ago been raked and burned. Hens pecked between the cobbles. There were dogs in the kennels and hawks in the mews for men lived here who hunted daily in the fields outside the city, returning mud-splattered and hungry, paying for their keep with venison and wild birds.

Late one afternoon the stillness was broken by the noisy honking of the grey goose's warning. Branwen looked up from scratching in the garden where herbs thrust new growth through the dark wet earth. There were riders coming through the alley. The low sun shone in her eyes as she stood up, shielding her face with her soiled hand.

"Thorkell," she breathed.

Suddenly the yard was full of men and noise—dogs barking in their kennels; sweat-covered horses stamping nervously, their harnesses jangling; the goose honking without respite; Ragnar and his men shouting as they burst out of the door behind her, swords drawn.

Thorkell stood in the middle of the courtyard. He pulled off his helmet and the late sun shone through his long brown hair. Branwen wiped her hands on a corner of her apron before untying it and letting it drop onto the bench beside her. Silently she stood waiting as he talked with the men he had left behind four months ago. At last he broke away and strode toward her.

He swept her up into his arms, carrying her through the door and into the small treasure room. He kicked the door shut with his foot and kissed her. There was anger in his kiss, a fierceness bred of worry and uncertainty.

"You shouldn't have come," she said unreasonably, her eyes shining.

"I should never have left you at Noak Hill," he growled angrily. "I should have taken you with me, to Normandy, if necessary."

She said nothing.

"Knut is adamant. He will not even have your name mentioned. Why did you do it?"

"Do what?"

"God damn it to hell. Bran, a mouse!"

His words chilled her like an icy wind. Numbly she stepped back, away from him, leaning against the small oak table where she kept his accounts.

"Was I wrong then?" she heard her voice ask.

"All he wanted was that small victory, Branwen. Couldn't you have sacrificed even one miserable mouse for the freedom to be my wife?"

"So," she said, "I must give up honor, too. Where will it end, this list of things I must stop being in order to be your wife?"

"Honor!" he snorted. "You were drunk and proud and you lost your temper."

"That may well be," she said angrily, "but do you doubt that I would do the same thing, right here and now, if I had to?"

"Branwen, where is the honor between you and a mouse?" Thorkell asked wearily.

"Does it matter to whom your word is given, my lord?" she asked gently. "I don't think so."

Thorkell stood silently, looking down at her. "So be it," he said at last. "But I know Knut well and he won't let this lie."

"He is a fool."

"He's no fool, Branwen. His strength grows daily in the land. Many a battle has been lost because a man underestimated the strength of his enemy."

"I'm not going to do battle with the king," she said.

At that Thorkell laughed. "So you will not do battle with the king! Well, I am relieved to hear it."

And she who could read his heart did not understand that the laughter sprang from dread. She did not yet sense the dark shadow of foreboding which hung over him. She did not know how well and deeply he had learned to be a Viking, a warrior who laughed at fear.

"Oh, Thorkell, I don't mind the king's interdict," she went on, oblivious. "If I am banned from his sight, the noblemen will avoid me as well; then I will be free from endless dinners and hunts and ladies' gossip. Is that so bad?"

Shaking off the shadow, he smiled at her and asked, "So you will be my sometime wife?"

"I am carrying your son," she said simply.

He stood looking at her for a long time until at last she felt his joy well up in her. "A son," he said. "How long I have wanted a son."

Branwen smiled. "You must wait a while longer, my love, until the summer is over."

She went to him, unbuckling his breastplate, her fingers tugging at the stiff leather straps. Eventually, when she had freed them, the breastplate dropped to the floor. He took her then in his arms and the chill worry of the last months disappeared. They clung together, feeling the bond which held them grow strong again.

Suddenly Thorkell set her down and, tilting her chin up so that he could see her eyes, he asked, "'A son,' is it? How are you so sure it will not be a daughter?"

"I am the last of my race, Thorkell. Have you forgotten? I will bear no daughter."

He frowned.

"I told you, you should have married someone else."

"Aye," he said mockingly, "but it's a little late now."

Just then there was a knock at the door. Branwen went over and opened it.

"Here is warm water for my lord to wash," Budda said timidly. "Bridey is preparing supper."

"Good," Thorkell said. "Set the basin down here. Is there wine, Bran?"

"Of course. Bring some wine, Budda. Have Jack open the new barrel which came last week," Branwen said.

The girl curtsied and ducked out the door. Branwen held the kettle while Thorkell washed the grime of a long day's ride

from his hands and face. He had only just finished when Budda
returned with a decanter and two goblets.

"Come on, we'll take it into the hall. Then I can give you
the news where Ragnar can hear as well. Godwin told me
Ragnar opposed the king's command in order to give you
escort from London."

"I begged him to stay in the city but he would not. He said
he had his orders from you. There was no swaying him. The
loyalty you have from your carles is very great. Don't be angry
with him."

In the great hall the carpenters had long ago finished their
work. A thick oak table ran the length of the room—pale gold,
newly oiled, not yet darkened with use. Trestle tables had been
hastily set up on wooden horses to serve those who had just
arrived. Forty men had ridden in with the Jarl of East Anglia
and the room was crowded with hungry men. The shutters
were opened to the clean April air and a great black rook sat
preening himself on a windowsill.

The fires burned brightly in the room for the cookhouse
hearth alone could not prepare enough food to feed so many
quickly. An iron cauldron hung over the flames in the end wall
fireplace, filling that end of the room with the smell of chickens and rabbits stewing in a sweet syrup of wine spiced with
raisins and currants, cinnamon, ginger, cubebs, and cloves.
Turned by a small boy who had come to live with them, the
carcass of a deer dripped and sputtered above the fire in the
central hearth. Baskets of thick dark trencher loaves, sent for
in the market, were set among the jeweled goblets from a warrior's treasure chests. Budda circulated almost gracefully
among the men, pouring the spiced wine.

With the knife he wore at his waist, Thorkell sliced a gobbet
of venison from the haunch spitted over the fire. Tearing at it
hungrily, he ignored Branwen's impatience. Not until he had
finished, draining his goblet as well, did he say, "We got back
last month."

"Three months is a long time to arrange a marriage, Thorkell," Branwen said.

"It was more than a marriage," he said, slicing off another
bit of meat. "Robert found the thought of ruling this island
himself very appealing. He and Emma had given the matter
considerable thought."

"He'd need a great army," Branwen said, incredulously, "and where would he get enough ships to carry such a force?"

"It would have cost him dear." Ragnar laughed.

"A fact I pointed out to him several times," Thorkell said, his mouth full. "In the end, though, it was Emma who decided. After the farce of her marriage to Ethelred, the thought of sharing both bed and throne with a man like Knut proved too enticing to turn down. She'll be here in July."

"And share his bed with how many others?" someone called out and the talk fell into ribaldry and laughter.

"And the Lady Aelgifu will be set aside," Branwen said bitterly.

"Not at all," Thorkell said, wiping his beard on his sleeve. "That is good food to put in front of a hungry man, my lady."

"Thank you. I'll tell Bridey."

"Here, Budda, give me some more wine, will you?" Turning back to Branwen, Thorkell said, "She's just given him a daughter, you know. Named her Gunnhilde. Knut is very fond of Aelgifu and isn't happy at the thought of sending her away. He believes that what he is doing is for the good of the country. It's some consolation to him. She's leaving for Northampton with Eric in a week or two."

"And you? What are you going to do now?"

"I thought I'd see some of this land the king's given to me, the east coast shires for a start. They've been without the king's justice for a long time and there are many who await judgment." He leaned back against the wall, stretching out his legs in front of him. "There are tax collectors to be appointed, roads and bridges to be repaired—you know—all the work which has been let slide while the countryside was at war. It will not all get done this spring," he said absently, watching Ragnar across the room, "but we'll get a start on it. Come fall, we'll ride through the shires along the western border."

"And do you want me to come with you? Poor Ragnar, he'll be desperate if you leave him behind again to guard me."

"Oh, no, my lady," he said, looking at her without a trace of a smile now, "you'll come. I'm not going to leave you by yourself again. From now on, you come with me where I can keep an eye on you."

"Yes, my lord," she said, laughing at him in spite of his seriousness.

"That's better," he said, pretending not to notice the laughter. "Ragnar," he called, "it's time you were back on the *Raven's Wing*."

A shout went up from the ten men of Ragnar's command. They would all be glad to get back on board the flagship.

"Take her out as soon as you can," Thorkell went on. "Bring her around the Dover headland to join the rest of my fleet on the Isle of Wight. I want those ships and men brought up to a level of performance and appearance not seen before in these waters. When you join Knut's ships at the end of June to sail across to Normandy, I trust you will teach them how a fleet should be turned out to escort a queen."

"Aye, my lord," Ragnar said with a grin. "We'll do our best."

They remained in Maldon less than a week after Ragnar left. Thorkell spent much of each day riding over the lands, forest and field, which surrounded the town. Tax lists were updated and reeves were appointed to collect the king's tax in the outlying shires. Often these were men whose families had been shire reeves for generations but occasionally, if the line had died out, new men needed to be appointed to fill the post. Bridges and roadways, especially the long beds across the marshy ground, were in need of repair this spring. It was always costly work and Thorkell found it necessary to meet often with the landowners whose responsibility it was to maintain them.

When they moved out at last, Thorkell and Branwen rode at the head of the column where the black and red raven pennants snapped in the early morning breeze. Overhead, Blaec was a speck of freedom high in the sky. Behind them, laughing and shouting to each other, rode the men who served Thorkell the Tall, Jarl of East Anglia, the sheen of their weapons and shields, the ornately worked silver and iron trappings on their war horses glinting in the sun. Brightly painted wagons, heavily laden with the treasure and provisions a jarl's household would use going from town to town, rumbled along in the rear.

Forty men rode out of Maldon that spring morning, each one heavily armed: some wearing hooded chain mail, others in stiff boiled leather breastplates and conical helmets, their faces hidden behind protective nose guards. They formed a professional mounted infantry no local lordling could hope to oppose. They drew their pay from the jarl. Free from the demands of owning land, they served in a military guild, a brotherhood of honor. And they were proud men. Their heads were high, their cloaks rich, their horses sleek and well fed. Their commander was one of the most powerful men in the land.

In addition to the carles who rode with him through the April sun, Thorkell commanded a fleet of forty ships, each one manned by thirty-two or more free fighting men whose shields decorated the gunwales. Although many of his men had been killed in the fighting during the past two seasons, the full complement had been filled by the remnants of his dead brother's forces. More than a thousand men now served him; and, because Viking tradition placed the king only first among equals, Thorkell's army was his own to command. His men would not hesitate to follow him, even in opposition to the king.

Now the forty who rode with him climbed almost imperceptibly out of the golden gorse of the Blackwater marsh onto the green of the low-lying downs where thick-wooled sheep dotted the land. They rode steadily for two days. Mile after mile the road continued over the rolling downs, crossing countless streams which meandered toward the sea not far to the east. Here free farmers worked the rich alluvial soil. This was the southern edge of the Danelaw, settled more than two centuries before by an earlier wave of Vikings who found good farm land, sparsely settled; and, sending back to Scandinavia for their families, stayed and prospered. Here the Viking tradition of equality pervaded the social and legal systems in a way which gave the Danelaw a special character of its own. Here the free farmer owned his own land, paid his tax directly to the king, and owed his lord much less burdensome service than was often the case in Mercia or Kent. Here a farmer could survive a bad harvest without having to trade his freedom for food as so often happened to cottars in other areas whose service to a lord crushed them to near subsistence level.

The arrival of the jarl and the men who served him was an event of no small importance in the fishing port of Ipswich. Filling three inns, the men spilled out into the streets day and night, looking for food and amusement. Generally well-behaved and disciplined, they still took delight in the local girls and the local brew.

In the years to come, there would be great halls, not only
here but all over East Anglia, to house the jarl and his men,
and there would be no need to put up with the discomforts of a
public house. Much of the land was empty; war had decimated
the population and those who were left could not work all the
fields. This spring, as he made his way through his new do-
main, Thorkell rewarded many of his men with large land
grants. These men would build and maintain estates where the
jarl would always find a welcome.

While Thorkell was involved long hours of the day with the
local officials, Branwen was free to wander along the Ipswich
salt marsh with only Blaec for company. She roamed far and
wide, attracted by the stillness of the salt pans and the spring
herbs which grew along the edges of the river. And the great
raven seemed genuinely happy to be free once more. The
glamor and excitement of court life had worn thin during the
years he had spent with Knut and he reveled in the chance to
spread his wings and ruff out his neck feathers, challenging all
comers.

Once, while Thorkell argued with the thegns and burghers of
Ipswich, Branwen followed the pathways through the countryside searching for the powerful shepherd's knot which grew
there. She knew it opened its yellow flower, like a wild straw-
berry's, in the hidden marshy places. Finding it at last, she
pulled only a few of the knobby roots, careful to leave enough
so the herb would continue to grow. In the evening when she
returned to the inn, she prepared a tincture from the rootstocks.
She worked quietly, away from the eyes of others, for there
was a kind of magic in the white flesh of the roots which bled
crimson when they were cut. Crushing the incarnadine pieces
with a pestle, she mixed the herb with alcohol, stoppered it
tightly and set it aside, knowing she now had an effective
weapon against the bite of sword or axe. There was no other
tincture with the power of shepherd's knot to stop bleeding.

In mid-May they crossed the sedge-thick fens from Norwich
to King's Lynn. The low land stretched as far as the eye could
see. The River Nar, its banks forgotten, spread out over the
land, moving slowly toward the Wash, still miles to the north.
Yellow swallowtail butterflies flicked through the patchy sun
as if to coax it out from behind the scudding clouds. The raised
causeway along which the men rode was in sorry condition.

Log crossings had completely disintegrated, and in many places the causeway itself had been eaten away by seasonal flooding. Watching the grey sky, heavy with rain, they hurried the carts across, afraid a downpour would mire them completely. Thorkell's face was stern. Branwen knew the lords of Lynn would pay a stiff fine for neglecting this stretch of roadway.

It rained, long steady days of soaking rain, while they were in Lynn. Growing tired of looking out the windows of the inn where they were staying, Branwen went with Thorkell to see the king's justice administered. She listened as the rain fell on the thick thatch overhead while the Bishop of St. Mary's brought a complaint against a man who had broken into his park and hunted there, killing the deer.

The clerk had only just read the charge when a mud-splattered messenger burst into the room. He pushed his way through the crowd toward the front of the room where the twelve sokemen sat with Thorkell. The jarl stood up to meet him.

"My lord," the Viking said, "I have ridden straight through from Portsmouth."

"That's a long ride, Ketel," Thorkell said, taking him by the arm and leading him out the side door.

Branwen, seated in the front of the gallery, followed them. Standing in the doorway, she saw Thorkell, ashen-faced with fury. She stopped, afraid to go nearer, knowing too well that the strength of his fury would overwhelm her.

With his eyes burning like coals under the blacksmith's bellows, he looked at her and said, "Ragnar's been murdered by commission of the king."

"Oh no!" she said. "It's not possible. . . ."

"Take this man to the inn. See he is taken care of. Tell Orm I leave at dawn for Winchester."

Branwen shuddered at his words. "I leave at dawn for Winchester," he had said. Suddenly a great gap had opened between them. She would not go with him. She knew that he would not ask her to. She had been the cause of Ragnar's death; he had paid for his loyalty with his life.

It was very late when he came to bed that night but Branwen had not slept. "Will you come back, Thorkell?" she asked in the stillness. She had grown afraid in the dark that he would abandon her rather than endanger his men further.

And Thorkell knew her fear, feeling its cold grip in his heart as well. He drew her close to him. Incredulous, she felt him smile as the child in her womb came between them. The anger and tension were momentarily forgotten. "How could I not, Branwen? Love is not wise, but like a fire, burns without caring what it consumes."

"Oh Thorkell, I do love you so."

He kissed her and there was no need for words between them.

In the dawn, as he dressed to leave, she asked, "What are you going to do, Thorkell?"

"We know who killed him. I will find them and seek the blood price."

"And if Knut objects?"

"He will not. The deed was shamefully done. Now he must live with his shame. He will not repeat his mistake again soon."

"You will be careful?"

"I will be careful, my love," he said and the words came strangely from his lips, as if he had not thought to say them ever before. "Where will you go?"

"To Cynewithe. Will you come when your son is born?"

"Before that, if it is possible. Tell Beorn he will have help with the harvest by the time the oats are ripe. It will be good to work the land once more."

"And when the harvest is in, we can go up to Maldon together for the winter. We were so happy there last year. Do you remember? Before we left for London?"

"I remember."

"In that house our child was conceived. He can grow strong there. They say the abbey school is a good one. He'll need good schooling so that he can grow up wise, like his father."

"It will be a while before he is ready for school, I think, Branwen," Thorkell said with a gentle laugh.

"It will pass quickly, Thorkell. I am afraid he will grow up too soon and leave us. Why does everything good have to end so quickly?"

"Branwen, he's not even born yet. Let's not worry about losing him just yet."

She finished buckling his breastplate. He leaned down to kiss her.

A little later, as she watched him ride away, she noted absently that the rain had stopped.

Chapter Seven

"Lady Branwen, Lady Branwen!"

She looked across the sunny, half-mown hay field and saw the figure of a woman coming toward her.

"Oh Lady Branwen," the woman said, smiling, "we heard you was back at Cynewithe." She hesitated then, as if she suddenly realized that it was not just one of the neighborhood women she had run out to meet. "Oh my lady—we thought—Ralf and me, we thought—would you like a cold mug of ale? 'Tis too hot to be out in the sun and you with child and all."

"What did I tell you?" Blaec croaked from his perch in the heavy shade of the old rowans. "You should see yourself, all red and sweaty. A fine sight for a jarl's wife."

The man haying with a long-handled sickle had stopped his swing and stood nearby listening. He was bared to the waist and an angry red scar ran across his belly.

"You remember Ralf, my lady. Ye saved his life, ye did. He were cut bad at Ashington but you fixed him up just fine. If it was not for you, he'd be long dead."

But Branwen shook her head, knowing it was not her skill which had saved him. The spear must have been spent when it cut him. It was just luck. If it had had the strength to pierce his intestines, he would have died no matter what she had done.

"We have a new bairn, my lady," the woman went on, taking no notice. "Hardly seems likely, what with him so bad hurt and all but you know how men are. We named her Branwen," she added shyly.

"Did you?" Branwen said. "Well then, I must come and
see her. And I would be grateful for a mug of ale. The sun is
hot this morning." She was carrying a basket of wilting herbs
which she had collected in the fields ahead of the reapers.

The woman's name was Goda and the cottage they walked
toward was large and thick-thatched, with a barn behind big
enough for a cow, Ralf's horse, poultry, and a pair of sturdy
oxen. Inside the cottage the air was cooler, moving gently
through the windows whose shutters were thrown back. A tiny
red infant lay crying angrily in a wooden cradle set carefully in
the shadows.

"Ralf will pull up the jug from the well," Goda said, hurrying to clear off a place for Branwen to sit. Then, picking up a
cloth, she started to wipe out three mugs which had been
sitting on the shelf along one wall.

"Here, let me do that. You take care of the baby," Branwen
said with a smile.

"Oh no, my lady—it will only take a minute. There," she
said and, setting three mugs on the table, she picked up the
crying baby. She sat down on the bench and untied the lacings
on her bodice. The hungry infant began to nurse with such
expertise that Branwen laughed.

"How old is she?"

"Three days, my lady."

"Only three days, yet see how she knows what she wants."

"Aye, 'tis a mystery how they are born knowing how to go
about staying alive. And you, my lady. You'll be having a
bairn of your own before long, I think."

"Not until the oats are harvested," Branwen said.

Ralf came in then, his coarse blue linen shirt mottled by the
water he had washed with. "Ye've met the wee one then, Lady
Branwen?" he said, grinning proudly.

"She's beautiful," Branwen lied.

"Aye, that she is," Ralf agreed. "We owe you much, my
lady, the wife and me."

"Not so," Branwen began, but they would hear none of it,
filling her mug and urging her to drink.

"The alewife's brew is good for you. 'Twill make the child
within you grow strong," Goda said.

They sat not uncomfortably together, almost like neighbors,
and spoke of the fine weather, saying how they hoped it would
hold until the hay was stacked.

"But mine will not get stacked with me sitting here all day," Ralf said, draining his mug. "I'll be getting back to work. Come and visit us again, my lady. It's an honor you do us and our house."

After he had gone, Goda rose and laid the now sleeping child back in the cradle, which she pulled to one side so that the sun would not shine on her face.

Branwen, watching her tie the lacings on her bodice, said thoughtfully, "How do you know what to do? You seem so easy with the baby. It's all so strange to me."

"'Tis not my first, Lady Branwen. There was another, a little boy, who only lived seven months," Goda said, looking out over the fields.

"Oh, I'm sorry," Branwen said.

"No matter, my lady. It's nature's way. I only pray we may keep our little Bran until she is grown."

"Goda," Branwen said hesitantly, "will you let me come and help you with the baby this summer, so that I can learn what to do when my own is born?"

"Haven't you ever had a little one to care for?"

"No, I can't remember ever having a baby in the house. I've often cared for infants when they were sick, and I've helped women when the hour has come for the baby to be born, but I've never taken care of one. Will you show me how it's done?"

"Aye," said Goda warily, "if ye be serious. It's a simple enough thing. I can teach you what you want to know."

And the pattern of her days was easily set. Each morning, just as the dew was drying on the fields, Branwen went out to gather herbs. Dried herbs lose strength rapidly and must be replaced each year in their season. The salt air, blowing in from the sea, nourished different healing plants from the ones she had known in Wessex. Opening her soul to the earth's voice, she let it teach her again, as it always had, which were the herbs she needed. And she marveled that she had ever thought she could wall off this part of herself.

Later each day, when the herbs had been spread out to dry, she would go to the farmer's cottage where Goda showed her how to care for an infant. The baby needed only to be fed and kept clean, her soiled linen washed and dried in the warm sun. And Branwen saw how the little thing fed on more than her mother's milk, growing on the smiles and warm noises that went with her caring. But, although Goda was pleased to see her, still there was always a distance between them, due in part, she knew, to her place as mistress of Cynewithe, but also to the stories she feared Goda had heard from Ralf. And often in the late afternoon, walking back along the cartway to Cynewithe, Branwen wondered how long it would take to feel at home here. And she longed to return to Thornbury where she had grown up, where people might still think of her as her father's daughter.

Few people were sick while the weather held warm and sunny, although once she used the crimson tincture of shepherd's knot which she'd had made at Ipswich when one of the men was deeply cut by a careless stroke with a sickle. And shortly after that accident she had to prepare a poultice for Trygg who pulled a muscle lifting and stacking the drying hay. Though he had come willingly, even proudly, with her from King's Lynn, still, here among the farmers, he seemed to need to prove himself and in the proving strained muscles not used to the work.

Late in the month, when the nights had grown very short, when the sun still shone at eleven o'clock at night, a great pile of faggots was built at the crossroads in the tiny village of Clacton nearby. Excitement rose as the time drew near for the lighting of the midsummer fires. It was a festival which had its roots in the dim past and although the priests had tried to Christianize it (saying the fires were lit to celebrate the birthday of John the Baptizer), still there was a part of the night which would not be civilized.

But the excitement her neighbors shared only made Branwen feel more isolated, more aware that she was not one of them. Two days before midsummer, in the evening while the others gossiped and visited together, she felt more than ever this sense that she was an outsider, an intruder. She went out and walked along the ocean's edge for a long time, until at last night came and she could sleep. That night, the dream she had dreamed before at Cynewithe returned. Once more she dreamed of Rynna and Tril in their cave above the sea. Once more, when she needed it, their world became a place of warmth and welcome and good company. And in the dream she taught them to use more of the wild herbs which grew along the shore and back in the woods behind the dunes. She began to teach them as well to listen to the voice of the earth itself. She woke

with the sun shining in through the open window and was sorry
that the summer night had been so short.

In the cookhouse, Budda was already at work, plucking the
wild birds Trygg had netted for the feasting that night. She was
humming to herself as she worked and Branwen smiled to see
her happy. It was a glorious morning, bright and already
warm. Branwen took a basket from near the door and went out
to pick the wild strawberries which grew in a fallow field
beside a small stream. She noticed that the flies were up as
well, buzzing around the gutted carcass of a stag which hung
from the cross brace nailed between two trees.

She was glad she had left early for as she worked the sun
grew hotter, shining out of a clear sky. Her head had begun to
ache when she finally finished filling the basket. She was
thankful for the cool shade under the trees. There was a stand
of delicate blue spikes of vervain which grew along the path
back to Cynewithe and she stopped to pick some. The women
called it enchanter's plant. Not far off grew the furry-lipped
blossoms of lavender motherwort and she picked some of those
as well.

Back in the shadowy courtyard, under the trees at Cynewithe, she washed the berries and put them in a bowl covered
with a clean cloth to keep the flies off. Then she began to braid
a chaplet of the vervain and motherwort for Budda to wear to
the celebration. It was pleasant, sleepy work. As her fingers
twined the stems together, her mind wandered nearer and
nearer the edge of her dream until the wreath she made was for
another woman in another time. When Trygg rode in with
Beorn and Wymer, the finished chaplet had slipped forgotten
from her fingers.

"Sorry to waken you, Lady Branwen. They're calling for
the stag now the cook fires have been built," Trygg stam-
mered.

It was long moments before Branwen could remember
where she was. Finally, as the men were laying the stag across
the back of Wymer's old rouncy nag, she rose and went to the
well. Drawing up the cool water, she splashed it onto her face.
Then she turned and took the lavender and blue wreath into the
coolness of the main hall where the sea breeze blew through
the open shutters. She left it on the sideboard and, taking her
wide-brimmed straw hat with her this time, went back out to

the lane which ran away from the sea toward the woods. She had promised to pick some blue larkspur that day. There was a popular belief among her neighbors that anyone who looked through the feathery fronds of the larkspur at the midsummer flames would not have any eye trouble during the coming year. It was a harmless enough superstition and Branwen was glad to have this work to do. She could hear the laughter and shouting as people passed by on their way to Clacton and she was not anxious to join them, not yet anyway.

The late afternoon sun was very hot here where the sea breeze did not blow. The woods were still and quiet as if everything that lived in them was hiding from the sun. She found great masses of blue larkspur growing beside a small brook now shrunken into unconnected pools. A pale fish gasped in one of the shallow pools, its gills opening and closing, clinging to life. Picking up a stick, she dug in the stream above his pool, channeling the higher water so that it could flow down to him. When she looked up, still holding her muddy stick, the unicorn was there—watching her.

"Oh," she whispered, "you have come."

The pale white beast stood unmoving, the whorl of his horn gleaming coolly amid the shadows. *The sun will kill the fish, Daughter of the Moon, for the fisher king is ill,* he said in her heart. *He is beyond your help.*

"Yet he lives," she said softly.

Nothing truly lives in the wasteland.

"This is not a wasteland," she said.

"To him who feeds in the Meadows of the Moon, this world has become a barren place," a voice behind her said.

Branwen turned and saw The Mother shimmering like the dew among the larkspurs. "Mother," she said, "I had not thought to see You. Tonight we celebrate the power of the sun."

"It is not His power you celebrate, but His defeat."

Branwen's eyes widened in disbelief.

The Goddess laughed, a cool sound like water falling. "So much has been forgotten," She said. "What was once elaborate ritual is now brought so low—a holiday whose meaning is not destroyed but desecrated."

"Why would the sons of men celebrate the sun's defeat, Mother?" Branwen asked.

"It was not the sons, My child, but the daughters who lit the first fires; they who feared the sun would go on growing hotter each day, burning down on the fields longer and longer until there should be no night, no time for the moon to shine and the sweet, saving dew to fall. If the power of the sun were not defeated, all living things would shrivel and die. And so, when the priestess who kept account of such things saw how the sun moved back toward the south, she proclaimed the world saved and a great celebration was prepared. Although, still fearing to anger the sun by feasting while he yet looked down upon them, they waited until the dark of night. Then the great fires were lit and there were songs and dancing and great rejoicing.''

"Ansgar told me that in the old days the king was killed at the midsummer festival.''

"And these same tales would have you believe a king was killed at midwinter as well. Those days must have had a rich supply of kingly men who cared little for life,'' the Great Goddess said with a laugh.

"Oh, Mother, where is the truth in it all? So many names and tales, each different and yet the same.''

"Truth is like an oak tree, My child. At first it stands strong and tall in the forest, but then the mistletoe finds it out and begins to grow upon it, penetrating the bark with its roots, sucking the life from the oak until all that remains is mistletoe. But when the oak dies, the mistletoe is doomed. And you, child, have come so late that all you can see is the twisted branch of the vine. The oak is dead and long rotted away. You can learn little of the truth from the convolutions of the mistletoe. Yet,'' She said, looking off into the forest, "another oak has grown up, though it, too, is doomed by the deadly vine.''

"And do I have to find this new oak?'' Branwen asked warily.

"No, Daughter of the Moon, let others do that. To you it is given to watch as the ancient mistletoe decays and is finally destroyed.''

"Destroyed?''

"This land will yield in the end to a conqueror who will crush the last of the mistletoe beneath his heel until nothing is left but the pale berries.''

"I'm tired of riddles,'' Branwen said with a sigh, "and I have troubles enough with Knut without worrying about another conqueror.''

"Your trouble lies not with Knut but with yourself, My dear. There are very few who have been able to live in two worlds."

"What happened to those who tried?" Branwen asked.

"It would not help you to know, child. You must work out your own destiny."

"And my son's?"

"Branwen, Branwen, the life which quickens in you is not yours. You are a chalice filled with the Water of Life poured from the Eternal Infinite. Do not come to think of this child as your own, for he is not, though you may have him to love for seven years."

"Seven years?"

The Goddess smiled.

"Yet it's a simple thing, to have a child," Branwen said wistfully.

"If it were simple, My daughter, would the healer be helpless when the infant is stillborn, the spark unlit? Who can give life to the dead babe? Who could help Godgifu's daughter? Neither mother nor father, neither priestess nor healer. Life comes from Eternity and, in the end, returns to that same stream. No, child, it is not a simple thing."

Branwen picked the petals from the flower in her hand, lost in thought. At last she said, "Tell me about my dream, Mother. Who are Rynna and Tril? What does it mean?"

"You dream of the ancient oak as it comes forth from the acorn, a tiny shoot with one leaf only. Do not fear it. As you are the last priestess, so must you be the first.

"The women who gather around you in the dream lived here on this shore one hundred thousand years ago. They are the beginning. Their daughters will be the first to know and fear death's sting. You will teach them, console them. You will show them how to count the days of the moon, as already you show them the healing herbs. You will share with them the language of all living things.

"From these women will spring the race of My priestesses who will increase in number and spread out over the face of the earth. Only after nine hundred centuries have passed will men, stumbling onto the knowledge of paternity, terror-stricken, overpower My daughters: chaining their souls with lies, shackling their bodies with laws. Out of fear did man first do this and out of that same fear does he do so still."

"And the race of Your priestesses was defeated," Branwen said.

"Yes, child. They were pushed back and back, eventually, over the millennia, back to the shores of this island from which they had first come forth. Here, along the edge of the sea, that race will die with you."

"Is there nothing to be done?"

"To turn back the years?" the Goddess asked. "Oh, no, My daughter, Our hour has passed and a new cycle spins round, and beyond that is a final one more brilliant than either which has gone before."

"Will I see this wheel of brilliance?"

"Not from this shore, child. Here it is far in the future.

"But now you must take the larkspur and go back. See, the sun is setting. They will be looking for you."

"Will I see You again?"

"Of course, Daughter of the Moon, I am never far from you."

As Branwen watched, The Mother faded until Branwen stood alone amid the tall blue flowers. All at once she was aware of a cool, tinkling sound. Looking down, she saw that the brook had filled. Clear water ran merrily over the rocks on its way to the sea. She saw the fish, almost motionless, near the bottom of a deep pool, half hidden by gathering shadows.

And the last priestess of the Great Earth Goddess gathered an armload of larkspur and went back to Cynewithe.

In London the late afternoon sun was warm. The smell of roses drifted in through doors which were open onto the queen's private gardens. When Thorkell came into the room where she was sitting with her women, she looked up at him and smiled. Seeing who it was, the women disappeared, melting away as quickly and silently as snowflakes in April, until only the flute player and an old woman who had been her nurse from childhood remained.

"You're early today, mon cher," she lisped. She had reverted to her older speech pattern when she was in Normandy and the habit seemed hard for her to break.

"I've only come to say goodbye," he answered, leaning down to kiss her cheek.

"Mais non," she cried, getting up angrily. "You can't be serious! You promised you would stay."

"I promised I would stay until you were settled. I've stayed almost two months. It's time I got home."

"But I need you."

"No, you don't. You and Knut are just fine now."

"He's just a boy! He's crude and . . . and . . ."

"He's young and he's a king, Emma. The rest is up to you."

"But it's so much easier when you are here."

"Only for you, Em. Not for him . . . or for me. And I promised Branwen. . . ."

"Branwen! Always Branwen!"

He sighed and turned away from her, looking out into her gardens.

"I'm sorry," she said, coming up beside him, laying her hand on his arm, leaning her head on his shoulder.

She was tall—not as tall as he, of course, but taller than most of the other women—only slightly shorter than the man she was going to marry—the man who was king now. She was almost thirty and still slender; her skin glowed with warmth, and there was a fascination in her eyes and in the confident way she moved, as if she always knew what was expected of her and how to do it with grace and elegance. It was a combination few women had—one which came with age and only to those rare women who could afford it.

"You'll do fine, Em," he said after a while. "He is like a boy discovering the sword he thought would be dull and wooden is fine, sharp steel. I've seen him, the way he looks at you."

"And what about me? When you've gone I'll have no one to talk to. Nobody understands me here."

"I understand you," he said and laughed, "and the games you play. Before the year is out you'll have civilized us all. The court will glow and sparkle with your touch. It will be just the way you wanted to make it when Ethelred was king."

"It didn't work then. What a dull, dreadful place this was in the end."

"But that was Ethelred. Knut may be many things, but never dull."

"Non," she said with a smile which faded instantly. "You've settled then with him—about Ragnar."

"Aye," he said with a frown. "It was a stupid thing he did.

He knows it. He's testing, Em. Trying to find the limits. He's never been a king before."

"And Branwen didn't make it any easier for him—in front of all those people."

"Branwen doesn't make it any easier for anyone," he said ruefully.

"Then why, Thor?"

"She's my wife," he said simply, "and I love her."

"I know," she sighed. "You've told me that a million times."

"Why do you keep asking?"

"Hope, mon cher ami. Hope."

He didn't say anything.

"Stay," she pleaded, "just a few days more, please."

"Branwen will be furious," he protested weakly.

"Please."

"Just until the end of the week," he said, "no longer."

A month later, when the midsummer fires were forgotten, their ashes scattered by the wind, Branwen, now big with child, wandered barefoot along the edge of the sea. She had ventured too far out only minutes before and a wave had caught her, wetting her coarse linen skirt so that it clung heavily about her legs. The late afternoon was hot and she welcomed the coolness of her wet skirts as she walked along the quiet stretch of narrow beach exposed by the ebb tide. Sandpipers chased the waves, ignoring her, running among her footprints before the lapping waves washed them away. Where the beach was at its narrowest the lowering sun cast a long shadow across the sand. Branwen looked up to see what caused it.

"Eadric," she said, the taste of hatred in her mouth like sour wine.

He sat, cool and precise, on horseback at the edge of the low gravel bluff. "Lady Branwen," he said, "may I join you?" Without waiting for an answer, he clucked to his horse and it stepped daintily down the edge of the bluff, sliding a little in the gravel.

Branwen turned back to Cynewithe, sorry she had come so far, for it would be a long walk back.

"My lady, I had hoped for a warmer welcome," Eadric said, laughing at her, "for old time's sake."

"For old time's sake, Eadric?" she said turning on him angrily. "For old time's sake? Surely the 'old times' I remember were better forgotten. My neighbors here still mourn for men who died because of your treachery."

"Men die every day. What difference whether it's this year or next?"

"Tell that to a child who can't remember his father, or a woman who sleeps alone."

"Ah yes," he said, his green eyes raking her pregnant shape, accented by the wet skirts clinging to her legs. "It's very becoming to you, you know. You always were a bit on the thin side, just a trifle too ascetic."

She glared at him. "Why have you come here?" she asked.

"I have a message for you from your Viking consort," he said.

"From Thorkell?"

"The Jarl of East Anglia sends his greetings, et cetera. He regrets he cannot be here himself. He hopes to be delayed no more than a week or two."

"Is anything the matter?"

"No," he said coolly, "only that the queen desires him to stay."

"The queen? Why? Isn't she happy with Knut?"

"Oh, she is quite pleased with the king, from all reports, but apparently she looks on Thorkell as an old and trusted . . . er, friend. I understand she finds the court a trifle cruder than what she is used to. It must be a relief to have Thorkell around."

"From what I hear of the lady she will civilize the king and his court soon enough."

"Yes, no doubt you are right." Eadric laughed. He did not dismount but sat astride his horse looking down at her. "There is an amusing story going around London, you know. It is said that the reason Thorkell took so long in Normandy last winter was that the lady preferred to wed the ambassador and not the king. It is said that she tried for some time to persuade Thorkell that together he and she, with Robert's backing, of course, could defeat Knut and take back what belonged to her sons."

At his words Branwen burst out laughing. "Oh Eadric," she said at last, "you are impossible. What a fool I was to believe

"No, not at all. In that ancient manuscript it was written that a virgin was a woman who submitted to the rule of no man, preferring to stand alone. Though she bore many children, if she remained independent of a man's support, she was called 'virgin.'"

"You lie to yourself, Branwen. You're not his wife—you never will be—no matter how many squalling infants you bear him. Can you deny it? Are you really a wife to him, as another woman would be? I think not."

"He doesn't ask it of me," she said, her voice hushed.

"Then perhaps he's not such a fool." He laughed, a short bitter laugh. "Indeed, I was the bigger fool to think that I could make you mine." He paused, looking at her. "Yet the flame was there once," he said, "and burns still."

And she knew, looking into his eyes, that it was true. "I want to hate you, Eadric," she said.

"Why?" he whispered, taking her awkward shape in his arms. "What is the rest of the world to us?" He leaned over to kiss her but she pulled away and he let her go.

She went up onto the dais and sat down on the backless chair there.

"Of all that I have done, I regret most that I did not take you when I might have," he said. "I can think of little else which would have changed so much."

Reaching out to touch the puddle of warm wax spreading out around the candle on the table, she said, "Why don't you go to Normandy? You would be safe there."

"The game's not over yet," he said. "The field of play is here. Who knows? My luck may change."

"I cannot help you, Eadric."

"Can not or will not?" he asked, the familiar edge of scorn back in his voice.

"Does it matter?" she asked.

After a while she added, "I won't ask Thorkell. I think if I ever once mentioned your name to him, he would know . . ."

"Know what?" Eadric said sharply.

"Nothing," she said, confused. "Just—he won't help you and if he knew you were here tonight he would kill you himself."

"Would he, Branwen? Cause or no?"

"Oh Eadric, I don't know. Maybe you're right, maybe I'm

not really his wife—but I'm not free either—certainly not free to sleep with you.''

''Do you want to?''

''No,'' she said slowly, ''not now. Eadric, I don't want to sleep with anyone now.''

He laughed. ''I'll wait, Branwen. The game's not over yet,'' he said again. He set his goblet on the sideboard and started toward the door.

''You don't have to go. It's late. Stay here.''

''Do you really think that I'll sleep in your hall and not in your bed? My dear Branwen, if Thorkell is going to feel obliged to kill me, for God's sake, let's be sure it was worth it.''

''I'm sorry,'' she cried suddenly.

''For what, that I let him have you?''

''No, not that, only . . .''

''Only what?''

She did not answer him. Only when he was gone and she stood looking at the empty doorway did she know that she was sorry for him, sorry that there was such bitter emptiness in him. Not until the night was quiet once more, not until the sound of his leaving had died away completely, leaving her alone, did she get angry with herself that she had let him make her care again when she had thought she would feel nothing but hatred for him for the rest of her life.

Chapter Eight

Her back ached; she could hardly breathe. She felt fat, awkward, trapped in a body which was no longer her own. When she talked to herself, the answer came from a small voice which seemed to have retreated to the uppermost part of her head, like a sparrow chirping in some monstrous storage closet, all crammed with boxes and bales.

She longed to escape, to leave the body which wasn't hers anymore, to let her soul fly free with Blaec high over the fields, but she was afraid, afraid that the baby would not be all right if she left him behind. And it wasn't his fault. She didn't blame him for the fetters of her pregnancy. Indeed, there was no one she blamed. And why should she seek to blame someone? She was glad to be having a child, a son, Thorkell's son.

So there she was, gross and ungainly, and no one to blame for it, no one even to complain to, for who would understand? Everyone was thrilled for her. Even Trygg, although he tried to keep it secret. The young carle had made a wooden cradle, one that could be hung from a beam or a branch. She had not seen it but she knew he had finished it, and that it lay, carefully wrapped, in the stable behind the sacks of oats.

And when she was short-tempered, which was quite often now, she met with such patience and forbearance and tongue-clucking understanding, that she would storm out, tramping for hours through the woods and fields or along the shore away from human company, until she was too tired to care.

Like the day Elsey had folded her bony arms across her

narrow chest, looked keenly at her and said, "Two weeks, my lady, two weeks. He will come with the full moon."

"Two weeks!" she had cried. "It can't go on that long. Every day I feel my womb tighten, and my hopes rise, but it never lasts."

"'Tis a good sign," Elsey said wisely. "Mark my words."

Branwen had laughed. "Elsey, do you know how many babies I have seen born? I don't need you to tell me what is happening."

Hurt, Elsey had looked down at the beaten earth floor.

"Oh, Elsey, I'm sorry. I didn't mean . . ."

"That's all right, my lady," Elsey had said with a sniff and a smile, "'tis hard to wait."

She had felt like screaming.

A few days later, in early September, she went out with Budda and Trygg to pick the wild grapes which grew along the stream edge; but she had slipped and lost her balance reaching too far, and they had sent her back to wait in the shade. Leaning against the rough oak bark, the cloying odor of the fruit sickening her, she looked up and saw the tall figure of a man striding across the oat stubble toward her, the sun shining in his hair. Thorkell had returned at last—a month later than he had promised. She struggled awkwardly to her feet. A sharp pain stabbed her side. She had moved the wrong way again. Damn.

"You've been gone a long time, my lord," she said as he stood grinning down at her.

"Too long, Branwen, too long. It was stifling in London, like waiting for a thunderstorm to break."

"Oh," she said, "I heard the new queen found you entertaining and would not let you leave."

"Nonsense, Branwen. Who told you that?" he asked, looking at her keenly.

"Does it matter?" she asked icily.

His face froze and he stood for a long moment, looking down at her. Finally he said, slowly and deliberately, "Believe what you wish, my lady, but I have not ridden all day to be welcomed thus."

When she said nothing, he turned on his heel and walked swiftly back across the fields.

"And you can keep right on walking, my great Lord Thorkell," she muttered softly. "If you think I am going to spend the rest of my life waiting for you to find time for me, you are very wrong." Angrily she brushed away the tears.

She stayed late with Goda and Ralf that evening. They had not heard of the jarl's return and were glad to have her stay, for an easy familiarity was beginning to grow at last among them.

"You know," Goda said as they were washing the supper things together while Ralf played with the baby on the fleece beside the fire, "you are positively blooming tonight."

Branwen laughed.

"Nay, 'tis true, lady," Ralf said without looking at her.

"Oh, I remember feeling as you do—a great lump—but still, there is a . . ." She stopped, seeing the tears come to Branwen's eyes. "Hush now, don't cry," Goda said, taking her in her arms. "Ralf, don't you have to tend to the animals?"

"Don't send him away, Goda. I'll be all right. I really must be going anyway. It's getting late."

"I'll walk with you, my lady," Ralf said uncertainly.

"No, really, Ralf, I'll be all right. It's such a short way."

"Of course he'll go with you," Goda said firmly.

"I'm sorry to be such a goose," Branwen sniffed.

"Nonsense! What's there to be sorry about? I was the same," Goda said, hugging her tightly. "A good night's sleep will work wonders. Walk carefully. The moon is bright enough." As they were leaving she called after them, "Be quiet when you get back, Ralf. The baby will be asleep."

They walked in silence along the moonlit cartway. She wondered if Thorkell would be gone when she got to Cynewithe. She dreaded meeting him. What could she say? She had every right to be angry with him. He had kept her waiting almost a month longer than he had promised. She had been left here alone, imprisoned in this mountain of flesh she dared not leave. It was not fair.

He was there. Slouched tiredly in a thick-cushioned chair in the great hall, he looked up when she came in. There were men already asleep on the benches around the room, she noted absently, not really seeing them. She smiled awkwardly at him, unwillingly, not knowing what to say.

"If you want I'll leave in the morning," he said, "or I'll stay. But I will not be held to account for my actions like an errant child."

His words tolled like a knell in her soul. That he should

leave, that it should be ended, was suddenly inconceivable to her. She could not bear to think of life without him. She turned away so that he could not see her face.

"You might have known I would worry when you did not come. You might have sent word," she said. Her voice was thick.

"Every day I thought I would be able to leave. Each morning it seemed pointless to send a message when I would be just behind the messenger," he said gently. She turned into his arms and leaned toward him. He bent down, gathering her carefully to himself, holding her quietly until the world should be right once more.

"Elsey said I must be patient with you, that the last weeks are difficult for the woman."

"I longed so many times to send Blaec to you," she said, ignoring his words, "to beg you to come quickly."

"It's just as well you didn't, Bran," he said, stroking her hair, his eyes fixed in the distance.

"Will you tell me?" she asked.

"Not now, my love," he said softly. "It is late and I am very tired. Beorn says they will start cutting the wheat as soon as the dew is dry in the morning."

Before she woke the next morning he was up and gone, out in the fields harvesting the wheat crop with Beorn and the free farmers who owed this service each year. How easily the men accept him, Branwen thought, watching him come home at sundown, sweat-soaked, laughing easily with them.

That evening Cynewithe was alive with ale-drinking men. The five carles who had ridden in with Thorkell had spent the day hunting with the dogs, so that there was no lack of game on the jarl's table. As they sat together in the great hall, Branwen smiled to see how skillfully the great Danish leader won the loyalty of the East Anglian farmers, speaking little, listening intently, until every one of them believed in his heart that the jarl valued his opinion and would be glad for his support. And Branwen, spinning quietly, laughed to herself, for she knew it was true and not just artifice.

A few nights later, when she couldn't sleep, she lit the candle and sat beside the sleeping Dane wondering how it was that just his coming had made everything easier. It was as if all her unhappiness had been an illusion. Now that he was beside her, she couldn't remember why it was she had felt ill-used;

now that he was beside her, she felt the world was theirs. Sights and sounds had become brighter, and even the rain which had fallen that evening had not been dull grey but shimmering crystal.

As she sat there in the dark beside him, she saw that being at Cynewithe, even for so short a time, had been good for him. The grey circles around his eyes had vanished as his skin grew dark from the sun. The softness which had crept into his body was hardening with each swing of the sickle. Only the grim lines about his mouth were still there.

In the morning, seeing him lost in thought, she went over to him and laid her hand gently on his arm. "Tell me," she said.

"What is there to tell, my love?" he answered. "He paid the blood price—easy enough for him—twelve thousand silver pennies."

"It's the price of a great noble," she said softly.

"He was captain of my flagship. Should his murderer have paid less?"

"But it doesn't please you?"

"It was too easy for him, Branwen. He would do it again without a moment's hesitation. I don't know where he will strike next."

"Why should he want to strike again?"

"Oh, I don't know." Then he laughed, ruefully. "Emma will keep his thoughts on other matters—for a while anyway."

She wanted to ask him then about the woman who was queen. For as long as she had loved him, Thorkell's name had been linked with Emma's. But the grimness of his face intimidated her and she said nothing. There were depths to him that she wondered if she would ever penetrate. She kissed his cheek and went out to the cookhouse to see about dinner.

Her labor began in earnest one morning a week later just as Elsey had said. All day she struggled with it. Then, when the full moon rose over the ocean that night, she held tightly to Goda's strong hands and delivered her son into the world.

Elsey, crowing with delight, washed him clean of his birthing. Wrapping him loosely in soft blankets heated by the fire, she laid him beside his mother.

"See if he will give suck yet, my lady. Touch his cheek to your breast."

Branwen did and felt radiant happiness flood through her as

he began to nurse. Suddenly, she cried out as pain twisted low in her belly.

"Hush now, 'tis only the after pains, child," Elsey said, wiping her face with a cool cloth.

"Ah," Branwen said as the contraction eased, "I had no idea it would be so sharp."

"Drink this, it will ease you," Elsey said handing her a goblet of warm wine mixed with rosemary and thyme.

"Where did you find the wine?" Branwen asked with a smile.

"My Lord Thorkell returned with some just before sundown, lady."

"I wonder where he went," she said.

While Branwen nursed the newborn child, the women cleaned her bedding, washing her and covering her with blankets of woven linen. They moved quickly, Elsey and Goda, so Thorkell would get a chance to see his wife and son before both were asleep.

He brought her flowers. She knew then where he had been all day, for they were upland white asters and did not grow near the sea but farther away. She had seen their blooms trampled and bloodied once, a year ago, beneath the fallen men at Ashington.

"We'll call him Hemming," Thorkell said tenderly, leaning down to kiss her.

"Our little bear," she said.

The Dane lifted his son gingerly, cradling him in his great hands.

"Tell Trygg we have no place for the child to sleep," she said, her eyes closing. "He will know what to do."

"He's a beautiful child, Branwen," Thorkell said and Branwen knew, for his heart spoke to hers as it always had, what he had no words to say—that there would be no way he could return a gift to her as precious as the gift she had given him. As long as he lived, he would be in her debt.

And she struggled to tell him that it was not so, that the child was not a gift to him, that he was her son, too, but she had labored long and hard and now the drugged wine pulled her easily into sleep.

When the baby was only a few days old, she saw that Thorkell was anxious to be gone, but she said nothing to him. He waited two weeks before coming to her one morning. She was working at the loom while the baby slept in Trygg's cradle hanging beside her, and looked up, surprised to see him for she thought he had gone hawking with his men.

"You are back early," she said.

"I didn't go, Bran. There are things to attend to here."

"You are leaving then?" she asked brightly.

"Aye." He nodded. "You'll be all right?" It was barely a question. "There is work which must be finished in King's Lynn and then further west in Hertford and Peterborough. I can't let it go any longer. I'm meeting Orm on the way. I'll send ten men back here to protect you and the child."

"There's no need, Thorkell."

"I hope you are right but I'm not going to chance it."

Branwen smiled at him. "Do you doubt me, after all you've seen?"

"No, Branwen, I don't doubt you," he replied evenly. "I would just feel . . ."

There was a sudden clamor in the courtyard, the sound of a horse and clanking steel. Thorkell moved in front of her, his sword drawn. His battle axe hung beside the door. Grabbing it in his left hand, he went out.

In the yard a great giant of a man sat astride a foam-flecked war horse. The giant's eyes burned from the darkness of his overhanging iron helmet. Even on horseback Branwen could see that he was as tall as Thorkell but much heavier. The weight of his swordstroke would cut through a man's armor like butter.

"I am Lady Branwen's man," the giant roared. "'Tis said you doubt I am strong enough to protect her." The stranger bellowed a deep laugh and swung easily out of the saddle, his sword in hand.

"You lie," Thorkell said. "The lady has no men but mine."

"Yet I tell you I serve her better than your own. Where are they now? What protection has she?" he asked with a sneer.

"Not much, I'll warrant. Still, it's your blood will water her courtyard," Thorkell said, advancing, his battle axe over his head.

The giant stood his ground, grinning at him. Even as the axe crashed through his shoulder, the giant's grin was unchanged. Nor did he seem at all disturbed by the split which healed as suddenly as the axe had opened it.

Pale beneath his tan, Thorkell turned his back on the giant and looked at Branwen who stood in the doorway.

"All right," he said, "I'll send no men."

"And you're not going to worry about me or the baby?" she said.

"No more than I can help, being new at this."

"Not so new, I think," she said. "You've trusted me before. He'll be quite safe."

The giant had vanished; the courtyard was empty. Elsey came out of the cookhouse and emptied a basin of dirty water over the cobbles.

Chapter Nine

"Damn," he said, stamping the wet snow off his feet as he came into the room. "Damn. It's colder than Freya's tits."

Thorkell looked up from the tax lists he was going over with his host, a thick-set dark Saxon with bad teeth. Recognizing the newcomer, he broke into a grin and said, "Eilaf, by the hammers of Hel, what are you doing here?"

"I've heard a rumor that you're outfitting a ship for a run up the Seine come spring, just like the old days."

Thorkell laughed. The Saxon looked appalled. At the sight of his gaping mouth, Eilaf laughed as well.

"He's not serious," Thorkell reassured the reeve. "This is Eilaf, an old friend, who is no doubt hungry as well as cold."

"Of course, my lord," the man said. "Welcome to my humble household, my lord. Please, warm yourself. I'll see about some food and drink. Only a moment," he added, backing toward the door.

When he had gone, Thorkell frowned and said, "He's an idiot. I've caught him twice cheating on these damn tax lists."

A maid came hurrying in. Her apron was soiled with more than one day's work in the kitchen. She held a bowl of water in her hands, grey toweling over her arm.

Eilaf washed his hands and then wiped them across his face, the water glistening on his dark beard.

"What brings you out in this weather? I thought you had settled in with your brother in Thetford."

"My brother is a proud father. Do you have any idea what

that means? All day long he talks about that mewling kid of his, as if he were the greatest thing since two-edged swords. I stood it as long as I could. When I heard you were at Newmarket, I decided to pay you a social call.''

"Well, good. I'm leaving for Maldon day after tomorrow. Then you can have the pleasure of watching me be the proud father.''

"Oh God! At this rate I may not wait until spring to set off for Byzantium.''

"Byzantium? Are you serious?''

"It's the only place left where there is a chance at some real fighting. The pay is good, they say.''

"Then you don't believe it's true—that we'll not fight again?''

"The men of Ashington? Oh, aye, it's true, all right. I almost got myself killed, finding that out.''

"What happened? Tell me,'' Thorkell said tensely.

"We can't strike a first blow. I can't describe the feeling . . . utter revulsion . . . a physical thing. I don't know. I just know it disappears, that feeling, after an attack has been made. Then I could strike back, but never press the attack—only defend myself. And hardly even that. How can you successfully defend yourself with a sword if you are not free to follow up with an attack of your own when the opening is there? Why I'm not dead, I don't know.''

"And yet you talk of going to Byzantium. Are you so tired of life?''

"Oh, I'm not going,'' Eilaf laughed with just a trace of bitterness, "not yet. Some day, maybe.''

"You need a wife.''

"Good God, don't you start. That's all I hear from Estrid. I have yet to find a woman who does not bore me very quickly.''

"You're right.'' Thorkell laughed. "I've got that to be grateful for, I guess. Branwen may be many things, but never boring.''

"But Branwen is yours,'' Eilaf said reaching out for the goblet the maid handed him. "I'll be hard pressed to find another like her.''

Thorkell laughed. "Thank God for that!''

Finally, when Eilaf had eaten and tossed the last bones to the dogs who had been watching him hungrily, he looked up at Thorkell and said, "Olaf told me you are going to London for the midwinter feasting." He drained his goblet. "He said you're taking Branwen with you."

"Aye," Thorkell said, leaning back against the wall.

"And the child?"

"And my son."

"And is it also true that Knut is to be his godfather?"

Thorkell's eyes narrowed. "It's true," he said.

"What does Branwen think?"

Thorkell stood up. Crossing the room, he stood with his back to Eilaf and said, "She doesn't know." Turning around to face Eilaf, he asked, "What's all this to you?"

"Why, Thorkell? Why push this?"

"Why?" Thorkell seemed genuinely puzzled, as if the question were meaningless, as if any fool would know without asking. "It's the only way I know to keep the boy safe. Branwen can only protect him while he is with her. How long will that be? A few years at best. Then? No, this is the only way. Knut cannot harm him once he has answered for him at the font."

"What made him agree to do it? Branwen's child?"

"My child," Thorkell said, pausing a moment before adding, "I asked him publicly, formally. He could not refuse me. He owes me that much, anyway."

"And Branwen? What will she say?"

Thorkell shrugged. "It will be all right. She'll understand. She'll see this is the only way."

Eilaf sighed and, putting his large strong hands on the table, he pushed himself up. He stepped carefully over the sleeping dogs and went toward the sideboard to refill his cup. Standing there, he stopped suddenly and said, "What about this other thing? That Knut wants you to marry Eadgyth when Eadric is dead?"

"Eadric is not dead and I have a wife."

"Is it worth all this? If you face him down on this matter, you risk losing everything."

"Look, Eilaf, what's on your mind? We've fought together long enough to at least be honest with each other. You've ridden long and far, in freezing weather. Suppose you tell me why."

Eilaf poured the goblet full and drank it down before turning to Thorkell. They stood there, ten feet apart; their eyes held and neither looked away. "Let me take her back to Thornbury.

That land will be close to Eadric's holdings in Cheddar which will be mine. I'll keep an eye on her. Her brother will too. Knut will gradually forget her. You can marry Eadgyth. Her lands and yours adjoin. It will mean great power for you. Knut needs you as his friend, the way it used to be. . . ."

"So you have it all worked out," Thorkell said, his mouth tight. "How many others know of this neat little plan?"

"No one knows but you and me, Thorkell," he said quietly.

"Then the matter will go no further. This is between me and the king. Leave it be."

"Very well—but the offer stands—when and if you need my help."

When Thorkell went up to Maldon to join his wife and son, Eilaf went with him. They stayed only a few days, time enough to talk, time enough to load wagons with chests of rich clothes and furs, treasure of gold and silver and precious stones—the train of a Viking lord who was on his way to attend the king's midwinter festival.

And when at last it was time to leave the city, Budda rode on one of the wagons with the jarl's infant son robed in fur against the chill. The jarl and his wife rode on ahead with Eilaf. Behind them rode the standard bearer, and Orm, captain of the house carles, who brought up the rear, each one fully armed, the horses' harnesses jangling over the frozen ruts.

They came to Noak Hill on the London road as the village church bells rang for vespers. The drawbridge was lowered this time, for the jarl and his men were expected, his way having been prepared by the marshal who had gone on ahead to see that all was in readiness.

"Welcome to Noak Hill, Lord Thorkell," Byrtric said, bowing gravely. He was a soft man, yet lean, ill-fashioned with flesh like grey putty. The lines on his face were deep and there was an emptiness in his eyes.

Thorkell swung out of the saddle and stood facing the lord of Noak Hill. "My wife, Lady Branwen," he said deliberately.

"Lady Branwen," Byrtric replied flatly, "of course. A pity your man didn't mention that your wife rode with you, my lord."

"Yes, a pity," Thorkell said. "Perhaps your wife will see to her needs—and the child's as well."

"Of course, Lord Thorkell," Byrtric said. "Show the Lady

Branwen to my wife's rooms," he commanded a liveried servant who stood at the door.

There was laughter and the sound of a recorder piping gaily as Branwen, carrying her son, followed the servant through the hall to the bright women's rooms beyond.

There she was greeted with a delighted shout. "Branwen! I didn't know you were coming." Godgifu, out of breath and flushed from dancing with the children, dropped a curtsey. "And you have a baby. Oh, let me see!"

"He's three months old now," Branwen said proudly.

"Three months! And see how big he is. Let me hold him. Look, this is Lord Thorkell's wife and son," she said introducing Branwen to the women who sat at the tall looms. "Isn't he beautiful? But we had no idea you were coming with the jarl. Why didn't your marshal let us know?"

"We thought there would be less chance of . . . difficulty, if no one knew ahead of time I was going to London with Thorkell."

"Difficulty? Oh, yes, I'd forgotten. Your quarrel with the king. Byrtric told me about that. We weren't supposed to welcome you into our homes—some nonsense like that. Well, most people must have forgotten by now and anyway I don't care. I'm so glad you've come! See the boys. How big they've grown. Say 'good day' to Lady Branwen, children."

The boys made sturdy bows and mumbled their greetings shyly.

"Good day to you as well, sirs," Branwen answered. "You've taken good care of your mother these last months, I can see that."

"Oh Branwen, so much has happened in a year. I shall tell you everything; but first, you must rest and have something to eat and drink. It's a cold day for traveling and from the way your baby is tugging at my dress he, too, is hungry. Won't you sit here in the last of the sun? Ola, run and fetch some wine and see what can be brought from the kitchen. We'll have supper right here and let the men entertain themselves in the hall."

They sat for a long time. The weavers left, going back to their own hearths in thatched cottages below the walls of Noak Hill. The piper left, too, sent for by the lord to play in the great hall. Budda helped the maid servants who built up the fire and lit the torches, serving cold meat tarts from the kitchen. Good strong wine, spiced and warmed in a thick crock, was set near the fire.

"You seem so happy here now," Branwen said, settling into a soft-backed chair, her baby nursing hungrily, easing the fullness in her breasts, swollen during the long afternoon's ride.

"Oh yes, Branwen," Godgifu said, her eyes sparkling.

"And Byrtric is good to you and the children?"

"Byrtric?" Godgifu laughed brightly, the sound tinkling through the thick oak rafters hung with dusty branches of dried herbs. There was an openness in her laughter which was not yet overwhelmed by a chill bitterness which clung at the edge. "Byrtric is always drunk. In the morning he is sick and by midday he is in his cups once more. Days go by and I think he forgets I am even here."

"And yet it doesn't seem to bother you."

"Oh no, Bran, it doesn't bother me." Her bright smile wavered and was gone. "Sometimes," she continued, "when I see him there, falling down in the courtyard with it, I am sorry for him and wish it weren't so. It's hard to see how the others despise him for it, but still . . ."

"But what is it then that pleases you?" Branwen asked, shifting the child to her other breast.

"Oh Branwen, for the first time in my life I am free. There is no one to tell me to come or go. I do as I please. When the household is kept going in spite of its master's lack, the people look at me—so that I feel proud, useful. Like a man, I am doing something, not just belonging to someone, not just being cared for like a valuable possession. It's a good feeling, Branwen."

"But if he's drunk as you say, day in and day out, he'll be dead before spring. Does he go out? Does he still hunt?"

"Sometimes he hunts and they say there is a reckless abandon to him then, a wildness that has already killed one horse."

"Then surely he will kill himself next. What will you do then? You must marry again and what will become of your freedom?"

"But Branwen, I don't want to marry again. Noak Hill has been willed to the boys, and the jarl must see to its maintenance while they are young. It is up to Thorkell what is to be done with me."

"Oh, I see." Branwen laughed. "And you're sure I will

speak to him and he will not arrange a marriage for you, is that it?"

"You will, won't you?" Godgifu's eyes were bright.

"You haven't told me everything, have you?"

Godgifu flushed.

"A lover! You've taken a lover."

"Not yet, Branwen. But there is one. Shall I tell you about him?"

"How not?" Branwen laughed.

"His name is Wulfmaer. He's the youngest son of Alfhere who owns much land to the north. He's tall and his hair and beard are dark. His voice is gentle, like his eyes. And when he looks at me I know he loves me as I love him."

"When do you see him? Does he come here?"

"Oh yes, he's often here. He serves Byrtric, hunts with him, sits at table with him."

"Then he must be of a good family. Why can't you marry him when Byrtric dies? Is he married to someone else?"

"Oh no, he doesn't have a wife. But if I marry him, love will die and I will be only his wife."

"But I married the man I love," Branwen said. "I don't love him less and I certainly don't feel I am *only* his wife."

"Don't you? Then you are lucky, luckier than most, I think."

Just then there was a knock on the door. Branwen took the sleeping infant from her breast and closed her bodice loosely. Budda went over and opened the door.

"Thorkell asks you to join him in the main hall, my lady," Trygg said with a bow.

Godgifu laughed.

"I am not *only* his wife," Branwen said, "but I am his wife nonetheless. Will you come?"

Godgifu nodded.

Turning to Trygg she said, "Tell him we'll be in shortly." She laid the baby in a cradle nearby which had been brought in for him.

"Old Megins will stay and watch over him," Godgifu said, indicating an old woman who was dozing in the corner. "Though she sleeps through everything else, the sound of an infant's crying wakes her quickly enough."

Budda brought a sleeveless fur house robe from the chest which had been brought in from the cart for the night, and held it for Branwen to slip into. The night was cold and away from the warmth of the fire the house, too, was cold. Branwen pulled off the fine gold hair netting which had bound her dark curls during the day of travel and Budda brushed them out quickly for her.

"You look just like a jarl's wife should," Godgifu said.

"Thorkell and I play the game for high stakes, Godgifu. I want to be his wife but the king denies it and that denial now threatens our son. I was content once that he should love me and I him, and thought, like you, that more was not necessary. Now, for my son's sake, I must be his wife. Come, let's go in. You can show Thorkell how well you stand on your own."

London lay like a dark smudge under leaden skies. The smell of wood smoke was thick around them as they rode through the ice-rimmed mud of the city streets. The cold and fitful rain had not kept many indoors; it was midmorning and the streets and shops were crowded with tradesmen and their customers. There was a certain richness to the crowd, more fur than might have been expected, trimming cloaks of wool, thick and new. The shops and stalls were filled with merchandise. The king was rich and the men who served in his army were rich as well. Booty and coin which had been wrung from the land in the past years were being returned through these streets of alehouses and shops.

In a small, richly furnished room in one of the better houses, a group of men stood around a low-burning fire, their hands holding heavily jeweled goblets filled with warm spiced yppocras. They were young men, their hair not yet threaded with grey, but already old enough to have the heavy shoulders of men who had wielded a broadsword in battle. Gold glittered on their hands and around their necks. Jeweled swords hung low over their hips, beautifully crafted pieces of masculine jewelry, not the swords they had worn to battle.

One man, blonder than the rest, his blue eyes steady, his voice rich with a Norse accent, said, "What kind of an order is this? What kind of king fights with tactics like a woman's?"

Then another man, a Saxon judging by his brown hair and southern pattern of speech, answered, "Do you expect him to fight my sister like a man, Hakon? Don't be a fool. Branwen should consider herself lucky to have gotten off so lightly."

"But to tell us we are not to speak to her when she comes into the hall this evening. It's, it's . . ."

"It's what? Shameful? Dishonorable? Would you feel better if he'd sent one of us with orders to kill her? She needs to be reminded that he is king, that she lives at his pleasure."

"And he needs this victory over her, God knows," a third man added with a laugh.

"A stupid victory. It makes me feel soiled behaving like this," Hakon answered.

"Leofric is right. Knut needs this victory. And what harm does it do? A few awkward minutes for Branwen? Would you say she doesn't deserve it, after the display she put on last Christmas?"

"No," Hakon answered slowly, "but I still don't like it."

"Well, like it or not you sure as hell better follow orders."

"Oh, I'll do as I'm told, you can be sure of that," he said bitterly. "But if she were my sister . . ."

"If she were your sister, you'd do just exactly what I'm doing. Trying to reassure the king that she is only my sister, no more. As far as I'm concerned, she's a royal nuisance. I'm glad Knut only wants this small triumph."

"What would we have done if he wanted more, I wonder?" Leofric asked no one in particular.

"Packed it all in and gone back to farming. And wouldn't that have been exciting?"

Branwen and Thorkell dismounted and Branwen, taking the infant from Budda, followed the jarl quickly out of the raw cold of the street through the heavy iron-bound doorway. Just inside they were met by the maid servant, who curtseyed low.

"Welcome to London, my lady," she said.

"Thank you, Gwen," Branwen answered. "We are cold and the baby is hungry. Is there a room ready for us?"

"Yes, my lady, this way."

She had not meant to fall asleep when she lay down on the draped bed to nurse her son, but the room was warm and Budda's voice as she and Gwen began to unpack the chests droned on like bees in the summer sun, and she slept. After a while the baby slept as well, milk pooling at the corner of his mouth and dripping onto the coverlet. She didn't hear Thorkell when he came in. Seeing her asleep, he left a message with her women that he would return at nightfall.

She slept for an hour while the women worked. When she woke there was a kettle of water steaming over the fire, soap and thick linen for washing. Budda had laid out clean clothes of deep blue velvet and silky white. Her chest of jewels, still locked, sat on a small table under a dark mirror. The baby gurgled happily from his cradle beside the bed.

Budda, seeing her awake, smiled and said, "There is good thick soup, if it please you, my lady, and fine white wastel."

Branwen sat up, suddenly hungry, and Budda brought the bowl to her. "Where is Thorkell?" Branwen asked between mouthfuls.

"He came while you were asleep. He said to tell you he'd be back before dark. Trygg says he's gone to meet with the king."

Branwen frowned.

"There's a woman outside," Budda said hesitantly. "She's come to speak to you. She says she's had word you might be needing a wet nurse."

"A wet nurse? Whatever for?"

"But, my lady, surely you don't intend to take the baby with you to all the feasts this midwinter?"

"No, Budda, I guess not. But still," she said slowly, "a wet nurse. I don't want to leave him with a stranger."

"I'll stay with him. He'll be fine, I'll see to that, you know I will."

So it was that when Thorkell returned long after dark, which came early at midwinter, Branwen, richly dressed, her hair loosely bound with strings of pearls, errant curls framing her face softly, was sitting in the great hall laughing with the carles who had gathered around her. She looked up when he entered and felt an irrational stab of jealous anger flare up in his heart. It was an old thing between them and she was pleased it had not died. She smiled at him, the radiant reassuring smile he knew was his alone, and he grinned back.

"The queen will have us join her for supper this evening, Branwen," he said.

"Now?" Branwen asked.

"Aye, lady, now." The way he said it silenced all her excuses and she rose to cross toward him. Trygg appeared with her long cape of northern grey squirrel. Thorkell took it from him and held it out for her, gathering her against him for a moment in its rich folds. "You look beautiful tonight. Emma will love you."

"You know too little about women, Thorkell. She won't love me at all."

"Nevertheless, Branwen, we are going." Half in jest, he said, "Perhaps they won't even notice us."

But Branwen could not laugh. "Not notice us? You must be mad. Everyone will be watching, wondering what entertainment I am going to provide this year."

His voice was cold, like a sword striking stone. "Then they will all be disappointed. There will be no entertainment tonight."

They rode a short distance through the city to the king's great hall. Groomsmen took their horses and they went into a room blazing with candles, warmed by the fires and the crush of people gathered there. A page came up to them and bowed. "The queen would speak with you alone for a moment, Lord Thorkell," he said.

Thorkell frowned. "Wait here," he said softly. "I'll be back shortly."

The minutes dragged by and he did not return. There were many people in the room she knew but, oddly, none seemed to see her. It was as if she had become invisible; worse, for a space began to open up around her, so that she was standing alone in an empty circle. Her brother was there, across the room, and she caught his eye. Godwin winked at her and then, incredibly, he turned back to the group he was talking with. Neither Hakon nor Leofric who stood near him looked her way. Eilaf was not there. She fought down a rising desire to turn and flee.

"Smile, Branwen. May they all rot in hell." His voice was smooth and low; his hand on her arm was warm.

"Eadric," she said quietly, her lip trembling, "aren't you afraid you'll catch what plague I seem to be carrying?"

"No," he said, raising her hand to his lips, holding her eyes with his own, steadying her. "I am immune to plague, having a fatal disease of my own."

"Well then," she smiled, "we make a good pair."

"I told you that a long time ago, Branwen," he said quietly. Then in a louder voice, he added, "Come, let me get you some wine. Our new king serves only the finest Norman wines. Even I am impressed with his buttery.'' His voice carried through the room which had suddenly become quite still.

"Well, my lord," she said gaily, "that is high praise indeed. I remember enjoying your wines many times. My lord, the jarl, has yet to find a butler who can keep wines as yours can."

They stood for a few moments speaking together over their goblets while the room came slowly back to life. Turning his back to the crowd, Eadric said, "He let it be known that none was to speak to you."

"So that was it." She laughed. "What a petty thing to do. I'd expected more from him than that."

"He walks softly while Thorkell wields such power in the land. He's not strong enough yet to take him. He's just biding his time, Branwen."

"That's not true. Thorkell stands at his right hand," she said disbelievingly. "He is his advisor in everything. When he is gone from the court there are messengers daily between them."

"He's too powerful, Bran. Knut wants to be king in his own right here, not first among equals as in Denmark; and Thorkell is standing in his way. When Knut is ready, he will challenge him, mark my words."

Before she could reply there was a blare of horns.

"The king," Eadric sneered.

Knut's eyes swept the crowd looking for her, expecting her to be alone, shunned. There was a blaze of anger in his northern blue eyes when he saw that Eadric stood with her. He turned to speak to Eric of Norway who stood beside him. She watched as the jarl nodded slowly, almost reluctantly.

"So," Eadric said, "the order is given at last."

"What order?" she asked. But he had no time to answer, for Thorkell was suddenly there with them.

"There was some mistake. The queen had not sent for me at all. I apologize for being so long."

"No matter, my lord," she said, slipping her hand through his arm. "Eadric has been good company."

"My thanks, Eadric," Thorkell said stiffly. "Now, if you will excuse us, we will join Knut."

Eadric bowed slightly. "My pleasure, Thorkell. Your wife

is most charming. I hope to see you again before you leave this evening, Lady Branwen."

"Of course, my lord," she said, puzzled, for there was an intensity to his request that was unlike him.

As they walked toward the dais where Knut and Emma stood talking to a group of courtiers gathered around them, Branwen felt the power of the conqueror. The crown had come to sit easily upon his head during the last few months. It was a simple, graceful thing, a wide gold band topped by four lilies; it had crowned the heads of the last two Saxon kings. He wears it as a sign, she thought, so we will all think he's king as Edgar was, just and rightful. Under the crown his eyes were cold. When he smiled, only his mouth moved. He seemed to stand apart from other men, as if the strength of his vision made reality pale. She saw in his face that what Eadric said was true. He would be king—powerful and absolute. He would not settle for less than that. She knew with dread that reality would have to come to match his vision, for the soul behind those icy eyes would never melt. In that vision there was no place for her. Her power was too great. He could not defeat her and for that he hated her. The wellspring of her strength was beyond his reach. He knew it and it was intolerable to him.

"Thorkell," the king said, "welcome to London. I'm glad you've joined us at last." Turning to her he said, "It's been a long time, Lady Branwen, since you last graced our court."

"You are very kind, my lord," Branwen said with a graceful curtsey, her full velvet spreading softly around her.

"Why, Thorkell," the queen said, her voice strange with its Norman inflections, "it is too true." Turning to Branwen, she said, "But you are just as beautiful as he has always said, ma cherie."

Branwen looked up at the queen, seeing her for the first time. Her hair and clothes were exquisitely done. It seemed immediately boorish to consider her plain, as if a pretty face were too common a matter for a queen. Her skin was flawless, smooth and white; her pale brown hair was veiled and caught round with a gold crown. Branwen felt uncouth, clumsy, like a child with dirty hands.

"Thank you, my lady," she said.

"You are looking well, Emma," Thorkell said with a smile. "The bargain we struck last year suits you."

"Yes," she said with a warm smile, "and fruitful as well. Your king is everything you said he was and more, is he not? Yes, I am glad we were met in the marriage bed, for I would not like to have met him on the field of battle."

When they were seated at table, Branwen found herself beside the queen. Eric of Norway sat on her right.

"You have a young son, ma cherie," Emma said. "The king tells me we are to be his godparents."

"Thorkell and I would be most honored if you would answer for the child," Branwen replied.

"But of course, we should be delighted. And when he is older he must come to us and be our fosterling; and, if the child I am carrying is the son we hope for, why then you and Thorkell must do the same for us."

"We would be honored," Branwen said, realizing too late that she was repeating herself foolishly. But the pipers began to play and her words were lost in the noise. She toyed with the food in front of her, noticing as she did that Eric, too, was not eating the supper he had been served.

"Are you well, Lord Eric?" she asked him quietly.

He looked at her blankly for a moment as if he were bringing his thoughts back from a distant place. "Quite well, my lady," he said at last.

"The food is very good," she said.

"You haven't eaten much yourself," he answered. Suddenly he said, "Oh Branwen, war is simpler."

"What's the matter, Eric? What has happened?"

"Tell me," he said looking at her intently, "what is the duty one owes a king? Must his every command be obeyed?"

"No," she said slowly, "only if what he commands is right."

"And if it is wrong? What then? And if it is . . ."

"What's the matter, Eric?" she repeated earnestly, touching her hand to his arm as it lay on the table.

"An unpleasant task is all," he said smiling at her. But the blackness of his mood would not give him up so easily and he turned away adding, "Still, I would as soon be done with it." After a moment, he seemed to come to terms with whatever tormented him. Turning back to her he said, "Come, you must dance with me. Then no one will notice that neither of us has an appetite this evening."

They joined the figure of the dance, the young dark-haired

woman and the greying prince, and when the pipers played they danced, changing partners several times. She ended at the far side of the room and began to thread her way back through the crowd to her place at table. A hand slipped firmly over hers and Eadric pulled her into the shadow of a column.

"I've got to talk to you, Branwen," he said, his face pale and tense; his hand was sweating.

"What is it, Eadric?" she asked, alarmed.

"The order has been given. I am to die tonight."

"Tonight?" she echoed, unbelieving at first, and then knowing it was true. "What can I do?" she said, frightened for him. "Would you flee? Shall I change your shape so that no one will know you?"

He laughed hollowly. "You could, couldn't you? No, Branwen. Not that. I shall not flee. Life does not mean so much to me that I would cling to it when it were better done. No, the game is over." His hand gripped hers hard. "Only I fear the dying, Branwen. His hatred is great. Who can say what torments he will delight in?"

"What do you want from me?" she whispered.

"I have seen you after the battle. Men call you the Angel of Death. Will you do less for me?"

She did not answer him, knowing suddenly the blackness Eric faced. Which of them would be the executioner? It was a special skill, one she knew the old warrior found hard. Was it possible the tales told of Viking vengeance were true? If they were, Eadric had every right to be afraid. She shuddered for the pictures in her mind were terrible indeed.

When she made no answer Eadric said, "Now, Bran. There is so little time left."

"If you wish," she said dully.

They left the hall and made their way quickly through the deserted corridor to a small room nearby. Inside the door he gathered her roughly to him. There were tears in her eyes but his were once more mocking, hidden behind the urbane mask he had always worn.

"Are those tears for me, Branwen? Who would have thought it possible?"

He kissed her and she held him for a long time, until his lips grew cold and he slipped from her arms.

She went out then, to return to the great hall.

*　　*　　*

When the dancing was done and the pipers silent, late in the night they found Eadric there, in the small room, crumpled on the fur rugs. The armed men who had accompanied Jarl Eric took the body to the king who was waiting for them, his back to the fire. His dogs, sated with the food tossed to them all through the afternoon, dozed at his feet. Emma and her ladies had gone and only a few of his personal attendants were with him. In one corner of the room Godwin and Hakon spoke in undertones, a pitcher of drink set carefully on the reeds at their feet. They stopped talking and stood up when the body was brought in and dumped on the floor. Knut went over and prodded the corpse with the tip of his boot until it sprawled out flat on its back.

"He must have taken poison, Knut. He was dead when we found him," Eric said.

Knut stood over the body, staring down at the dead eyes. "Poison," he said slowly, "I think not." His voice was very cold.

"Then what, my lord?" one of the carles asked.

"Then what, indeed!" Knut said. "Look at his face. No poison leaves a man looking like that. Where have we seen men's faces which looked like that, Eric?"

"We've seen a lot of dead men," Eric hedged.

"You tell me, Godwin Wulfnothsson, where have you seen dead men's faces that looked like that?" Knut's voice rose as his fury built.

"I saw a man whose eyes looked like that," Godwin said. "He died when my . . ." He flushed, and then turned pale.

Knut's face contorted with rage. "When your sister killed him," he screamed. "How does she dare?"

"What difference does it make? He's dead, isn't that what you wanted?" Eric said quickly.

"Dead? I wanted him killed, damn it! Killed, sniveling, pleading for his life, knowing he was through, finished, dead. I wanted him *killed*—not this!" he shouted.

His voice hung in the stillness and no one dared move. Knut shuddered and when he spoke again his voice was cold, his command falling on them like ice. "Strip the body. Throw it over the city wall. Let the dogs gnaw his bones."

Some of the men picked up Eadric's body.

"Leave me, all of you," Knut said. "No, not you, Eric. I want to talk to you."

When they had gone Knut said, "Did you know of this?"

"No," Eric said. "She acted alone. He must have known. They were friends once, although I thought . . ."

"What am I going to do about her?" Knut said, sinking down onto a bench, his hands hanging between his knees. "Everywhere she goes she challenges me. And what of Thorkell? What of his fleet?"

Eric was an old man; his hair was thin and grey. His beard, thick and grizzled, framed a firm mouth. He had lived a long time, more than forty years, and most of that time he had been king of Norway. But he had risked it all to come south on one last adventure to help his nephew win the island Swein had conquered. He'd been unlucky then and lost his gamble, losing Norway to Olaf in his absence. His age, his sacrifice, his experience, all made him not easily intimidated by the twenty-two-year-old man who wore a crown and lost his temper over a fool woman. He had agreed in principle that Eadric deserved to die and, having gone that far, felt compelled to accept the order to kill him, but it was not an order he liked and in accepting it he had subtly but surely acknowledged Knut's power over him. But he knew full well the debt Knut owed him and how far he could go on that credit.

"You're a fool if you think she controls Thorkell. That man will never be a puppet, not hers and not yours. Even without her you would be hard pressed to control him."

"He threatens me."

"He does not."

"A thousand carles whose first loyalty is to him; a fleet of forty ships whose strength nearly matches mine, whose fighters are older, more experienced veterans than most of mine. I tell you, his very presence is a threat!"

"If he had wanted to move against you, he would have thrown his lot in with Emma and Robert a year ago."

"Yes," he said thoughtfully, his eyes glittering. "You're probably right, Eric. I'm just tired this evening. It's been a long day."

Eric wasn't convinced, but he accepted the king's words and bade him good night.

After he had gone Knut turned to his personal attendant, who stood waiting with the fur-lined sleeping robe Knut would wear to bed when he stripped off his court clothes, and said, "I'd like to trust Thorkell, I really would, you know. We were good friends once. But then that woman came along. Of course, if he were to give her up, as I gave up Ealdgyth—for the good of the country—marry Eadric's newly bereaved widow. . . . Yes, we've talked about that, Thorkell, haven't we, old friend? Just how loyal are you, I wonder?''

Then he stripped off his clothes and wrapped the fur cloak around his hard young body and went to the small room where a pretty girl sat up on a high, heavily draped bed, waiting for him with a shy smile. Godwin had found him this charming child. Interesting man, Godwin. Odd that he should have such a sister. He seemed so simple and easily controlled. An ideal courtier, never sure of his place, always eager to please. Yes, a good man to have around. Perhaps he would take care of his sister. . . . No, that would be pushing too hard. Still, when Thorkell married Eadric's widow, Knut would have Godwin take Branwen back to the west country. Away from East Anglia. Away from Thorkell.

Yes, thought Knut, I'll make her Godwin's problem. I'll give him a girl as he has given me one.

He went into the bed chamber grinning.

Later that week, the young priest of St. Paul's, Father Stigand, baptized the baby beneath the cathedral's ancient vault. They named him Harald in honor of Knut's brother, King of Denmark.

After the ceremony was over, the king and queen, godparents to the great jarl's first-born son, went back to Thorkell's hall. A great crowd of thegns, Danish and island-born, came with their wives for the feasting. Godwin was not among them. There was a chill in the air which could not be banished. Even the butt of Norman wine was not enough to turn formality into friendship.

Smiling politely, serving her guests graciously, Branwen hid the bitterness which grew in her heart as she saw that families who had always welcomed her as her father's daughter were cool and distant. Why had they come? she wondered. Was it curiosity or were they afraid to offend the powerful Jarl of East Anglia? She found herself suddenly sorry that Blaec had stayed in Maldon. If he were here, their guests need not go home disappointed. The great rook might at least have swooped low across the crowd, perhaps cawing in a particularly evil sort of way. But no, it had been too cold; he would not fly and disdained to ride, even within her cloak. He was getting old, she thought, irrationally angry.

Only the queen seemed friendly enough; as if perhaps she hadn't heard what tales the others told; or perhaps, Branwen thought, she was simply more professional, her own feelings hidden beneath the role she played. Once during the interminable afternoon the queen came to sit beside Branwen as if they were old friends.

"I have heard that your home in Maldon is lovely, ma cherie," Emma said in the accent so many had suddenly acquired.

"Thank you, my lady," Branwen answered. "Perhaps you know it. I have heard you often went to Maldon."

"Mais oui, I have good friends from my brother, the Duke's court, who had built a house like the ones we have at home—I mean in the Norman style—just across the square from the cathedral," the queen said, smiling warmly.

"Why then, it must be the very place, my lady, for there is no other like it in the city."

"Well, I congratulate you on your *bon chance*, Lady Branwen. My friends were very sad to give it up when they returned to Normandy. We all thought it one of the most pleasant of all the great halls."

"And so do I, my lady! Indeed, I had not thought to love a house as I do that one. Perhaps one day you will come and visit us there," Branwen said sincerely, recklessly accepting the queen's warmth as genuine.

Knut, standing nearby, turned to a serving girl and watched intently while she refilled his goblet. There was a look on his face, like the look a child might have who has suddenly discovered a very clever way to hurt the baby.

Chapter Ten

They went back to Maldon during the January thaw which came early that year but not early enough to suit Branwen. The atmosphere in London was frigid. She was not invited anywhere; people shunned her; there were no old friends anymore. There was no word from Godwin. Thorkell saw him occasionally among the men at court but he never came by to visit them. Eilaf came, though; he seemed to think the whole matter ridiculously funny and Branwen found herself looking forward to his visits, relying on his laughter to lift the gloom. Leofric stopped by, but only briefly one evening. He had nothing to say of any consequence and after a while their conversation grew strained. She was relieved when he left.

Thorkell seemed anxious to get away, too, but it was several weeks after they had returned to Maldon before she learned that his reasons were not the same as hers. One day when there had been a particularly thick sheaf of parchments in the message pouch from Knut, she sat with Thorkell in the quiet treasury room as he went through them. She spent the time going over the household accounts, until she could no longer ignore his increasing annoyance. She looked up as he pushed himself away from the table and began striding angrily back and forth across the room.

"What's the matter?" she asked.

"It's this damn business of the fleet again. He just won't let up. He is going to dismiss his men in the spring and expects me to do the same. And then," he added, slamming his hand down on one particular pile of parchments, "it's the same old thing about Ealdgyth. What the hell am I supposed to do?"

"You can't do anything now, can you? Don't worry so. In the spring you can go to him, talk to him. He still needs you, you know that. It will work out."

"Maybe I should go now, not let it drag until spring."

"But he's gone to Salisbury. And the weather's awful. Be patient. He'll be in Oxford by June. You can talk to him then. Besides," she added with a smile, "I like having you here."

"I suppose you're right, Bran," he said, ruffling her hair, "but June is a long way off. I don't like having it all hanging over me like this."

And then one cold rainy March afternoon, Thorkell came bursting into the small warm room they used as a nursery with a new letter from Knut. He was grinning. "I leave in two days, Bran, as soon as the wagons are ready and the ships have come round from the south coast. He's levied the Danegeld—72,000 pounds of silver from the countryside. London's been assessed over 10,000 pounds. He's going to make her pay in full for holding out for Edmund."

"Not one to forgive and forget, is he?" she said with a small laugh. "But whatever will he do with all that money? That many silver pennies will make a mountain."

"He's going to pay off his fleet, send them back to Denmark."

"So," she said slowly, "and what of yours? Is he going to pay them off as well?"

"He can't dismiss my fleet," Thorkell said grimly. "I will take the men out to collect the tax in East Anglia. One third will be mine. It will pay the men's wages for another year at least."

"You seem awfully glad to be going, my love. Is it so tedious, this quiet country life?"

"No, Bran, it's just that . . . after a while. . . . Well, damn it, it's almost spring. I can't just sit here forever, can I?"

"Of course not," she said with a smile. "I'll do in the winter, when there's not much else going on, but come the good weather and you and your friends are off, looking for adventure."

"Is it all that bad?"

"No." She laughed. "I'll see to the packing. You'll need some warm clothes. There is talk of more snow."

She did not go with him to collect the king's tax, for the baby was too young to leave behind and the weather was too poor for him to travel with her.

In the beginning Thorkell's fleet of forty longboats anchored off the coast. Their presence was sufficient threat to insure the collection of the heavy tax without trouble. But the carts, heavily loaded with sacks of pennies, proved impossible to move for any distance over the muddy roads, and so the shallow draft Viking ships began to sail far up the flooded streams to take on the weighty bags.

It took a month and when it was completed the Blackwater below the walls of Maldon was so thick with ships one could walk across from deck to deck with hardly a sight of water between. Several longboats, damaged by hidden rocks or heavy debris carried down the rivers by the spring floods, were run up on the beach for repairs.

Although their crews worked quickly, anxious to complete the work and collect their year's wages in silver coin, there were still two boats overturned on the gravel when word came down the coast that Viking pirates had been raiding north of the Wash. The messenger, his face flushed from his wild ride, changed horses in Maldon and rode on. Before he was gone an hour Thorkell's fleet was on its way down the Blackwater toward the open sea to meet this challenge to the authority of the new king.

Branwen stood on the pier with the baby in her arms to watch the *Raven's Wing* go by, its tall chieftain high in the bow. He seemed so mighty she dared not wave. He began to leave me while the messenger was still talking, she remembered sadly. His face hardened so quickly, so easily, and he became a Viking once more. She sighed as she turned back from the river and began to trudge slowly up the hill along High Street toward the cathedral, its blocky profile black against the sky. She hugged the baby closer. He was the only part of Thorkell which would ever be truly hers, she thought.

It was a weary climb and the child had grown heavy in the past months. Budda offered to carry him, but Branwen shook her head. They stopped to rest on a low stone wall which ran around the field beside the town house of one of the wealthier traders. The bulk of the house beside them gave them shelter from the raw winds and the spring sun was warm. They sat for long minutes, watching the townspeople make their way back to their homes and shops after the excitement of the fleet's sudden departure. Budda was sniffling into a corner of her apron.

"I think Trygg would be glad to know you are crying for him, Budda," Branwen said gently.

"Why should he be glad that someone as ugly as me should cry?"

"Perhaps he doesn't think you're ugly."

"Then he's blind!"

Branwen sighed, knowing it was futile to argue. She would leave it for Trygg to handle when he returned.

March became April while they waited. The swallows were nesting under the bridge once more. The marsh was golden with gorse. She grew restless and spent long hours roaming the meadows with Blaec. The great raven, too, was restless and easily annoyed. He scolded her fiercely one afternoon when she muddied her skirts and boots, crossing Weir Bridge toward Burleigh Abbey where the sweet myrtle grew.

'Tis most unseemly, he croaked, *for you to walk about unattended, your clothes filthy, like any country wench.*

Branwen stopped and looked up at him, perched on a branch shadowed by the soft new green leaves. "Do you know what?" she said thoughtfully, "I think you have a guilty conscience."

He ruffed out his neck feathers importantly. *Nonsense,* he said.

"It's spring; you're a bird. You should be nesting."

I've taken a mate, he protested, *a trifle young perhaps, not quite as good as the old bird back in Wessex, but serviceable. She has laid a clutch and broods even now.*

"But that's just it, Blaec," she said. "What are you doing here with me? You should be bringing her tidbits, hovering protectively. What if she is attacked by some other raven who wants your nesting site?"

What raven would dare? he said, drawing himself up on the low branch, his wings thrust out menacingly on either side, glaring beady-eyed at her. *Nay, what other bird, falcon or harrier, would dare touch my mate as she waits for my nestlings to hatch?*

"Nevertheless, your kingship," she said, turning away and starting off down the path, "you know where your duty lies and, no matter what you say," she added, looking back over her shoulder at him, "I think you have a guilty conscience and it's making you irritable."

Weeks later, Trygg returned, his shoulder bound, his linen shirt opened importantly. Branwen was in the shaded cloister naming things for her son who listened to her with great eyes, reaching out with fat fingers to touch her lips as they moved.

"So you shall have a battle scar at last, Trygg," she said as he bowed before her.

"It is nothing, my lady," he said proudly.

"It doesn't look like 'nothing,'" she said, smiling.

"I have a message from Thorkell, and letters as well."

"How is he?"

"Well, lady. He wasn't hurt. Though we captured forty-seven pirate longboats in three weeks. And we never lost a single ship," he added importantly.

"That's wonderful," she said. "But where is he? When will he be back? Where is the fleet now?"

"The fleet's gone north to patrol the coast until the summer's end. Thorkell is with the king in Westminster."

"Westminster?" she said with a disappointed sigh.

"Aye, my lady." He went on hesitantly. "The Gemot has been called to assemble from all over the land. They meet in Oxford in two months. He bids me tell you there is work which must be done though he is sorry to miss the spring with you here and . . ."

"Yes, go on," she said when he stopped.

"He is truly unhappy that he cannot return, my lady."

"Is he, Trygg? I think he is too busy with larger matters to think of me, except to hope I will accept what he does quietly and without making any trouble. You said there were letters for me as well?"

"Aye, my lady," he said, handing her a sheaf.

"Budda," she said to the young girl with the harelip who sat, her handwork forgotten in her lap, "go with Trygg. Draw him a draught of ale. You might do well to bathe his shoulder with an infusion of woundwort as I've shown you."

After they left she opened the packet of letters. They were filled with maneuvers and strategy. She looked through them quickly. There was no mention of his feelings toward her nor his relations with the king. They were the letters a thegn might dictate to a scribe while the room was full of men. She folded them up and later put them in a corner of her jewel chest. One day perhaps Harald would want them.

Two days later, before the hot weather arrived, when the mosquitoes would rise in great clouds off the marsh and the sewers in the street would breed armies of black flies, Branwen gave orders that the great hall in Maldon be closed and the household moved to Cynewithe on the coast. Only Bridey and Jack remained behind to see that the work was done over the summer. The rooms would be swept bare so no fleas could breed among the broken reeds on the floor. Windows would be polished, shutters repaired, the walls whitewashed, the hearths swept out. Even the barns, emptied of all but the chickens and Jack's old horse, would be cleaned out and rested for almost six months. The sheep and pigs which belonged to the jarl were taken out to the fields and woods by the sokemen who owed him service.

Soon after Branwen arrived at Cynewithe, half way across the island, the king held court in the ancient cathedral town of Westminster. Each morning he rode out to hunt in the private forests west of the city. They were often a gay crowd, riding out of the city, especially if they took out the hawks and harriers. On those mornings many of the high-born women went with them, dressed in fine clothes, riding their small gentle horses, accompanied by grooms and serving women. If the weather was bad, or if the king wanted to hunt deer, the group was smaller. It was very small one grey morning when rain fell steadily. Knut and Thorkell found themselves playing some kind of game—to see who could stick it out longer. By eleven, they were soaked to the skin and far from town. There were three small thatched cottages at the crossroads just ahead. Smoke drifted slowly up from one roof and although it wasn't cold, still the magnetism of a fire proved impossible to resist and they went into the house to dry off. Standing in front of the surprised cottar's fire, they laughed together about their stupidity—even the deer had had more sense. They had seen no signs of life since getting separated from the dogs an hour ago. When the cottar's wife brought them fresh cheese and warm new bread, she seemed to hesitate as if there were something she wanted to say.

"Yes, what is it?" Knut asked, not unkindly, but his abruptness subtly reminded her that he was a great man and she was hardly worth much of his time.

"Begging your pardon, your kingness," the woman said awkwardly, "but it's the queen, sir. Has she had the baby yet?"

"No, not yet," he said smiling more warmly at her, "not for a few weeks, she says."

"We're all prayin' for her, y'know."

"Thank you. I'll tell her you said so," Knut answered, dismissing her.

"That reminds me," Thorkell said. "I'll be owing her a gift before long. What do you suggest?"

"Well, they say it's unlucky to cross that bridge ahead of time," Knut said, "but there is one thing I know Emma would like."

"Oh?" Thorkell asked.

"Yes, it's that house of yours in Maldon. I don't suppose you could . . ."

"The Maldon house?" Thorkell said.

"She used to go there, it seems. It holds good memories for her."

"Yes . . . I vaguely remember Branwen mentioning that. Well, of course she shall have it. I'll write to Branwen tonight. She may not be too pleased," he added frowning.

"Splendid," Knut said, suddenly very interested in the cheese set on the table. "I know Emma will be delighted."

Later that night, when the hall was empty except for the thegns snoring on the benches along the walls and a servant who slept standing up, leaning against the wall, two men sat together, a battered pitcher and two goblets between them. They leaned on their elbows, supporting heads heavy with drink and the late hour. They were old friends and they had spent the entire night getting to the point they were now, when each thought the other drunk enough so that he could talk freely without being blamed too much for what he said.

"Remember when we put that toad in Sigvaldi's bed?" the older man said.

"Yeah, you made me do it," the king said, laughing. It was apparently an old joke between them.

"You were the smallest. It was easier for you to get in and out without being seen."

"Remember how he roared?"

"And they turned Jomsburg inside out trying to find out who did it."

"Well, the commander's bed. How did we have the nerve?"

"I think it was Hemming's idea."

"As I recall, your brother was full of good ideas."

Thorkell said nothing, filling up the cups, instead.

"It was his idea, too, that you take me viking with you, that first season you were given a boat," Knut said.

"I wasn't 'given' a boat. I worked damn hard for that chance."

"Yeah, and your brother being commander didn't hurt either. There you were, proud as a jay, and you got stuck taking me along."

"Well, I'm not sure I was stuck . . . king's son and all. Still, I suppose if anything had happened to you there would have been hell to pay."

"From Swein? Don't be an ass. He had Harald. He didn't give two figs for me as long as I didn't disgrace him too badly."

"Do you really think that's true?"

"It's true. He told me more than once."

They both emptied their cups. This time Knut filled them.

"But I didn't disgrace him, did I? We fought like bloody savages that season, didn't we?"

"It was never quite the same after that," Thorkell said, somewhat maudlin.

"What? The murder and the rapine?"

"Aye. The first few times it was loud and wild and no one really noticed what was happening, what we were doing."

Knut lifted his goblet, watching the other man over the brim.

"But after that," Thorkell went on, "it got to be work and nasty, brutish work at that, better avoided, if another way could be found."

"Not everyone felt that way."

"No, you're right. Your father loved it to the end, didn't he?"

"Oh yeah, it was right up his nasty, brutish alley. He could never understand you, though. And when you went over to Ethelred over that stupid archbishop, he thought you were off your rocker for sure."

"What did you think?"

"That you were and still are a stubborn son of a bitch."

"Thanks."

"No, I mean it. I don't know what I'm going to do with you. Once you get an idea in your head, there's no changing your mind."

"That's not true and you know it. What bothers you is that I won't give in when you want me to do something I know is wrong."

"But that's just it, Thor. I'm the king. You're supposed to be my most loyal, trusted, oldest friend and advisor."

"And now you don't think I am."

"Oh, I know you are, that's the funny part. Any of a hundred other men, more I suppose, would smile at me one minute, 'yes, Knut,' they'd say, and then when my back was turned they'd plunge a knife into it. But not you. I'd know you were my enemy, wouldn't I?"

"I wouldn't stab you in the back, if that's what you mean."

"Well then, why can't you just do as you're told?"

"Because it isn't right. The fleet is mine. It isn't yours. What I choose to do with it as long as it's no threat to you is none of your damn business. And while we're at it, my wife is mine, too, not yours to choose."

"What good does it do me, being king, then, if you don't have to do what I tell you?"

"Oh for God's sake! Tell me to collect your taxes, tell me to fight your battles, tell me to enforce your laws, build your roads, send tribute, whatever belongs to a kingship. But leave it at that. Leave me what is mine."

"You were such a hero to me once. It's hard being your king. I want to keep looking up to you but I can't."

"Be careful you don't begin to take this kingly business too seriously. You're a better man than I would be as a king—God knows I had enough chances to make my own bid for the throne—but that doesn't mean that you're a better man than I am, Knut."

"Yes, I am, you bastard. Wait and see." He laughed.

"I'll wait."

Eilaf was in Oxford, too, but he found constant attendance at the court a tedious burden and escaped whenever he could. There was one tavern in particular which he frequented and everyone knew that if he were needed it was at the Sign of the Dove they would be most likely to find him.

One night, while the rain came down in buckets, a group of thegns stood in the common room enjoying the fire, which drove the damp chill from the summer night, and the alewife's brew, which was at its peak this time of the year when the grain was ripening. Eilaf was throwing darts and winning when his attention was distracted by a conversation going on between two men he knew vaguely, having seen them in the crowds around Knut.

"I wonder what she'll do when she finds out." One of the men was laughing.

"I'd give anything to be there—raise an army of mice, and drive the old girl screaming from the room, I'll wager."

Eilaf walked over to collect his darts slowly and thoughtfully.

"Maybe she won't care about the house. After all, she and Thorkell can have any other place they want."

"She may not care about the house but you know as well as I do that she won't let him turn her out."

"But the message we're to give her is supposed to be from the queen."

"So, what difference? She'll be off to Westminster and then there'll be hell to pay. I can hear Knut laughing already. Thorkell will have a fit."

"And so will everyone else. No one knows about this yet. The rest of the court will judge her harshly, for disturbing the queen so close to childbed and all."

"Knut will finally put her in her place."

"You can say that again!" He laughed.

They were still laughing as they finished their drink and went out again into the night.

Eilaf went back to throwing darts but his mind was no longer on the game. He lost repeatedly until he threw up his hands in disgust, bought a round, and left.

Branwen had been at Cynewithe less than a month when Jack rode in. His poor old nag stood with heaving sides in the courtyard while the man, grown paunchy and bald, said, "There's men come to Maldon, lady. 'From the queen,' they says. They says the queen wants yer hall and we're to get yer things packed and moved out."

Branwen paled. "What did you tell them?"

"I told 'em, my lady, we couldn't do anything until we

heard from the jarl himself, but the jarl is up to Oxford, my lady. . . ."

"There's been no word of this from Thorkell. What did they say?" Branwen asked intently.

"Why, they laughed, my lady. Said, 'suit yerself but ye better be out within the week or there'll be trouble,' they says."

"There'll be trouble for sure," she said quietly, "but you'd better see to your poor horse. Take him round to Wymer there beside the barn and then tell Elsey to fix you something to eat. Where's Trygg?"

"Right here," he said, walking through the alley between the stable and the storage shed. "They said someone rode in. What news?"

"There's been trouble in Maldon. Jack is here but he won't be able to ride back today even on a fresh horse." She told him what Jack had told her and then said, "I want you to go up to town. They've given us a week, but that may not be long enough."

"Long enough for what, Branwen?"

"I'm going up to Westminster. I'll talk to the queen. That hall in Maldon rightly belongs to the Jarl of East Anglia. She can't just toss him out on the street like a common gebur."

"Why not let Thorkell handle this?"

"He's busy. And besides Oxford is too far. It would take too long to get word to him."

"I'll come with you."

"No, I need you in Maldon. There are two things you can do for me there. Those men who have been sent to take over the hall—it might be a good idea if they heard rumors—you know, how I can wither a man with just a stare, command the birds in the skies to peck out a man's eyes—you understand, Trygg? Not openly threatened but late in the evening when the ale cups have been emptied many times, just a story now and again may slow them down."

Trygg laughed. "Aye, Branwen. It's easily done. What is the other?"

"I don't know how long I'll be, Trygg, or what the queen will say, but we can't have our things just lying in the gutter. You will have to inquire discreetly for a place to store them if they have to be moved. But try not to let anyone know," she added, "that we are even considering the possibility."

"Aye, lady. Still I don't think very much of your riding all the way to Westminster by yourself."

"Why, then I'll take Blaec." But then, knowing that his concern for her was real, she smiled and added, "Don't worry, Trygg. I'll be all right, really."

"Aye, lady," he said slowly.

"But you must leave at once. I don't want to leave Bridey alone overnight."

Later, after he had gone, although the summer sun was still shining and would not set for many hours, the baby, now nine months old, was given a supper of soft cheese which he loved feeding himself as he sat, quite steadily she noticed, on the high stool with the curved back and sides which Trygg had built for him. Harald had grown up in the last few months. He ate many things now that two teeth gleamed top and bottom when he grinned. Indeed, he had grown up too much. He would never accept a wet nurse now as he had, reluctantly enough, when he was smaller. In the kitchen, Branwen watched while Budda coaxed him with sweet, weak wine which he drank slowly, one sip at a time from the cup she held to his lips.

"He'll be all right, you're sure?" Branwen asked again.

"Of course, he'll be fine. See how well he does. And if he fusses, I'll rock with him until he falls asleep."

"Still," Branwen said with a sigh, "I hate to wean him so abruptly. Poor Harald," she said tousling his baby golden hair tenderly. "I think you would have been better off if you'd been born to someone else."

"Nonsense, lady," Elsey scolded. "He'll be fine and will grow up to be a great lord like his father. But you," she said, frowning, "your breasts are going to be awfully painful, I'm afraid."

"I'll get Budda to bind them tightly for me tonight when they're empty. I have brought in some sage. Make me some strong tea. It will help dry up the milk." Feeling tears prick her eyes, she bent over the baby saying, "Come along, Harald, let's go down to the beach."

Budda let them go without scolding although the baby would get all wet and sandy and have to be bathed again before bed.

And as she stood on the sand watching the child concentrate on the beach pebbles and shells he discovered, picking them up and tasting their saltiness, she felt as if this night she were moving inexorably closer to her own death. She had had a baby and had been his whole world for a while. Now that was done. Only one final time would she feel the milk in her breasts let down, would she feel the peace which came over her then as her son was nourished by her body. There was an ending tonight, a closing of a part of her life.

It was fifty miles to Westminster and she rode out of Cynewithe when the sky was only beginning to lighten in the east. Her urgency was keenly felt by her small stallion and Beornwig trotted steadily for several hours while the sun rose overhead. They stopped a little before noon in a sunny meadow filled with the scent of wild angelica. She sat in the shadow, along the edge of the wood, and watched the horse graze hungrily in the sun. Blaec flew down and she gave him some bits of the trencher and cheddar she had brought with her.

It's still many miles to the crossing you are headed toward this day, the raven said.

Beornwig looked up, a bit of purple crane's bill trailing from the side of his mouth. Walking across the meadow toward him, Branwen told him, speaking the forgotten language of man and beast, what the raven had said. The horse shook his head, his harness jangling, and she knew he meant to be off.

"You'll grow thin and your coat will lose its shine if you don't take time to graze each day," she said, reaching up to stroke his nose.

Beornwig pawed the ground.

She smiled. "Well then," she said, "if you're willing, we'll go on."

They did not stop until they came at sundown to an abandoned cottage Blaec had found hidden in the woods. There a young screech owl was just waking for the night. She spoke to him and he was intrigued that she should do so. He told them that few men ever left the main road near here to venture into the woods. He readily agreed to warn them if anyone approached while they were sleeping. They had come more than halfway that day and slept bone weary until the owl returned at dawn and they set out once more.

Branwen ached, climbing into the saddle. Her breasts, filled with milk, were so tender that every movement of her arms was painful. The anger which had given her strength the day before had faded with the miles. She was sorry she had come. It would have been better to have sent word to Thorkell. Then she could have stayed at Cynewithe with Harald. Poor baby, he must be so unhappy. But she had come too far to turn back now. She would see it through, although what she would say to the queen she did not know. She leaned forward carefully, running her hand over Beornwig's neck, sensing the same weariness in him, knowing it was determination alone which kept him going, trotting along steadily, eating up the miles, while Blaec gloried in the sun overhead, keeping watch for them. Those they met along the road never saw the woman who rode alone for she had woven an illusion and they passed only a young country lad riding on an errand for some lord, a very ordinary sight.

They stopped to rest at midday along a stream. Branwen picked her way through the brambles and tall bracken to a place well away from the road. She slipped out of her tunic and gingerly unwrapped the linen bindings. With a sigh of relief, she sank into the cool water and began gently to massage the hard sore lumps in her breasts, watching the water whiten from the milk which she wasted upon it. When the engorgement had lessened to a dull ache, she sighed and reached out to pull the bindings, stiff with dried milk, into the water where she washed them before rebinding herself with the cool wet cloth. Then she dressed, combing her wet hair and braiding it loosely over her shoulders.

There were wild berries beginning to ripen in the sunniest places and she ate what she could, grateful for their juice, which softened the twice-baked simnel bread Elsey had packed.

Her heart was lighter as they set out again for Westminster. She understood at last why she was going. Laughing, she chided herself for believing her earlier lies. What a fool she had been to try to convince herself that Thorkell would care tuppence for the house in Maldon. He would have given it to the queen with an easy heart, confident that his dignity and power among men was based on his deeds and not his property. No, she thought, smiling ruefully, I want the Maldon house and Knut knows it for I told his bloody wife as much myself.

She hummed distractedly, letting her mind roam free, fluttering like a butterfly over the meadows of her mind, until a brilliant blossom attracted it and the butterfly settled upon it.

So her thoughts settled on how she could meet Emma and what she would say to her.

She was smiling to herself as she rode along the road from Cynewithe to Westminster, confident that she was cloaked in the illusion she had spun earlier. It was an odd little smile which flickered at the corners of her mouth for she was imagining herself a dragon—not too large; quite a beautiful dragon, really; green scales glistening like jewels; a dark pink mouth with just a wisp of steam—lying at the end of the rose garden where the queen would find her when she went out with her ladies.

Suddenly a voice beside the road called out to her by name. "A penny for your thoughts, Lady Branwen."

Startled, she lost control of the illusion and a dragon—not too large; quite a beautiful dragon, really; green scales glistening like jewels; a dark pink mouth opened gently with just a wisp of steam curling around the gleaming white teeth—stood looking at the man who had been leaning against a tree. A raven sat forgotten on his forearm, picking at the food he held in a gloved hand.

"I only offered a penny, my lady. You needn't have gone to such trouble," he said with a weak laugh.

The illusion shimmered and dissolved. Branwen sat astride Beornwig staring at him in amazement. "How did you know it was me?" she asked at last.

"You hide yourself passing fair, my lady, but the bird gave you away. He has a fondness for dates, acquired at the king's table, as I recall."

"How did you happen to be beside this road with a sack of dates, my Lord Eilaf?" she asked patiently.

"I was waiting for you. I thought you might need some help."

"Perhaps I do, but I didn't expect to find any."

"Ah, but that's all the better."

"I don't understand," she said, puzzled. "What do you know of all this? Why are you here?"

He looked at her, his clear eyes guileless. "Lay it to what you will," he said, "boredom, loyalty to Thorkell . . ."

"Loyalty to the king?" she suggested softly.

He paled, the blood draining out of his face. "Would you think even that?" he asked angrily.

"My lord, I don't know what to think."

"Trust me, Branwen," he said.

After a moment she said, "I will, Eilaf. Why, I don't know, but I do trust you."

"Good," he said. "There's an inn not far from here. We can talk there. And get some grain for Beornwig; he looks hungry," he added.

A little later, disguised once more as a boy, she sat at a back table in the common room of the inn and ate hungrily while Eilaf, watching her, drank from a thick mug of foamy ale.

"You know," he said, "it's really disconcerting to sit here with someone who looks so . . . er . . . ."

She looked up at him, saying nothing.

He started over. "How are you planning to get in to see the queen?"

"I come and go as easily as I please," she said, wiping out the wooden bowl with the last crust of bread.

"She's just had a baby, you know."

"No, I didn't know that. Is she all right?"

"As far as I know, she's fine, but no one goes in to her rooms except the women who serve her. She would certainly think you very ill-mannered to just suddenly appear in front of her."

"It can't be helped. I've got to see her and soon."

"There is another way," he said. He leaned across the table, his chin in his hands, his face close to hers. He spoke rapidly, intently. "There is a grey-haired gentlewoman attending the queen. She is seldom in court, preferring the quiet of Northumbria. She's only here now as a witness to the royal birthing. Her name is Gytha."

"Eric's wife," Branwen said softly.

"She is Knut's half-sister," Eilaf went on as if he hadn't heard her. He leaned back, refilling his mug from the sweaty pitcher. When Branwen said nothing, he went on, "Eric has spoken to her of you. She wants to meet you. She wants to thank you herself for the murder you spared the old jarl."

"It was such a small thing," Branwen said.

"Eric is an honorable man, Bran. Though he has lost much, he hasn't lost that yet. Knut deliberately sought to humble him by asking him to do what a butcher might have done as well."

Branwen winced.

He looked down at the scarred table top. "I'll take you to

Gytha tonight,'' he said. "That way your husband will have no cause to doubt me,'' he added with a grin.

Watching him pay the innkeeper for their supper, Branwen thought, how like a boy he is. Although his shoulders are those of a man who can wield a broadsword one-handed, his eyes are so bright, eager, so like a boy's. And his pale hair, so thick and unruly. How like him it is, refusing to submit to more courtly ways.

She met the old noblewoman, Gytha, that evening and the next day, when the newborn Harthaknut suddenly became ill, crying fretfully and refusing to nurse at his royal mother's breast, it was Gytha who told the queen that Branwen was in Westminster.

"Is she?" Emma said.

"I've heard she is an expert healer," Gytha answered. "Perhaps she will know what is wrong with the baby."

"*C'est vraiment*, ma dame," said one of the young women attending the queen.

"She's called the Angel of Death," said another, rising in alarm.

"She can make herself disappear. 'Tis said she vanished from in front of the whole court once."

"It's true. I was there. I saw her."

"And she talks to a raven."

"But certainly, I have heard all these rumors." Emma laughed.

"Nonetheless, she is a fine healer and knows the use of many herbs," Gytha said quietly.

"Well," Emma said with another little laugh, "you know how mon cher Knut hates her. Perhaps we shouldn't call her right away. But if the baby is not better soon, then . . ."

"Would you care for more wine?" Gytha said, offering Emma a second goblet of the rich red wine, so interestingly spiced, which she had given the queen before, during the night, when she wakened to nurse the baby.

Throughout the long morning the baby cried, sucking miserably on his tiny fist but refusing his anxious mother's milk until at last Emma asked that Branwen be sent for.

When Branwen came into the queen's rooms, the bright summer sun was streaming through the tiny panes of long glass windows which opened onto the gardens beyond. The waiting women who had come with Emma from Normandy were standing in small groups, staring at her, this small ordinary-looking woman they had heard such strange tales about. The room was silent except for the thin wail of a little baby. Emma lay in a great bed, propped up on gleaming white pillows.

Branwen curtsied deeply. "He has a good loud cry, my lady," she said.

"It does wear one down after a while," the queen lisped. "Whatever can be the matter with him? My other babies were both so quiet."

"Perhaps he inherited his father's strong will," Branwen said with a warm smile. "Shall I see if I can quiet him?"

"You may try but . . ." Emma lifted her hands hopelessly.

Branwen took the infant from the woman who held him. "Hush, little prince," she said, walking with him toward the windows. Great banks of bright yellow celandine bloomed close against the panes. She reached out ever so gently to touch the bedlam of the infant's mind. He seemed to quiet in her arms but the rustling of the waiting women disturbed him and he began to cry again.

"Perhaps if there were fewer people in the room," Branwen suggested.

"Leave us," Emma said distractedly.

When they had gone the baby grew quiet. Branwen smiled as his tiny mouth opened into a wide yawn. "Crying is tiresome work, isn't it?" she crooned. The infant closed his eyes. Branwen leaned down to lay the sleeping prince in his richly draped cradle.

"Bring him here first," Emma commanded quietly.

"He's only sleeping," Branwen said with a wry smile, taking the baby to his mother.

Reassured, Emma smiled and said, "When he wakes, I pray he will wake hungry."

Branwen went back and laid the infant in the cradle, covering him loosely with a delicately embroidered sheet of finest sandal. "The woman said he has not nursed all day," she said.

Emma nodded.

"Then you'll have too much milk for him when he wakes up," Branwen said.

"You're right, I know," the queen said. "Bring me the cup—là."

When Branwen handed her the cup Emma saw that the bodice of Branwen's tunic was wet, the infant's nearness hav-

ing caused her own milk to let down, leaking through the linen
bindings.

"But, ma cherie, what of my godson? Where is he?"

"I left him at Cynewithe, along the sea."

"But I think you left him suddenly," Emma said. "Whatever could be so important to bring you all this way?"

"You don't know?"

"Know? What should I know?"

"Your men are in Maldon with orders that our great hall
should be given over to them."

"Mes hommes? C'est impossible," Emma said, looking up
from the cup now nearly filled with milk

"They say their orders are from the queen."

Emma was silent, thoughtful, until at last she sighed, closing her gown and handing the cup to Branwen who emptied the
bitter milk quickly into the slop jar.

"Men are such truly curious creatures, *n'est ce pas,*
Branwen?" Emma said. "They have such an exalted view of
themselves."

"Some more than others, I think." Branwen laughed.

"I will, of course, have an order drawn up immediately and
sent to Maldon. My men—or those who claim to be my men—
will leave you in peace."

"The king will be very angry with you."

"And I with him," Emma laughed. "He speaks of you most
bitterly but can tell me no reason for his hate. 'Tis most curious. Can you tell me?"

"It's not so easily explained, I'm afraid. Perhaps another
time. Now I think you should sleep while you can."

"Yes, you're right. I'm really very tired. Strange how he
quieted right down for you," the queen mused.

"Not really so strange. He was worn out from a long morning's crying."

"And you think he will waken hungry, no?"

"When he wakes up he will nurse eagerly, I promise,"
Branwen said with a smile.

"How can you be so sure?"

"I have seen babies behave like this before," Branwen lied.
"He has no fever; his eyes are clear and unclouded by pain.
He'll be fine."

"Still, I wish you'd stay," Emma said settling down into the
pillows.

"Of course, if it pleases you."

When the young prince woke, he nursed hungrily and, filled with warm milk, slept again.

The queen's scribe prepared the document she ordered. She signed it that night, sealing it with wax, her own ring pressed into the soft surface.

"Shall I take it myself?" Branwen asked.

"Must you leave? What if he grows ill again?"

"He won't, my lady," Branwen said. "And it's probably just as well I don't stay too long. The king will only be angrier with both of us."

"I suppose you're right. I'll caution my women to say nothing of your visit. I wonder if he'll ask me to explain the order sent to Maldon?" she asked with a laugh.

Believing she had defeated the king once more, Branwen rode to Maldon with a detail of the queen's guard. She did not know that she had sprung a trap which had been very carefully set for her.

Chapter Eleven

There was a stranger seated in the sun outside the barn door when Branwen arrived back at the jarl's hall in Maldon. He looked up at the sound of her footfall but his eyes were clouded and he knew only the sounds his ears heard. His heavy boots were worn through, bound with strips of rawhide. The thick dark wool of his breeches, too, was worn and filthy. Only his coarse linen tunic, belted around the waist, showed signs of recent laundering. He looked like a man who had been outfitted for a journey long ago.

I hope the end of his journey is not too far off, she thought, looking at him. It doesn't look as if he can go much further.

And then she knew him for what he was. For there, leaning against the side of his low stool, was a battered leather harp case. "A harper," she breathed, almost afraid he would vanish.

"Aye, Branwen," he said, rising from his seat to stand facing her, his head held at an odd angle.

"You know me?" she asked.

"I was sent to find you. The pynkyrdd sent me from Caernarvon."

"To find me? Whatever for?"

"You know where lies the key to tune the harp of Taliessen."

"The key to tune Taliessen's harp," Branwen said, tears springing suddenly to her eyes. "Yes, I know where it is. It hangs on a gravestone where the wind is salty and smells of the sea."

162

"Will you take me to it?"

"It is all there is to mark a prince's grave," she said sadly. "Do you have to take it?"

"It belongs in the western hills. It belongs with the harp. It belongs to Taliessen."

"Taliessen is dead."

"Only in this world," he said gently. "Only in this world."

"I will take you," she said.

They sat together through the twilight and when it grew very dark, Branwen did not light the candles. The harper never noticed the darkness. Sitting with him that night, in the warm summer darkness, she heard for the first time the songs which lived in the Welsh hills, tales from the far off time when the High King's sister-son ruled the Old Tribes after him. Sitting there in the warm summer darkness, she heard the story of Bran the Blessed, last of the High Kings of the Old Tribes, Penardim's son: Penardim, sister of Beli, who had been High King. The harper sang of the new tribes coming among them, sowing the seeds of change, stirring black thoughts in young men who would be their father's sons, who would keep their father's power from passing to a cousin, by blood and the sword if need be. And into the tale was woven the giving of Branwen, sister of Bran the Blessed, to Matholuch, High King of Ireland; a wedding arranged by a brother without her consent, a thing never known before among those people. And though it was late when he put down the harp that night, the tale was yet untold of the misery which lay ahead for the High King's sister in the country of Matholuch the Spineless.

These were the tales which had always been sung in the halls of chieftains, high in the wild hills of Wales. There, amid the crags, the ancient mysteries had lingered late, hidden from the destroyers from the east—the Roman soldiers, the Christian priests. There, like a glowing ember hidden in ashes grown cold and grey, the mabinogi still kept the tales of a way of life which had lasted along the western edge of the world, thousands of years longer than it had in the high civilizations of the Mediterranean and beyond.

She took the blind singer with her when she set out for Cynewithe a few days later. There had been no further difficulty over the jarl's hall. The men who were there to take it over accepted their new orders with the indifferent shrug of those accustomed to obeying without asking for explanation.

Now, as she walked with the blind man through the dappled shade where the road cut through a small copse crowning the last hill before the sea, she no longer thought of her troubles with Knut or her meeting with the queen. Her mind was filled with curiosity about the harper beside her and the strange tales he sang for her in the dark.

"Who is the pynkyrdd at Caernarvon? Why did he send you to me? How did he know I had found Eadric's key, Taliessen's key?" she mused to herself, unaware that she asked the questions out loud.

But the blind man's ears were keen and he heard her questions.

"The pynkyrdd," he said reverently, "is the master, a singer of magic who knows a new song for every night. In the days when the High King still sat on his throne in the western hills, the pynkyrdd sat ten seats away and when he sang, it was from the front of the hall."

His blind eyes stared and Branwen knew he was seeing that other world where magic was still part of life, where reality had not yet won its grim triumph.

After a while, he went on. "He is a very old man now and there is none to take his place. None of us who live with him at the old school will ever master what he has known. There are those who whisper that the pynkyrdd is Math the Ancient and that his death will mark the ending of the old ways."

"Why did he send you to me? It wasn't just the key, was it?"

"He knew of your need."

" 'My need'?"

"The answers are easier for some, Branwen."

"Will you stay?"

"For a while."

"Will you tell me your name?"

"Caradoc," he said.

She had heard the end of the tale of Bran the Blessed; she had listened to the wonders of Pwyll, Prince of Dyvved, and Rhiannon of the Birds who had left faery to come and live with him; and she had sat, her hands stilled from her needlework, as he sang of Arianrhod and the son who had been tricked from her by Gwydion, son of Math.

These were the epics of the Welsh, collected by the mabinogi, the harpers; and Branwen, listening to the singer, felt the magic of his words, a magic which time had not yet dulled. Listening to the singer, she felt that weird sense which comes to everyone now and again, the weird sense that she had heard it all before, somewhere, somewhen. Rhiannon, coming to Pwyll, as Annuvial had come to Caedmon; songs of another Branwen in the long forgotten past who could talk to the birds. And she knew, listening to the singer, that these were the songs of her people, that she had more in common with these dim figures than with the bright faces in the world around her. And she began to think that the unease she often felt with people was only because in one sense everyone was a stranger to her. Her own people, the ones who thought as she did, who asked the same questions, searched for the same answers, were all gone. She was alone, a stranger in this land. Only a few in this time and place would ever be able to learn her language, and her thoughts could not be voiced in theirs. Thorkell was the only one. Would there ever be another? And why Thorkell? What a strange choice for the Goddess to make for her. But then, smiling a little, she was very glad it was Thorkell, very glad he loved her, and she thought how much she missed him. It had been so long since she had had word from him.

In August, when the great assembly at Oxford at last broke up, Thorkell came to Cynewithe. Branwen stood in the courtyard, her son in her arms, and watched the arrival of the jarl and his men. Blaec perched behind her on the thick frame of the door. He would not come nearer while she held the child in her arms, having lost two iridescent tail feathers to young Harald already.

"You've been gone a long time chasing pirates," she said smiling up at him, her eyes squinting in the summer light. "Your son and I have missed you."

Suddenly she felt his anger, not hot with the flash of temper, but cold. Like ice, his fury formed around her.

"What is it?" she gasped, clutching the child to her.

"Not here," he said, his voice tight.

She turned and led the way into the great hall. Her hands were shaking as she sat the child down beside the basket which held his toys.

She could not speak. Leaning back against the edge of the table for support, she looked at him.

But he had turned away from her. "I have come to take my son," he said.

Fighting down the desire to laugh that he would dare say such a thing to her, she remained silent.

But he felt the laughter in his heart. Furious, he whirled to face her, his hands clenched at his side. "By what right do you dare interfere in what is between me and the king?"

"I do not know what has angered you, my lord," she said, her voice cold.

"Not know," he whispered. "Did you think you could write to me so?" He flung a worn letter down on the rushes at her feet.

Slowly and deliberately, she leaned down and picked the parchment up. She glanced at it briefly and laid it on the edge of the table. "I never wrote this letter, if that is what you think."

"Would you lie to me as well?" he hissed

"I have never lied to you. If you choose to think it of me, the door is open. You need not stay."

"I have come for my son."

She thought, so it comes to this already. We are to struggle against each other. And if one of us loses, how can the other win? Then in a voice as quiet as the summer breeze, she asked, "If you think I am a liar, are you so sure he is your son?"

"Enough," he shouted. He leaned down and picked up the baby who began to whimper. He started toward the door. But as he approached, the heavy oak door swung shut and the iron bolt shot home, although no hand came near it. He turned back to her. Branwen stood gazing out the window.

"Just one thing before you go, my lord," she said.

He waited.

"Tell me what happened, to make you so angry with me."

"The great hall in Maldon was to have been a gift to the queen on the birth of the prince," he said bitterly. "Knut wanted it so and I agreed, knowing it would please her. It seemed a small matter."

"You might have sent word," she said, turning to face him, her eyes snapping.

"A messenger was sent and returned with your reply," he said coldly.

"Never," she said. "I had no word from you or anyone concerning this matter until Jack rode in and said the queen's men were at the door with orders to take possession of the hall."

"And just where did that letter come from?" he asked, nodding toward the table.

"Not from me," she said, "not from me."

"Yet it is in your hand, with your seal upon it."

"I sent no letter," she said.

"Oh, God, Branwen, how can I believe you? Who would do such a thing?"

She said nothing, feeling the deadness where their trust had been. Like an arm or a leg suddenly gone numb, there was no feeling in that part of her heart, only a bleak deadness.

"Why?" Thorkell asked, setting the baby back down on the floor where he began to toddle eagerly toward his mother.

"The king seeks to drive a wedge between us."

"Didn't he know the truth would come out?"

"He doesn't care. The damage is done. It won't be the same between us. Now there is an ugliness, a bruise, that we must be careful to avoid. How long before there is another?"

They walked for miles along the sea edge that afternoon until the hurt between them eased. At first they walked without speaking, with only the sound of the sea and the cry of the wheeling gulls to keep them company. Somewhere along the shore she slipped her small hand, strong and capable, into his large, rough, callused one. His hand closed around it but he said nothing. She was almost running to keep up with his long strides but he did not seem to notice. When at last they came to the flooded salt marsh where the Blackwater emptied into the sea and they could go no further, she went over and sat on one of the dry rocks along the marsh edge and waited. The sun was lowering in the west.

"What are we to do then, Bran?" he asked at last.

Tears sprang into her eyes for the first time that afternoon. "We can't let this come between us, Thorkell. We can't let him win."

"Is it only that?" he groaned.

Then she was in his arms and what they whispered amid their tears and caresses not even the seagulls knew. There is a kind of healing which loving brings. It is not without some truth that the act of love is called a little death—bitterness and anger can die in those moments, leaving wounds that will heal in time if not picked open again. So, Thorkell and Branwen loved each other and cried a little—frightened and sad because what they had thought was rock had been so shaken.

In the morning they sat around a table set out in the sunny courtyard beside the cookhouse. The fifteen thegns who had ridden in with Thorkell the previous day were standing in small groups, waiting for him to be ready for the morning's hunt. Beorn had come in from his holding that morning, and old Wymer, and Trygg with Budda and her mother, and Caradoc, the blind harper—all came in hungry for the news from Oxford.

Watching the baby trying to catch the old brown hen who was pecking at the cobbles, unconcerned by his toddling pursuit, Branwen felt again the bittersweet realization that the baby was the only part of Thorkell she could ever really hold on to. It was something she had felt before but this morning it seemed frighteningly true. There was no real way to be sure of Thorkell's love. It had been too easy for Knut. Oh, it hadn't lasted this time, but what of the next, or the time after that? It would come, she knew with quiet certainty, that time when she would lose him. But not his son, not Harald. Harald would always be hers, her baby. No one could take him from her.

Between bites, Thorkell was telling the others how all the great landowners, ealdormen, and bishops, called to assembly by the king, had gathered in Oxford. Most numerous among them were the powerful landowners who led the local shires, some owing fealty to the king but many, especially the Saxon thegns, powerful noblemen who owned vast holdings, held no office which the king could take away, and were as free as any man to speak their minds about public questions. For the past two hundred years, since before the reign of Alfred the Great in the ninth century, the king had been counseled by his thegns and ealdormen, as well as bishops and ecclesiastical leaders. This was the Witena Gemot which Knut had summoned to give legitimacy to his claim to the throne. Throughout the history of the island, this body chose a successor whenever the succession was disputed. These were the same men, many of them, who had called Ethelred back from exile when Swein Forkbeard had died.

"With their approval," he said, "Knut can claim his right to the throne by virtue of conquest and election. It can't be easily set aside now, even by one who might bear a blood tie to the old Anglo-Saxon line.''

"Don't let the baby chase the old biddy like that, Budda," Elsey scolded, suddenly noticing young Harald.

"Don't worry, mother, he can't catch her," Budda whispered.

"She won't lay an egg today, mark my words," the old woman said in the too-loud voice of an old woman whose hearing had begun to fail.

"That old hen hasn't laid an egg since Whitsuntide." Budda laughed.

"Why then haven't we put her in the stew pot before this?"

"You'd have to stew her for a month," Budda said leaning over and patting her mother's gnarled hands. "But hush now, you're interrupting Lord Thorkell's story."

And indeed, Thorkell had turned around and was watching them, a smile flickering across his face. When they were quiet, he said, "A lot of men were raised to positions of great power in the land this summer, Branwen. The Gemot confirmed Leofwine's right to the lands which Eadric held in Mercia."

"That's no surprise," she answered, tossing a handful of crumbs to the hen.

"Eilaf was given the traitor's land in Herefordshire."

"Hereford is a long way from East Anglia," she said, looking down at her hands. "We won't see very much of him anymore, will we?"

"No, I suppose not," he said and then he added, "Your brother was made Jarl of Wessex."

"What!" Branwen said, stunned. "You're not serious. You can't be."

Thorkell walked around to her side of the table. He put out one hand, drawing her to her feet. "Aye," he said. "It's true. Godwin's been made the new Jarl of Wessex. He's come a long way, Bran."

"But Thorkell—Jarl of Wessex?" she repeated. "It makes Godwin the equal of any man in the kingdom."

"Even to the Jarl of East Anglia?" Thorkell said with an easy laugh.

"Why not?" she said, still incredulous.

"He's the king's man, Branwen," Thorkell said, turning to Budda who refilled his cup. "As long as he pleases the king, he will hold power, but it will be many years before he can stand alone.''

"I'm afraid you underestimate my father's son," she said, shaking her head.

"Do you think so?" He laughed. "Perhaps."

She wanted to ask him then what new honors he had been given, but it was still too near, too raw a wound. She could not ask what he had gotten from Knut—any more than a wife can ask her husband what gifts he has received from his mistress. Only later, when she was decanting some wine with Trygg, did she learn that Knut had dismissed his own fleet, all but the fourteen ships of his house carles. But Thorkell's fleet had been left as they had always been, under Thorkell's command, safeguarding the shores of the island. That battle he had won anyway.

But while they were still sitting together in the morning sun, Wymer asked the jarl, "What did they accomplish? All those great men together for so many months?"

Thorkell laughed a little and said, "We spent most of the time discussing which set of laws should be used to govern the whole island, now that it is united, more or less, once again."

"Wasn't no easy thing, I'll warrant," old Wymer added sagely.

"It seemed impossible for a time, you're right. But after a month or more, with the harvest pressing, it was agreed to adopt a code based on the laws of Edgar's time."

"Edgar's time! That was fifty years ago. A lot's changed since then," Beorn said.

"It's a start," Thorkell said, pulling up his boots. "No one's really happy with it, except Knut, I guess. He's started to work on a general proclamation which should be ready this winter or maybe by spring. Are you coming with us this morning, Beorn?"

"Aye, if ye're riding north, that is. There's a matter I've got to be tendin' to up there."

"Well then, north it shall be."

She walked with him to his horse. Just before mounting, he turned to her and said, "I forgot to ask you about the harper, Branwen. Where did he come from? Has he been here long?"

"Not long. He's Welsh. His name is Caradoc."

"Welsh, is it? That's a long way for a blind man to come."

"Yes," she said. "But he had his reasons for coming and it

was not to see me. Wait until you hear him sing this evening. He's really the best I've ever heard."

"Even better than Elfheah?" he teased gently.

"Poor Elfheah. You know, I think they had met, Caradoc and Elfheah, several years ago. Elfheah went to Wales, did you know that?"

"No," he said, swinging up into the saddle. "Keep your fingers crossed we get a deer. You'll be hard pressed to feed us for long if the hunting is not good."

"Keep my fingers crossed, with an army like this! Don't be absurd, my love. Have a good morning," she added, reaching up for his kiss.

That evening, while they feasted on fresh-killed venison, the baby sat on his father's lap picking raisins from the bowl of pudding set in front of him, dripping the meat sauce down the front of his white dress onto his father's knee. And if Branwen noticed, she never mentioned it. Not until the child fell asleep, listening to the harper, did she take him gently out of his father's arms and off to bed.

The song the blind man chose that night was a far different one from the cycle he had been singing for Branwen. It was a song he chose to suit his audience, thegns of a Viking chieftain, the Jarl of East Anglia. This night, the singer out of the hills of Wales sang of Ragnar Lodbrok, famous among the Viking heroes, who had ravaged the lands from the Orkneys to the White Sea. For years he had laden his ships with treasure, leaving death and destruction all along the shores. When at last fate turned her face from him, he was captured by Aelle, King of Northumbria, and thrown into a pit of poisonous snakes to die. Even more than his years of successful raiding, the way he faced death earned him a place forever in the sagas of the Vikings. Defiantly, standing amidst the writhing adders, he had laughed and sung his death song. And when death's agony gripped him, he had cursed the Northumbrian king who was standing on the pit's edge. "How the piglets would grunt if they knew how it fared with the old boar," Ragnar Lodbrok said and then he spoke no more. It was late at night when the harper sang of the revenge taken by the four sons of the great hero and Branwen knew this was the death Eadric had been afraid to face. King Aelle, taken alive by Ragnar's son, Ivar the Boneless, was condemned to die the "blood-red eagle";

his flesh and ribs laid open in a wedge-shaped pattern, his still-breathing lungs torn out by the avenging son.

Branwen shuddered. She was glad the child was asleep. It was an awful story; one to color many dreams.

It was only two days later when the king's messenger brought word that Harald had died, childless. The throne of Denmark's was Knut's. Thorkell was summoned to Winchester.

It was raining, a warm summer rain, and the night sky was black. Only the edge of the sand glowed in the dark as they walked once more beside each other where the waves whispered beneath their feet.

"I'll have to leave at sunrise. It's going to be a long time, I'm afraid, before I get back. Will you come with me this time?"

"I'll come," she said, "but not until Knut's gone. And then only to be with you," she added, "not to be a jarl's wife."

"Won't I ever have a wife as other men do?" he asked.

"I can't be any different, Thorkell. It was a mistake to think I could. If you wanted a wife like other men, you should have married someone else."

"When will you understand," he asked, turning to grip her shoulders with his powerful hands. "I couldn't marry anyone else. I love you more than life itself!" He pulled her close against his wet tunic.

"I know," she whispered. "I know."

There was a cloud of dust along the road from the north one day not long after Thorkell left. As it came closer Branwen could see that it was a large group of riders, dark-haired Saxons riding with Danes. And with them were women, serving women riding on carts and two ladies on palfries. One of them was a girl whose golden hair shone unveiled in the summer sun.

Out in the field, Branwen raised a hand to shade her eyes as she watched the column move along the road. "It's Godwin," she said to Budda, who stood beside her holding the basket of raspberries they had been gathering. "What's he doing here?" She reached down to pick up the child who sat intently and unsuccessfully trying to catch ants with his awkward fingers. "Come along," she said, hoisting him to one hip, frowning because he was wet and she would have to greet her brother with a wet patch on her skirt.

"I'll carry him," Budda offered.

Branwen shook her head. "No," she said, "run on ahead. That's quite a crowd to have to feed on short notice. Your mother will need some help."

Trygg met her on the path home. "The Jarl of Wessex sends greetings to his sister, Lady Branwen."

"Did he tell you to say that, Trygg?"

"Yes, he said to say just that."

Branwen laughed. "Go back and tell him, 'the Lady of the Ravens will be with him shortly.' And see if you can draw some wine from the good butt we laid down last month. Nothing but the best for the Jarl of Wessex. Oh, and Trygg," she called after him, "who else is with him?"

"Lord Ulf, and his wife, Estrid, his sister, Gytha, and his son, Swein."

One big happy family, she mused to herself after he had gone running back down the path. What are they doing here?

She and the baby slipped unseen into the cookhouse at Cynewithe where Elsey and Budda were trying to cope with thirty unexpected guests, the cooks and serving women who traveled with them, the boxes and baskets of provisions unloaded from their wagons in the courtyard.

Branwen stood in the doorway, marshalling her forces, setting a plan of action in her own mind. Suddenly Trygg burst in looking for help in serving the wine he had just decanted in the buttery.

"Budda," Branwen said, her voice deliberately quiet and slow, "put on a fresh cap and apron and see to our guests."

"But, Branwen . . ."

Ignoring her, Branwen turned to Trygg and said, "Go tell Beorn we'll need some help. Two or three women, I think. Tell him to send word to the swineherd, too. We'll need a good beast before nightfall or first thing in the morning at the latest. There will be feasting tomorrow. Oh, and Trygg," she called after him, "stop at Ralf's cottage on your way back. Goda has made a cheese. I saw it setting the other day. Tell her I'll make her a coverlet of finest down for the new baby if she lets us have it this afternoon."

Turning back to Budda, she said, "Bring along the kettle.
I'll get fresh linen out of the chest for you."

A few minutes later, Budda, neatly capped and aproned,
went into the great hall to serve wine to their guests and fresh
peary to the serving women who were not in the kitchen with
Elsey. Branwen watched her go, confident that the girl had
learned her lessons well and could be counted on to do the task
with some grace and the attention to detail courtesy demanded.

Then Branwen washed young Harald, splashing warm water
from the kettle into the basin. While she dressed him in his
infant dress, she cooed to him gently so that he would be quiet
and not start to fuss, frightened by the excitement. But she
didn't have to worry; his father had been gone only a few days
and Harald was still used to having the great hall filled with
guests. He seemed quite easy about his role and went out alone
on unsteady legs to stare at the strangers.

He was in the middle of a circle of admirers when Branwen
came into the room. Godwin, standing a little apart from the
others, looked up as she came in. She wore a simple linen
tunic, dyed deep purple, almost black. It had been stitched
from cloth which she had found amid Thorkell's treasure
chests. She had never been able to match the dye which had
been used on it, never quite able to catch the richness of tone.
On her breast she wore the gold enameled raven she had had as
a gift from the jarl when their son was born. Its wings out-
spread, like a Roman eagle, it hung suspended by its wing tips
from a fine gold chain of square links. Its great hooked beak
was open and a gleaming red jewel, set for the eye, glared
balefully.

Godwin bowed to her. "The Lady of the Ravens," he said
with a flourish.

"My lord, the Jarl of Wessex," she replied. "Welcome to
Cynewithe."

He laughed then and embraced her.

With his arm still draped across her shoulder, she turned to
greet her other guests: Knut's sister, Estrid, and her husband,
Ulf.

"And this is Gytha," Godwin said.

She was a beautiful young girl, her long hair like spun gold,
hanging in loosely braided plaits over her shoulders. Her skin
was creamy and her blue eyes deep and intense. She looked at
Godwin with such unmasked admiration, as if he were the

most wonderful man in the world, that Branwen wanted to laugh.

"Gytha and I were betrothed last month. We've come to ask your blessing before we go to Denmark with Knut. We'll be married there this winter."

"Why, that's wonderful!" she said. She hugged Gytha saying, "I'm so glad. I hope you'll both be very happy."

Gytha looked at her, her eyes shining. "Oh, are you truly? I was afraid you would be disappointed that he didn't choose a Saxon woman. And I know you hate Knut so."

Branwen laughed. "Of course I am happy my brother is going to marry you. And I don't hate the king—he hates me, and I'm not quite sure why," she added.

"He thinks you cost him the kingdom at Ashington," Estrid said. "It's that simple."

"That's ridiculous," Ulf said. "I've heard all that talk as well. He claims he saw you stand on a small rise and cast some sort of spell over the army so that no one could fight. Some kind of nonsense like that."

"But that was so long ago. The kingdom is his. Edmund is dead. What more does he want?"

"He's afraid of you," Estrid said, coming over to stand beside her at the window. "He's afraid you can move against him any time you want. Isn't that what makes men enemies? A simple thing like that?"

"And you, Lady Estrid, you're his sister. What do you think?"

"Are you afraid that we are all your enemies just because my brother is?"

"No, I'm sure she doesn't think that, do you, Bran?" Godwin said hastily. The conversation had gotten serious too quickly.

"No, of course not," Branwen reassured them with a smile.

But Estrid laid her hand on Branwen's arm and looking at her intently said, "I envy you, you who have the power to stop men from killing each other. But it is not the envy that can turn to hate. Don't ever think that."

"I wish that power were mine as well," Gytha said shyly.

"I wish it were every woman's," Estrid said, turning back to the children.

"Not every woman hates a battle, nor does every man love one," Branwen said softly. "Will you have some wine?"

Later that evening, when the work was done and the company settled and quiet, the harper sang. Branwen and her brother sat together on the bench in the back of the hall speaking quietly, not wanting to disturb the others.

"I hear you are the king's man, Godwin, and have great honors heaped on your head."

"Not as much the king's man as Knut may think," he said. "He's already sorry he made me Jarl of Wessex."

"Oh?"

"He misjudged me," Godwin said with the same wicked grin she remembered suddenly from when they had been children. "He thought I was no more than a useful Saxon thegn, currying favor."

"You gave him plenty of reason to think that. For more than a year you've acted the part well enough."

"Still," he said, "it was simple-minded of him to be so easily deceived."

"Not simple-minded, Godwin. I just don't think the subtleties of politics come naturally to him—any more than they do to Thorkell."

"He's learning fast." Godwin laughed. "Faster than Thorkell."

"I don't think Thorkell will ever learn. I don't think he wants to."

"No, I don't think so either, Bran. And I'm afraid it's going to be a problem for him. War is a simple game, peace is harder."

"You play the game well enough."

"Why not?" He stopped to drink deeply from his jeweled cup before going on. "The strength of Wessex is mine now, Bran," he said earnestly, setting the cup down on the table. "The Saxon thegns are loyal to me and only by my nod to the king. It surprised him when he suddenly realized that that's true. He really had no idea."

"I tried to tell Thorkell when he was here," Branwen said with a smile.

"Thorkell knows I am a Wessex man. He knows Father was a Wessex hero. What no one seems to be ready to believe is that Edmund is still loved in the shires. He's become a kind of folk hero. Ironside, they call him everywhere."

"And you're a hero because you were his friend through it

all, good times and bad. And the fawning hound Knut threw a bone to turned into a mastiff after all,'' she said.

"No, Bran, not quite. We are still friends, Knut and I; he wants to trust me and I make it easier for him than Thorkell does.''

"Do you, Godwin?"

Across the room Ulf pushed his dogs aside with his foot and stood up. Watching him, heavy-set, his face flaccid, his eyes small, she thought of his brother who was always so bright and eager for life. How unlike Eilaf he was. She felt a twinge of pain then, thinking of Eilaf, hearing his laughter, remembering the keen intensity of his eyes, so amused with the world they saw. Did he know? she wondered for the hundredth time. Was he part of Knut's little plot? He must have been, she thought sadly.

"You two are close this evening,'' Ulf said, walking across the room toward them. "Has he told you how he changed Knut's mind about having Thorkell marry Ethelred's widowed daughter?"

"No, Ulf, I have not,'' Godwin said wearily, his distaste for the man only thinly veiled.

"Why not? You know, Branwen, you are lucky to have such a clever brother.''

"What did he do?"

"Well, I'm sure you know how Knut wanted Thorkell to wed Eadgyth,'' he said.

"Yes, Thorkell told me. What happened, Godwin?"

"Let Ulf tell it, since he started,'' Godwin said, turning away to fill his goblet.

"There was a terrible row in the offing. We could all sense it, knowing how Thor feels about you and all. Still, the king had given up Aelgifu to wed Emma,'' he added.

"Yes,'' she said, "but what happened?"

"No one knows, really. One minute it was all tense between them and then Godwin spoke to the king alone and it was never mentioned again.''

"Is this true?" she asked her brother.

He nodded.

"What did you say to him?"

"Only what was true,'' he said. Suddenly he looked at her and grinned, that same boyish grin she had seen earlier. "I reminded him that the blood of Saxon kings runs true in Eadgyth's line.''

"The blood of Saxon kings?" she asked.

Godwin said nothing.

"So any son of hers . . ." she said thoughtfully.

"Knut's clever. I wouldn't be surprised if his thinking was much the same as yours. Anyway, the matter was dropped."

"Whose idea was this? Yours or Leofric's?" she asked with a laugh. "He's always been good at this kind of thing."

"We only had your interests at heart, Bran," he protested.

"Of course," she said. "I'm very grateful." She reached up and kissed his cheek.

Later, as they sat listening to the harper singing the long and complex tale of Rhiannon's wedding to Pwyll, Prince of Dyvved, the first branch of the Mabinogion, the song she had asked him to sing, she looked across the room to where her brother sat with Gytha now, his arms around her, lost in the song.

How professional you've gotten, she thought, how clever. Did you think you would charm even me with your smile? It must work with most people. You're very good at it. You didn't speak out against Thorkell's marriage for my sake at all, did you? Her land and Leofwine's are interlaced, aren't they? And why should either of you want a son of Thorkell's to have a claim on the throne?

Chapter Twelve

She stayed at Cynewithe late that year, reluctant to go up to Maldon. She wondered if the pall which hung over the great hall could ever be removed, if she and Thorkell would ever recapture the quiet conjugal joy they had found there once—when it had been their home, the one they had made together. Now it belonged to her. She had, in the end, taken it from him even as she had fought to keep it from the king. Although the harvest had been gathered and the festivals celebrated, although she had long since given a golden harp key, Taliessen's key, to the blind singer, still she lingered at Cynewithe.

The weather held unseasonably warm. The ground turned to mud instead of icy rime beneath the frequent November rains. There was a lull in the round of farm chores for it was the season to drive in the hogs from the oak forest where they had been fattening on pannage of fallen acorns. But this year the swineherd delayed, keeping the hogs out, waiting for the hard frost. At Cynewithe they could not salt away the meat nor smoke the sausages and hams while the weather was so warm. There was too much risk of having the meat spoil.

Wymer and Trygg filled their days with chores often put off, finally rebuilding a storage barn which had taken on an alarming tilt. There was even less than usual for Branwen to do. Few were sick enough to need her help, and the endless handwork of carding and spinning and weaving could as easily be left for another.

The sun shone brilliantly one afternoon. Restless, she called to Blaec and went out, leaving Budda, pregnant at last with Trygg's child, to watch over her son napping on his cot. She walked slowly through the little wood near Cynewithe, listening to the quiet of the empty trees, their leaves all fallen and brown on the forest floor. Through the leafless undergrowth she could see the brown marsh which lay beyond the wood.

As she walked out onto a low causeway between pools of dark water, she heard the whisper of the wind passing across the dried grasses of the meadow. It was an old sound, the sound of the wind, the sound of dying, the year ending, the circle coming round one more time. Walking through the empty meadow, she heard the grasses whisper to each other, whispering of the emptiness of life, new life springing so proud and eager out of the moist ground each spring, glorying for a season in the warmth and pride of tall green growth, only to turn sere and brown as the wheel turns steadily on and on. She felt this endless turning of the seasons—not flowing like a river—the turning, always turning, like a millstone, time going round and round until the years blurred, ground down into dust. And in that blur of years, she felt herself merge with her mother, the twenty years which separated them as nothing in the great gulf of time. And the kinship grew until she became one with an endless line of women who had lived with the same small joys and sorrow, feeling themselves grow older, wondering why.

In the sky, the raven was a distant speck. On either side of the causeway there were black water pools where the November rains had flooded the grasslands. Under the dark water the grass still stood in bunches. These were the pools where the faery folk lived. Were there sprites here, she wondered? Did they hear the voice of the dead grass? She turned her eyes away from the drowned meadowland, unwilling to see that the pools were empty.

The women of her kind had been caught in long ago turns of the wheel and she walked alone until the late afternoon fog began to blow in from the sea. Chilled by the raw cold, she turned inland toward the high ground, away from the fog, so that she could find her way more easily back to Cynewithe. But even along the high ground the fog thickened until she gradually lost all orientation.

Wrapped in the muffled silence of the grey fog, she walked on looking for the glow of cottage fire, listening for the sound of evening chores at one of the nearby farmsteads. She walked for a long time, seeing nothing, and hearing only the scurrying sounds of the small animals around her.

Suddenly, through the grey formless mist, she heard a scream. Long and drawn out, it went on and on until it seemed no human being could have breath left. And then it stopped and all was still once more. Branwen hurried toward the sound, knowing what it was. She had walked only minutes when it came again, closer this time. Somewhere ahead of her in the mist a woman labored to give birth. Before the scream came a third time, Branwen stood before a poor cottage, its thatch rotted, the door only a ragged piece of cloth. Two children stood huddled against each other beside the doorway. A small man leaned against the side of the house, his back to her. He did not seem to hear the children call out when they saw her come out of the mist. He didn't move. A woman came to the doorway of the cottage, though, pushing open the drape with one heavy arm.

"Who be ye?" she asked. "What do ye want here?"

"I heard a woman cry out in labor. I can help. I have some skill."

"She be dyin'," the midwife said, spitting. "There be nothing not you nor nobody can do for her."

It was the cold tone of her voice, and the look of horror on the children's faces as they listened, that roused the anger which smoldered in her, the unreasonable anger she always felt at the suffering of women in childbed. It seemed so wrong, like a torture imposed on them by some hidden monstrosity.

"Wicked woman," she snapped, "how dare you say such a thing! It may well be that she will die, but there are worse things than death and those at least I can turn aside."

Just then there was another awful scream from the darkness beyond the door. Branwen pushed the midwife roughly aside and went in. A hen squawked as she crossed the small room to where the woman lay.

"It will be all right. I've come to help now," Branwen crooned as she leaned over, brushing the woman's hair back from her face with her fingers.

From sunken eyes the woman looked up at Branwen in despair.

Without taking her eyes from the woman's, Branwen said to the children, "How long has your mother been like this?"

''Two days,'' the bigger one, sexless in rags, answered in a small voice.

''Oh Mother,'' Branwen swore, her heart wrenched by the other's suffering. Suddenly the birthing pain seized the exhausted woman again, plunging her into the maelstrom of agony. In the moments which followed, Branwen reached out, easily touching the other's mind, blocking out the pain, causing her to go down into the shadowy depths of her mind, beyond the threshold of feeling, where sleep, too long denied, would hold her fast, for a little while anyway.

''She'll not wake in this world again, you mark my words,'' the midwife said, watching from the door.

''Go away,'' Branwen shouted.

''I'll not go.''

''Get out of here.''

''Who do you think ye are, comin' in here like this?''

''Go away,'' Branwen commanded, pushing her from the cottage with the fury of her will. ''Get out of this house!''

The woman hesitated a moment, turned, and then went out, disappearing into the mist.

''When your mother wakes up, she will need a good strong soup, for she is working hard and needs strength. You must kill the hen and clean it. Then we will cook it for her, and for you, too,'' Branwen added with a smile. ''Has it been a long time since anyone has fixed you something to eat?''

The smaller child started to cry.

''Hush, now. Everything will be all right, you'll see. But you must help. We need that chicken for the soup. And do you think you can find some more wood?''

''Yes, lady, we'll help, won't we, Bryl?''

The little one sniffed bravely, wiping his runny nose with one filthy hand.

While they obediently cornered the squawking hen, Branwen turned back to the sleeping mother. Pulling aside the dirty cover, Branwen examined her to see what was hindering the delivery. Two days was much too long. The woman only moaned softly as Branwen found one tiny foot lodged in the birth canal.

She stood up and walked over to the fire smoking in the middle of the small room. Absently she rearranged the few sticks, making them flare up for a moment. There were two small logs by the door and she added those, too, so that there would be a hot fire for boiling the soup. She sighed and then turned back to the heaped up straw which served as a bed. By the now brighter light of the fire she saw that the straw crawled with vermin. With a shudder, she thought of her own clean linen and the rosy-faced babe who slept on a cot beside her. Then she emptied herself of all thought but her resolve to help the woman who slept here. Nothing else mattered.

She drew in from all the corridors of her mind until only a bright light shone strongly in the core of her being. Then the light reached out, touching the raging incarnadine darkness, the chaos of the unborn child's mind. There, darkness and light struggled with each other, but the light was too strong and gradually the infant's mind yielded to her. Just then the body of the woman bore down once more, pushing and squeezing. In the firelit cottage Branwen cried out, sharing the unborn infant's pain.

When the contraction eased, Branwen's will, holding the dark mind, withdrew the tiny foot from the birth canal. Once the foot was free, the infant turned easily in the womb. Branwen withdrew, fleeing, as the contraction tightened against the infant once more, this time pushing its head toward the light.

While the children stood in the doorway, a chicken, headless, dripping blood on the sill, hanging forgotten from one grubby hand, the baby was born. Branwen cried then, laughing, too, as she held out the tiny girl for them to see. Their father pushed in past them, his face aged, grown old early from too many disappointments.

"It's a girl," Branwen said happily to him.

"Who be ye?" the man asked, his eyes narrowed.

"My name is Branwen," she answered carefully.

"There's sommat wrong with her leg," the man growled.

"Aye," Branwen said slowly. "It may grow straight but it was twisted in the borning and may not be right ever."

"I'll not have a cripple around the place," the man said, "and a girl besides. There's mouths enough to feed."

"What are you saying?" Branwen asked slowly.

"I'm saying 'twere mebe better ye had let it die."

"And your wife, too?"

He shrugged. "She be a good woman oncet. Now she does little enough but complain, whining at me night and day."

"You bastard," Branwen said, thinking of the life this woman led here in grinding poverty made worse by drink and the constant sexual duty without joy, unending chores made almost unendurable by constant pregnancy. "You bastard," she said again, her voice dropping to a whisper, "have you given her no cause to complain?"

For an instant, seeing the hatred without fire in his eyes, she pitied him, burned out, wasted, only the shell of a man. Then one of the children began to whimper and the man whirled, kicking out at it with a heavy foot. Branwen saw in that moment that the evil in this cottage lay not only in the waste of a man's life but more in the waste of the lives around him which he was destroying.

Carefully she wrapped the newborn in the meager strips of grey rags which had been prepared for it. The baby yawned and fell asleep as Branwen laid her beside her mother on the verminous straw.

"I will not permit you to harm the babe," she said at last, turning back to the man who sat on the low stool staring into the fire.

He didn't look up.

"Nor the children, nor their mother," she added.

"Mind yer own business, woman," he growled. "This here be my house and what I do be none of yer concern."

Branwen took the chicken from the child's hand and began stripping feathers from it. "Listen carefully," she said, her voice low. "The day you harm my sister or my sister's children, your manhood will wither, shriveling within your loins. You will get no more children on her or any other woman."

The man looked up at her and then slowly and deliberately spat into the fire.

"You don't believe me, do you?" she said.

He grinned at her toothlessly. "Do ye take me fer a fool?"

"You are a fool," she said. She passed her hand out over the low fire and suddenly it blazed up, forcing him back off the stool, tongues of fire lashing out at him, pushing him back toward the door. He turned there and with a cry ran out into the darkness. She let the fire die back. He was a simple man and she knew that this small magic would be enough. He would believe her now.

She would tell Beorn to see to it that they had what they needed from the excess at Cynewithe. In the spring there would be work for them on her lands. These people at least she could help, although there were countless others who waited in the shadows, beyond her reach.

She stayed long enough to see the woman waken, take the newborn into her arms where the baby sucked hungrily at her mother's thin breasts. There was soup now for the woman to drink and then there would be more milk.

When she went out of the cottage, a thin moon cast pale light along the roadway home. The fog had gone back to the edge of the sea. The raven croaked and fluttered down from the branch of a tree where he had been waiting for her. He settled on her shoulder as she started off toward Cynewithe for he would not fly at night.

Pretty high-handed, if you ask me, the raven said when the light of the cottage disappeared around a corner behind them.

"What do you mean?" she asked absently, her thoughts elsewhere.

You take that Goddess business pretty seriously, don't you?

"Blaec," she said, a warning note creeping into her voice.

But he went on heedlessly. *You really do believe you are some all-powerful priestess, don't you?*

"That's enough," she said, pushing him off her shoulder. He fluttered to a low branch beside the path. "I've no wish to listen to your ravings tonight."

And you were going to be his wife, like any other woman, have you forgotten? he mocked.

"Stop it," she cried. "Stop it."

I told you you couldn't do it. I told you so.

"Leave me alone, oh king of birds, or you will end your days a croaking frog in a dark marsh."

Or I will wither your manhood within your loins, he mocked. *High priestess, indeed!* And he flew off through the darkness toward Cynewithe.

His words hung in the air, like ghosts haunting her. It was true. She had never even noticed. When had she stopped trying to be like other women? Oh Mother, she prayed, I never decided not to try any longer. It just . . . "What am I to do?" she whispered.

All around her was the quiet stillness of late night. Far off an owl hooted.

It rained for three days, steady cold rain which kept everyone indoors. When they woke on the morning of the fourth day, the sun shone thinly in a winter sky. There was ice on the puddles in the courtyard. The swineherd would be moving his pigs at last toward Cynewithe. She was glad they were packed and ready to leave for she had no desire to stay once the work of slaughtering had begun. It was hard grueling work and it stank.

As it was they left before noon—a motley crew. Budda was driving the cart with the blind harper beside her. He would leave for Wales in the spring, content to spend the winter with them in Winchester. Young Harald, filled with excitement, was tucked in between the rolls of bedding at the back. Branwen and Trygg rode on ahead.

Stopping in Maldon for a few days before going on, they made Winchester in less than three weeks.

Thorkell had arranged for them to stay in Eric's great hall while they were there. The jarl and his wife were in York for the winter and were delighted to have her use their house; in fact, it had been old Lady Gytha who had suggested to Thorkell that Branwen would be more at ease here than at Thorkell's residence which had, in the king's absence, become the center of the kingdom. Although many of the noble-born—those who had not gone with Knut to Denmark—were, like Eric, out of the city on their estates, Thorkell's hall was filled with officials and advisors carrying on the day to day work of the government. And, of course, Emma was there as well, presiding at table, entertaining with her women. For Branwen to move openly among them while the king was gone would only infuriate Knut. It was far simpler to set up her small household here, in the residence of the Jarl of Norway. Here she would be free to do as she pleased by day, knowing that Thorkell would come, glad to get away, when the day's work was done.

Branwen and Thorkell shared a supper of cold pork pie and raisin cake one night soon after her arrival. Picking at the raisins in the dark cake, she asked him, "Why didn't you tell me Godgifu had remarried?"

"Godgifu?" he asked, looking up.

"Of Noak Hill," she reminded him.

"Has she remarried? Oh yes, I'd forgotten. There's always such a list to be approved, Bran, I can hardly be expected to remember them all."

"I stopped there on the way here, you know."

"How is she?" he asked absently, a trifle bored.

"You shouldn't have let her marry him. I told you when we were there last year, she didn't want to marry again."

"Her signature was on the petition form, I'm sure. She hasn't got anyone else to sign for her but me as jarl. I didn't sign the petition, did I?" he asked frowning.

"No, my love, she signed it," Branwen said sadly.

"Well, what then? Does she regret it already?"

"Oh, Thorkell, she never goes out of doors anymore. She told me she spends all day in the women's room, weaving."

"What's wrong with that, Branwen?" he asked, a note of annoyance creeping into his voice. "Many women are content with that."

"She gives no thought to the boys, nor to the running of the estates."

"But, Branwen, the boys are old enough now so that they must learn from men and perhaps she realizes the management of Noak Hill is better off done by a man."

"She isn't well, Thorkell," Branwen said, not hearing his words. "It is driving her mad."

"It never took much to drive that woman mad, Branwen," he said turning back to the pork pasty. Then, having no wish to talk about Godgifu any further, he turned to Budda and said, "You're finding your way around the market now, I see."

Listening to them, Branwen tried to put Godgifu from her mind but worry for her friend was like a dull ache which could not be forgotten. Why was Godgifu so close to the edge of madness? Why did Thorkell so easily, without any question, blame her? Was Godgifu guilty for being driven mad? Like blaming a woman because her husband beat her, surely the blame lay elsewhere.

The next morning, with snow blowing through the streets like fine, white down, she bundled her son in the fur robes which had been a gift from his father. Last year they had reached down to the ground but now they were barely at his boot tops. They left the smoky solarium and walked through the mud-icy streets of the city. The child, delighting in the freedom, ran on ahead, darting into alleys, following the sights and sounds that caught his attention. Branwen followed, pleased to see him exploring so confidently. His father should see him, she thought. He shows so little fear. Eventually, following the child's random wanderings, they found themselves in a dark quarter, where the streets were narrow and badly drained, smelling even in the cold from the garbage and offal piled in them. There were children in the streets here—thin, grey-faced, many of them, their feet bound in rags to keep them warm for lack of proper boots. They gathered in groups staring at her son in his fur and he grew suddenly shy, waiting for her to catch up with him, taking her hand. As they turned a corner back toward the market street which would lead them home—to their warm fires and full bowls—she heard a child coughing, the small, tired sound of one who has been coughing for a long time, who has given up hope of ever stopping.

She heard the sound all evening and as she fell asleep, nestled against Thorkell's back, burrowed beneath the down coverlets, she resolved to go back in the morning with some celandine for the child's cough.

That was how it started that winter. The word quickly spread and she found that there were sick enough to need her from sunup to sundown.

Firewood was hard to come by in the city and expensive to buy. Many of the homes she went into were cold and dark by afternoon when the morning fire for cooking had died out. None of those she saw were starving; still none were well fed either. Cheese, milk, eggs, a bit of meat, dark bread—these were all stretched thin to feed more people than she would have thought possible. Always the women ate last, often going without so that a child might have a few bites more. And often the newborn infant died for lack of a mother's milk so that her living children became even more precious to her and she gave them more of her portion, until at last she fell ill, unable to resist the infections around her. Pneumonia, diphtheria with its dread smell of apples, measles smelling of freshly plucked feathers, the flux, miscarriage, they all killed women who could not fight them. Branwen gave them what she could, but they would not accept her charity, refusing the bread or cheese in her basket even while they accepted the medicines she brewed for them. All the apothecaries in Winchester came to know her as she searched out the cure-alls she needed during those weeks.

One overcast morning as she stood beside the door pulling on a thick woolen cloak—arguing with Harald, for the weather was too threatening to take him with her this time as she usually did—a messenger handed her a letter. It was unsigned and said only, "Once I bought a boy a meal at an inn outside the city walls. If the lad does not think too ill of me now, I will meet him at the inn on Bow Street this afternoon."

Frowning, Branwen stuffed the note into her pocket. "Tell the man who sent this that the boy he asks about will come if he can," she said to the waiting messenger.

Turning to Budda she said, "If it clears later take him to see his father. You'd like that, wouldn't you, Harald?"

Smiling broadly, the boy nodded.

"But mind you," she added, "only if the sun shines. I've enough with coughing and sickness among those who cannot stay warm and dry. I'll not have you sick just because you choose to go out when you were better off inside."

"He'll be fine, my lady," Budda said. Turning to the child she added, "Trygg will be back soon and then he will make you that fine hoppity-horse he promised."

It snowed most of the day although the temperature held just above freezing. Branwen was shivering from the cold, her boots wet through, when she hid herself under the old illusion and went into the smoke-filled inn on Bow Street. Eilaf sat alone in the far corner watching some men who were throwing darts. She went close to the fire, hungry for its warmth. After a moment he got up and came toward her.

"It's a cold day for roaming the streets, lad," he said. "Let me get you something to warm you from inside."

She nodded, struggling not to be glad to see him again. What part had he played in the quarrel over the Maldon house? It was hard to see how he could be other than Knut's man. Still, his eyes were clear and without guile. There was still a childlike openness in them that was out of place with the strong angles of his face, and the power of his man's body beneath the thick wool of a winter tunic. Holding the warm cup between her hands, she listened as he spoke rapidly, earnestly.

"I overheard two men I knew slightly, talking idly at an inn I often ate at while we were in Oxford," he said. "They were laughing together about how the king was going to put the Lady of the Ravens in her place at last. He had sent word, they said, that the queen needed her fine house in Maldon. They laughed, guessing what you would do. But I thought I knew and was off at dawn along the road to Westminister." He paused, watching a group of men come in and shake the snow off their cloaks. "I was set up," he said with a wry smile. "Intrigue is not for me. I am easily deceived and it was many months before I even discovered that I'd been used. I'd have come sooner, if I had known," he added.

Branwen said nothing, looking down at the dark spiced wine in the cup she held between her hands.

"So," he said, "you don't believe me." He stood up, set his cup down on the table and turned to go.

She reached out and touched his arm. "I believe you, Eilaf," she said slowly. "It is so like Knut. How well he knows his men, using each as it pleases him."

He turned back to her; an open grin flashed and faded. He put his hands on her shoulders and said, "I would never knowingly bring you harm, Branwen. This I swear by Odin's eye."

She shivered at the strength of his oath. "I never believed you would," she said, "not in my heart."

He looked as if he were about to say something but he hesitated and then said only, "Come on, you're cold and wet. I'll take you home. You can't get sick now. There are too many in the city who need you."

"How do you know?" she asked curiously. She had thought her movements unnoticed outside the quarter in which she worked.

"Everyone knows, Bran. Many eyes watch your movements, some because they care for you, others because they do not."

He lifted her into the saddle in front of him. Mounting, he took the reins on either side of her, leaning close around her so that she was sheltered in the folds of his cloak. Grateful, she leaned back against the warmth of his body.

"Do you know," he said as they rode through the empty streets toward Eric's hall, "it's easy to forget that you are only a young boy out too long on an errand. With a little effort I can imagine myself riding through these streets holding the most beautiful woman in the kingdom. But then," he said, looking down at her, at the young boy she was, "I see that I'm not. Pity."

"What does the most beautiful woman in the kingdom look like?" Branwen said lightly.

"Oh," Eilaf answered, "she has dark thick curls and great dark eyes that can see through any man. And her skin is white with roses stolen from the garden where I first saw her a long time ago, when we were both much younger.''

Branwen turned in his arms and looked up at him, all trace of illusion vanished. Their faces were very close. "Thank you for that, Eilaf,'' she said slowly.

They had come near to Eric's hall. He drew rein and said, "You'd better get down here so no one will see us together. Rumors fly quickly in the dullness of a winter court.''

She looked back once as she walked away from him. He held his stallion in close rein as he watched her leave him, though the animal pranced on the snowy road, anxious to get back to his warm stable. She waved.

Thorkell was waiting for her when she came into the solarium. He stood looking out the window toward the south where crimson streaks across the darkening sky still remembered the setting sun. His back was toward her and he did not turn as she came in. "Where have you been?'' he snapped.

"Is anything the matter?'' she asked, her heart pounding with sudden guilt.

"The town is full of it,'' he said, turning to face her. "You go out daily into the worst streets and dingiest hovels. Why, Branwen? Why can't you stay here?''

Oh, it's only that, she thought, relieved. "Budda,'' she called, sitting down on the stool beside the fire, "bring me some dry stockings and my other boots, will you? Oh Thorkell, I'm chilled to the bone today.''

Thorkell said nothing as Budda came in with young Harald galloping behind on his new stick horse. It was many minutes before she had to answer him. Not until they both stood together with jeweled cups of mulled wine did she say, "Do you really want me to stay here all day, waiting for the sound of your footsteps beyond the door?''

"Other women do as much. And they find work to fill the hours.''

"Oh,'' she said archly, "like spinning, and weaving, and fine needlework. And perhaps you would be kind enough to send back the harper to help us while away the hours. Don't ask it of me, Thorkell,'' she said. "If there were a need I would gladly do it but what goods we need I can buy with coin from the draper. My skill is as a healer and as a healer I will work.''

"And my son,'' he asked, "he goes with you?''

"I wish you wouldn't call him 'my son' like that. He's my son, too. I only take him in good weather. I didn't take him out today, you saw that."

In her heart she felt his pain and was sorry that she had hurt him again. But a small voice whispered angrily asking why she must feel pain at his pain, why she must labor under this burden of guilt when she hadn't done anything wrong.

"Even in good weather," Thorkell was saying, "those streets are miserable places for the child to go. Who knows what can happen to him there?"

"He's safe with me. You know that. Besides," she said with a tentative smile, "he really should see that there are children who don't wear boots and furs. If he's going to grow up to be like his father, don't you think it's a good idea to learn what kind of people he will have power over?"

"And if I forbid it?"

"Ah," she sighed, "we come to this again, so soon." After a moment she asked, "And do you forbid it, my love?"

"No, Bran," he answered, "but for God's sake, be careful."

"I wish I could be a better wife to you, my love," she said, touching the line graven beside his mouth.

He turned away, not yet ready to forgive her completely. "Well, perhaps you can. The queen has asked me to bring you to dinner in a few days, for the lighting of the Yule log. Will you go?"

"Of course," she said with a smile. "Emma and I are old friends."

But Branwen did not attend the queen that year, for when the time arrived for the start of the great midwinter feast Branwen tossed delirious, burning with fever, in Jarl Eric's small guest room.

They built the fire of willow wood so that the smoke which hung below the rafters smelled sharp, like the tisane brewed in the black kettle to bring down her fever. Budda sat beside her bed holding the cup of willow tea to her lips and the fever would lessen so that Branwen's eyes cleared and she knew for a little while where she was, but then the fever would mount anew, filling her head with strange sights and sounds till she would cry out in fear. Then Thorkell would take her hand and brush back the damp hair from her face, calling to her, trying to go where she had gone. But the way was blocked with fire and he could not pass.

For three days he sat beside her, listening as the small dry cough grew deeper and more frequent, watching her slip farther and farther from him.

And there was another, too, who came when he could, waiting in the solarium—Eilaf, the laughter gone from his eyes but not from his lips, cheering the others, bringing them back again and again from the edge of despair. He was the link during those dark days between Thorkell and the business of the country. He carried messages back and forth, shielding the tall Dane from the demands which others would have made on him, asking of Thorkell only what he knew the other could bear.

It was Eilaf who sent Trygg to make the rounds of the apothecaries to search out what cures they had: milkwort and celandine for her cough and rare myrrh and saffron; dropwort and goat's rue, ginseng—more precious than gold, but what matter—to bring down the fever. But it was no use, for her lungs sickened and the dread smell of apples hung around her bed.

Late in the night of the third day Eilaf sat alone, holding the sleeping Harald on his lap, staring into the dying fire in the great stone fireplace at the end of the room, while the others waited beside her bed. He felt he had no right to go in there, to stand with them, to wait, to listen to the labored breathing which drained the last spark of life from the woman who would never know that he loved her. Here the stillness was broken only by the sounds of the fire settling and the child's soft sleeping.

Suddenly there was a knock on the outer door. Eilaf frowned. It was late for anyone to be about the streets. He set the child down gently upon the pallet which had been made for him outside his mother's room. A pair of jeweled battle axes hung on the wall. They were of an ancient design, unlike the one he used in battle. He took one down and hefted it. It would do in close quarters, better than a sword. He slid the bar back and opened the door, standing in the shadow to one side. But he needn't have worried for there was only an old crone dressed in black. In her gnarled hands was a covered basket such as he had known Branwen to carry.

"You're too late, granny," he said hoarsely.

"Nay, lad," she said, "her time is not yet." She stepped past him, into the room. The door shut heavily behind her.

"Have you come to make my mother well?" the little boy asked, sitting up in his bed. "The others say she will die."

"What a pretty child you are," the old woman crooned. "Lie back now and sleep."

With a great yawn the child did as he was told. His eyes closed and his breathing quickly took on the deep regularity he was too young to feign.

"And you," the hag said, turning to Eilaf, "you are tired out from the grieving you dare not show. Go home and sleep. Return at moonrise tomorrow."

Eilaf said nothing. His eyes were filled with confusion as her hold over his mind warred with his own will which would have him stay.

"Go home and sleep," the crone said again. "When you come back her fever will be gone and she will know you."

Mechanically he set down the axe and lifted his cloak from the peg. Buckling on his sword, he glanced around the room once and then turned and did as the crone commanded.

When he had gone, she crossed the room and her step was strangely light for one of her age. Pausing at the threshold, she listened for a moment to the rattle of the sick woman's breathing. "See to Thorkell," she said quietly to Budda who stood beside the door. "See he has wine and a place to rest beside his son."

Budda looked at the crone. Her eyes showed briefly the same confusion which had flashed on Eilaf's face.

The old one went on, "Your man as well must sleep. There is no place for men here tonight. See to it and then return here and keep watch." She waved her hand—a little gesture, almost like brushing away a fly—and the three watchers obediently left the room.

"Now, Child of the Moon," she said, smiling down at the figure on the bed, "did you think we would let you die so, alone and untended?"

Setting the basket on a little table, she opened it and drew out a small packet. She turned back the folds of fine linen. Silver green leaves lay within, glowing like jewels in the moving light from the fire. She looked at them for a moment and the light made her face almost young once more. Then she gathered up the leaves and crushed them between her hands, letting the pieces fall into the low willow flame.

The fire paled, its heat vanished and the light it gave off became steady and white. The shadows became the shadows of moonlight, sharp and dark. The low smoke cleared and a dark coolness, like dew falling, spread through the room.

Then the crone crossed the room to where a small door led to the garden and the street beyond. She opened it and the cold December night pushed in. She cackled and said, "Not so fast, not so fast. This room is open to a different breath tonight. You must remain without."

And the winter night, too, did as she commanded.

She spread her arms then, and seemed to grow taller, straighter. "Come, Breath of Life," she prayed. "Here in spring moonlight lies the last of those whom you shall cure."

Faintly at first, then louder, came the sound of unhurried hoofbeats. The crone smiled. Leaving the door open, she withdrew to stand to one side, half hidden in the shadows. The pale light from the hearth bathed the bed where Branwen lay. And then the unicorn was there, his horn glowing in the strange, unearthly light. He tossed his head, his mane rippling along the pale velvet of his powerful neck. He went up to the bed and gazed down for a moment only. Then he dipped his horn, touching it to the chest that rose and fell so laboriously drawing breath.

Branwen shuddered and the rasp of her breathing stopped.

In the doorway Budda cried out, "What have you done?" Unthinking, uncaring of anything save that Branwen should not die, Budda ran toward the bed and pushed the unicorn aside. Her hand grazed his glowing horn.

Branwen's eyes were open. She looked at Budda and a slow smile spread across her pale face. "Your lip," she said softly, "he's healed you, too."

"Oh Branwen, you're alive," Budda cried. Tears filled her eyes and she buried her face in the coverlets which lay on the bed.

The unicorn turned and made his way toward the door. He paused for a moment and, looking back at her with his lavender eyes, said in a voice so soft in her heart, *I am only the messenger. The sacred Breath of Life comes from Her Who sent me.*

"I know," Branwen said softly. "Thank Her for me."

The old woman had taken her basket and stood beside the unicorn. As they started to go Branwen called out, "Wait, please."

The hag looked back from the other side of the doorway.

"Your basket," Branwen whispered, "leave it here. Please."

"We give you life, the unicorn and I. A gift from the Mother. And you ask for more!" the crone cackled.

"Not for myself. I wouldn't ask for myself," Branwen said, suddenly ashamed. Her eyes filled with tears so that she did not see the crone set the basket down beside the door. When she had blinked away the tears the doorway was empty. At that moment, too, the fire winked out, leaving the room into darkness. A cold wind blew in the open door, scattering the ashes. Budda ran to close it.

Chapter Thirteen

Eilaf came early the following evening, just as the moon rose in the darkening sky overhead. Budda was serving Trygg and Harald a late supper in the solarium.

"They say you are better, Bran," he said, standing beside her bed, his hands playing awkwardly with the heavy gold chain he wore around his neck. "You gave us a bad time." Although his voice was light, in his eyes she saw what misery the last days had been for him.

"Eilaf," she said. Her voice was very soft for the healing magic was gone now and, although the fever would not return and her breathing was easy, it would still take many weeks before she would be strong again. She held out a hand to him and he took it in his own strong ones. She saw there was a white scar across the back of his sword hand. She had never noticed it before. "Sit here with me," she said. "You seem so far away up there."

Eilaf's laugh was a trifle forced, but he sat down, saying, "Thorkell can't come tonight. It won't be possible for him to get away until very late and he doesn't want you to wait."

"Yes, he told me this morning. Poor Thorkell, how much trouble I cause him. They tell me he stayed here for three days and nights and would not leave although there were so many things he should have been doing."

"He loves you, Branwen," Eilaf said quietly. "The rest could wait."

They were quiet for a time and then he said, "We had almost lost hope."

"I know. I'm sorry," she said, reaching up to touch his face.

He took her hand and kissed the palm roughly. There were tears in his eyes.

"Silly Eilaf," she said tenderly, "you mustn't cry. I'm well now or soon will be. Will you come and see me often?"

"I'll come whenever I can," he said.

"Good," she said looking up at him. Her dark eyes were sunken and rimmed in shadow, her face was pale, her dark hair tangled and disheveled from days of burning fever.

He leaned down slightly, just a small movement, as if he were going to kiss her, but then stood up abruptly, letting go of her hand. "I've got to go now, Branwen," he said hoarsely. "Is there anything I can bring you?"

She looked away toward the wall where a coarse brown basket was set on the table between the gleaming silver candleholders. Without looking at him she said, "There is one thing."

"What?"

"Will you go among the people I was working with? Will you tell them what has happened and where I am? Tell them how to find that little door there; that they must come here now if they need me."

"Oh Bran, they won't come. It's a long way, not measured in miles."

"You're right, I know. Still, if they are desperate enough some of them might come. Will you go?"

"I'll go," he said.

"Thank you," she whispered, her eyes growing heavy even as he watched. "Come back soon."

"Aye, my lady," he said and then he turned and left her.

When Budda came in a few minutes later to see if there was anything that needed doing, Branwen was asleep. She went over to the table to blow out the candles. A small looking glass hung on the wall there. She smiled at her image, straightening her cap. She did not remember ever looking any different. Whatever did Branwen mean about my lip being healed? she wondered. It must have been the fever. She blew out the candles, bent over, awkward now in her eighth month, added another log to the fire, and went out.

The weather turned mild in mid-January. One brilliantly sunny afternoon when Eilaf came into the room, Branwen sat dressed in a loose dark velvet robe, the collar trimmed with sable. Her hair was braided and coiled around her head. Thorkell had brought her long strands of tiny pearls only the day before and Budda had woven them through the braids for her. She sat by the window embroidering odd flowers across a coarsely woven work shirt she had made for Thorkell to wear at Cynewithe.

"You look every bit a chieftain's wife," Eilaf said with a grin.

She smiled, happy to see him. "I'd rather be a young boy out running errands in the sun today," she said.

"It's just as well you're not," he said, "for I've brought you a special visitor."

"Shall I come in then?" the queen said, standing in the doorway.

"Oh, my lady," Branwen said, standing up. The handwork dropped to the worn rushes which covered the floor.

"Mais non, Branwen, you must sit down," the queen said. "You've been so ill. We were all quite worried about you and were so glad to hear that you are slowly getting better now. Sit. Please sit. And I shall sit here beside you. Eilaf will go out and keep Father Stigand company. We thought many people at once would be too tiring for you, didn't we, Eilaf?"

"Oh, much too tiring," Eilaf said. He leaned down to retrieve the needlework for Branwen and as he handed it to her their eyes met and he winked.

"Thank you," Branwen said to him with a warm smile. Turning to Emma, she said, "It's very kind of you to come."

"Oh, not at all. I am so bored. Mon Dieu, never have I been so bored. I had looked forward to seeing you and when you could not come. . . . Here I am. Oh Branwen, this winter is without end."

"The king will be back soon now. He must be finding the winter just as long without you, you know."

Emma laughed, brittle, crackling laughter. "But of course, you've not heard. It's not the kind of thing Thorkell would want to talk about. The king, he is living with that other woman, Aelgifu, and is in no hurry to return, they say."

"It can't be true."

"Certainement, it can be. Is he not a king, to do as he pleases?"

"Then you must take a lover," Branwen said firmly, feeling

her hatred of Knut mount afresh. Why was it that, just as she began to feel she could walk the same ground he did, he always came up with some new way to anger her?

"You're right, of course," Emma said looking at her closely. "Many times have I wanted to. Winter nights are long without a man, are they not? There is a chill no other bed-warmer can chase away."

"But then, why not? There must be many men . . ."

"There is one," the queen said with a little smile, "but he loves his wife and has refused me many times. It has become an old joke, one we even laugh about together now."

Branwen knew she meant Thorkell. She had heard rumors about Thorkell and Emma for almost as long as she had known him. Suddenly intent on her needlework, she said, "He is a fool. His wife would not begrudge him to you."

"Is she so sure he would be hers once more when I have no more need?" The queen's tone was cool, with a taste of bitterness.

"Oh Emma," Branwen sighed, laying down her needle, "there is such pain inflicted on us all by this 'belonging' of one to another. Surely Thorkell does not belong to me any more than I belong to him, even though we love each other and find it hard to be apart. Still, I wish he were free and being free himself, free me."

"So," the queen said with a knowing smile, "you would take a lover, too."

Branwen laughed. "I can only remember the hunger which ached in me once. The fever seems to have burned it all out of me. I wonder if it will ever return. It seems strangely peaceful without it."

"You would loan me the husband you do not desire, is that it?" Emma laughed.

"But, he is not mine to loan," Branwen protested. "Only in his own mind."

"Oui, in his mind," Emma said, lifting her hands in a pretty gesture, "and I think there is no changing it."

"No," Branwen agreed, "there is no changing it. We won't ever convince him that he's wrong no matter how hard we try. And I can't even imagine trying," she added with a laugh.

"And Knut, what would he say, do you suppose? He would be understanding, no?"

"No," Branwen laughed. "He'd never understand. Men place such stress on fidelity. Ours, of course, not theirs."

"'Twas ever thus, I think," Emma said. "How else would the poor things know their own children?"

Branwen stood up, placing her needlework on the table beneath the window. "Once, very long ago," she said gazing out at the brown of the winter garden, "no child knew his father nor did it matter. Women lay with whom they pleased and bore each child as a gift from the Great Goddess. Only through the mother was blood traced and property passed. Sons grew up and left home to make their own way in the world as hunters, artisans, or warriors. Only the daughters remained at home to inherit and carry on the family line. It didn't matter how many men they loved."

"What a strange tale," the queen said and laughed. "Your harper sings of such a time as well. I've listened to him many evenings when he sings at Thorkell's fireside."

"Those songs are lost to women everywhere now; only a few old men in the last hills of Wales can still sing them and when they are gone . . ." Her voice was soft and very sad for she remembered in her soul the ways which had been lost and would die forever when she went at last to join the Mothers. How sad that women should accept as natural the way of men—should think there could be no other way.

Just then the young priest, Father Stigand, came in. "I will only stay a moment," he said. "I don't want to tire you."

"Oh Monseigneur, what a wonderful fable Branwen's been telling me . . . of a time when women ran the world." Emma laughed, not unkindly, never dreaming what pain the laughter cut in Branwen's heart.

"I've heard the harper sing of such a time," the priest said. "I wondered as I listened how such a great change could come about. How can it be that the nature of women is so changed that she can no longer lead but must be guided always by the men around her: first her father and then her husband?"

"How do you know so much about the nature of women, Father?" Branwen asked.

"Certainly if women were meant to be equal with men God would have told us so, yet He has not."

"Perhaps you have never heard the Deity speak in a true

voice, Father. Perhaps you've only heard what you've been told to hear.''

"But my dear Branwen," the priest said patiently, "Christ came to redeem mankind. He was the Son Whom the Father sent to save man from his sins. How are we to think of women when clearly they have no place, at least no primary place, in the Godhead?''

"But my dear Father Stigand," she said innocently, "perhaps Christ came to save mankind precisely because womankind did not need redemption?''

Eilaf laughed aloud.

Branwen wondered where the idea had come from. She couldn't remember thinking such a thing before.

"What a novel thought," the young priest exclaimed. "Surely you don't mean what you say. Christ came to redeem mankind—the word is used in its broadest sense, including women as well as men. No one ever meant to exclude women from the work of redemption.''

"But what you meant and what the Deity meant in sending a redeemer may, in fact, be two different things.''

"My dear, you are mistaken.''

"Is she?" Eilaf said. "I'd like to hear her out. Go on, Branwen.''

Her mind racing, Branwen asked, "What was the message of Christ to the young lawyer, Father? Didn't he say all we had to do was love one another?''

"Yes, but . . .''

"And what would you say was the place of women throughout the ages, Father? What is her fundamental role?'' she asked, knowing suddenly where her argument was headed.

"To bear and raise children—under the guidance of a husband, of course," he added hastily.

"And if she chose only to raise and bear children, without the guidance of a husband, surely life would still go on.''

"Life, perhaps, but what of civilization? All the great thinkers and leaders have always been men.''

"But what of civilization, Father? What is civilization but the accumulated knowledge which enables one man to have power over another?''

"But Branwen, isn't it true that woman's role has always been to bear and raise children?" Emma asked gently.

"I wish I weren't so tired," Branwen said, sinking down

further in her chair. "This is so very important. The place of women which is the very root of life itself is to bear and raise young. Every woman feels that this is true, whether she bears children or not. It is the deepest wellspring of womanhood, this connection to new life. And, Father Stigand," she said, firmly, "it is a connection of love. That is why womankind did not need to be redeemed. The primary and most fundamental feeling is that of mother love. Even the animals have it. Women cannot lose what is the heritage of their soul. We needed no Christ to tell us that love is the greater good, not the desire for power which proves so fatal an attraction for men. Feed the hungry; give drink to the thirsty; clothe the naked; shelter the homeless—women have always done these things."

"And fathers, Bran, don't they love their children?" Eilaf asked gently.

"Some do, but it doesn't come naturally to them. Men love children because they are possessions, a key to power. The more a man possesses, the stronger he becomes. That's why when a man marries a wife he locks her away, like some precious thing, behind the walls of his house."

"Why is this hunger for power only true for men and not for women?" Eilaf asked.

"Oh, Eilaf, I think you will be sorry you asked."

"You mean it gets worse?"

"It gets worse," she said. "Do you remember what happens in the spring when the young are born into a flock? There is rejoicing over the female young but the males are slaughtered early, or castrated to be fattened for later butchering. Only the biggest and strongest of the young males will be kept to service the females."

Eilaf groaned.

"I told you," she said gently, looking up at him. "It is a lesson learned very early and passed from father to son. The need for power is the same as the desire for life. And it is a need womankind does not share. Every woman is valuable but only the most powerful man is."

No one spoke.

"Christ came to tell mankind," she went on, "that they must grow away from the animals. They must stop being afraid. They must learn to love. They must become more like women, whose nature is love, who has had to be love for the race to survive."

"But this is wonderful," Emma said, clapping her hands together.

"Have you told Thorkell all this?" Eilaf asked.

"No." She laughed.

"Good," he said. "I won't tell him either."

"And I certainly won't tell Knut," Emma said.

Chapter Fourteen

She left Winchester when word first came that Knut had set sail from Denmark. Refusing to nourish the hatred which had grown between her and the king, she fled to Cynewithe.

But the warnings she had heard and ignored, warnings that she couldn't have it both ways, priestess and wife, that she couldn't have both worlds, were not empty words. Magic, too, has its price. There are no easy answers. Shadows are caused by light, so the power for good which was hers admitted into the world the darker power for evil. She caused by her very being the cold flames of darkness to grow up around her. But the dark fires had smoldered low for too long. She had forgotten to fear them.

Blaec, who had stayed behind when she went up to Winchester, was dead. Wymer had found him one morning in the courtyard, lying frozen where he had been tossed during the night, a silver pin stabbed through his heart. Knowing what the great rook had meant to her, the old man had chopped out a shallow grave in the hard ground and buried him where the eglantine grew in the garden each summer. Three iridescent feathers had fallen loose as he was burying the raven. Wymer had saved them for her with the silver pin—silver, to ward off a witch's dark power.

"Who would do such a thing?" she asked when they told her.

"I dinna ken, my lady," old Wymer said, shaking his head slowly.

''Nor me,'' Elsey added, bending stiffly over the stew pot. ''We don't get·about much any more, not since the old man took sick. Ye must ask Beorn.''

So, when the steward drove in with a load of firewood late in the day, she went out to meet him.

''I'm worried about those two,'' he confided when they had greeted each other. Nodding in the direction of the cookhouse where Elsey and Wymer sat together, he said, ''They need someone looking after them now. You'll have to see to it. Ain't right leavin' them alone any more. Not with him bein' sick and feelings running the way they are.''

''What is it, Beorn?'' she asked. ''What's happened?''

''I don't rightly know, 'my lady. Ralf says it's an old woman's doing. Spreading lies she is. And then there's that family ye asked me to see to. They're all dead, you see. The father took an axe to the whole lot of 'em and then hanged hisself in the barn. There's them that's blaming you fer it. But why they won't tell me. Tarred with the same brush, I reckon,'' he said ruefully.

''What's to be done then, Beorn?'' she asked.

''I cannot say, my lady, but I worry about the old ones here. There's murmurings. It's said in the village that they deserve what the raven got.''

''And you, too, no doubt,'' she said thoughtfully.

''Oh no, not me. Them kind only strike at the weak ones who can't fight back.''

''Perhaps, Beorn, but there are other ways, I think—a hayfield set ablaze just before harvest, a cow poisoned. No, Beorn, it will have to be stopped.''

Beorn shook his head. ''I dinna think it can be.''

''I'll think of something, Beorn. I won't leave you here again until it's settled.''

''Aye, lady,'' he said, frowning.

The next day she was no closer to an answer. She wandered through the yard at Cynewithe noting absently that Trygg was mucking out the barns. He had a great pile of manure stacked up on the wagon ready to be spread on the fields. She wondered, looking at it, how long the old man had let the job go.

She came at last to the little room behind the cookhouse where Penardim had kept her herbs—where she, too, had put a few away in other seasons. The bunches of dried flowers which hung from the beams were thick with dust and crumbled as her movements stirred the air, sifting through the stillness like the first silent flakes of snow. In the drawers where other cure-alls had been stored—the leaves and rootstocks, the flower heads or bits of bark—all were gone to grey-green powdery dust.

"An herbalist needs to stay in one place, it seems," she said aloud to no one. Picking up a dusty handful which had once been the flowering umbels of pale boneset, she let the detritus sift through her open fingers. It doesn't do any good to pick what grows beside the road. And she stood still, there in the dusty gloom of the seldom opened room while memories flooded through her—of days she had spent long ago gathering herbs with an old man, far away, in another part of the land. Ansgar. How much she owed him. What would he think of her now? What would any of them think? What had become of Wulfnoth's daughter? How had she changed so much that people hated her, killing the raven because of her, killing Blaec? After a while she went out of the room, closing the door carefully behind her.

In the kitchen Budda was scouring the kettle with wood ash and sand while young Harald was poking at a half-dead fish swimming awkwardly on one side around the top of the fish barrel. Elsey was rocking contentedly with her new grandson in her arms.

"I'm going for a walk, Budda," she said.

"Me, too, Mommy?" her son asked eagerly, dropping his stick.

She bent over and gathered the tow-haired toddler in her arms. "Yes, you, too, if you like," she said, hugging him.

They walked together down the road toward the chapel which lay beyond the crossing. There was a bright sun in the morning sky and the wet spring earth steamed beneath its warmth. Everywhere new growth was pushing up. In the distance she could hear the larks arguing about their nesting sites. They passed several people from the village as they walked. Some greeted her courteously but there was one who turned aside and, though his hands were hidden from her, she knew he made the sign against the evil eye.

Near the churchyard there was a patch of ground thick with white mayflowers. She stopped for a minute and picked a few, binding them together with their three-lobed leaves. Harald picked some as well and she tucked his into the bunch she held in her hand, though the stems were too short to catch.

In the churchyard she stood silently looking down at Elfheah's grave. She stood without speaking for a long time. Finally Harald asked, "Why are we here, Mommy?"

"I had a friend once. He's dead now."

"What's 'dead'?"

"Oh, Harald," she said looking down at him, "when someone is dead it means they have gone very far away and we shall not see them again."

"Is Daddy dead? He is very far away."

"But we shall see Daddy again."

"And will you never see your friend again?"

"No, Harald, I will never see him again," she said.

"Who he is?"

"He was a harper, the brother of a king."

"Harald, like me; for the brother of the king is Harald, and he is dead."

"No, my little bear, his name was Elfheah and he was the brother of a different king. Now, run and play. Pick some of those pretty flowers, there, for me."

She watched him trot off obediently to pick the yellow-green wood spurge which grew along the old stone wall beside the churchyard. A golden brimstone butterfly gloried in the sun, fluttering among the blossoms.

"Oh Elfheah," she said silently to the man who slept beneath her feet, "how far we have come. I am grown older now. Not nearly as fragile as I was then. But, Elfheah," she said, tears springing to her eyes, "then I could have understood their hatred; now I cannot. I have done no harm that they should hate me now."

But she knew she lied and she answered herself with a bitter voice. *They hate you because they fear you.*

They have no cause to fear me, she argued with the bitter voice.

Oh really? Remember how you drove that old midwife back and out of the cottage. You were very angry with her. She would not forget you quickly nor forgive you easily.

But I only acted out of love, she pleaded with herself.

What's the difference? You frighten people because you have power over them.

I don't want to have power if people will hate me for it. Oh Elfheah, what am I to do?

"Mommy, Mommy, look. See what I have for you."

She looked as he opened his grubby fat hands, revealing the crumpled, crushed gold of the butterfly. She started to cry.

"Don't cry, Mommy," the child said solemnly. "He'll be all right, you'll see. I'll fix it. Look."

"Oh Harald," she cried as one wing came off in his eager fingers.

"It doesn't matter," he said, dropping the pieces and wiping his hands on his coarsely woven child's dress.

"No," she said, "I don't suppose it does, not any of it, in the end."

She leaned down and placed the flowers she had brought beneath the already lopsided wooden cross which marked the dead harper's grave.

Ralf was cleaning the rabbits he had found in his traps when she came into his yard early the next day. The night frost was not yet out of the ground and what would be mud in an hour or so was still hard underfoot.

"We heard ye was back, Lady Branwen," he said tossing some scraps to his dogs.

"How have you been?" she asked.

A fair-haired child peered out from behind the shed. "That must be little Bran," she said.

"Aye," he answered, his eyes on the fields around them.

"Are you afraid someone will see you talking with me?" she asked, laughing.

He looked at her, anger in his face. "Aye, lady, 'tis well enough for you to laugh. You who come and go as you please. We must live here. We can't leave."

"Do you want me to go away, Ralf?" she asked disbelievingly.

"Leave us alone, Lady Branwen. That's all I ask."

"Very well," she said, turning away. "Goodbye, Ralf." She walked with quick, angry steps across the field, blinking back her tears.

That night after dark, Goda came. She came alone, going into the cookhouse, for she was afraid to knock on the door of the great hall, not knowing what Branwen would say.

Budda came into the hall where Branwen sat stitching a tiny dress for Budda's baby. The children, worn out from the clean, fresh air along the sea, slept beside her.

"Goda is here, Branwen," Budda said. "Will you see her?"

"Of course," Branwen said, laying down her needlework. "Where is she? In the kitchen? Stay here with the children, will you?"

Budda nodded.

In the kitchen Trygg was just finishing his supper. He had been late getting back after seeing to some Cynewithe sheep Beorn had asked him to move into a higher pasture. The low land was still too wet for lambing, which would begin any day now.

Goda stood beside the fire warming herself, for the spring air had turned chill when the sun went down. "I come to say we're sorry, my lady," she said, looking down at the floor. "It's just that Ralf is near out of his head with worry these days."

"What is he afraid of, Goda?" Branwen asked.

But the woman merely looked down at her feet and would not answer.

"Oh for God's sake, what is he afraid of? Tell me," Branwen said.

"It's the wee girl," Trygg said, his mouth full. "There's them in the village saying you marked her when she was born."

"Oh, I see," Branwen said, sinking into the chair beside the table. "What are we to do?" she asked hopelessly.

Trygg said nothing, mopping up the thick gravy in his bowl with a crust of Budda's good dark trencher.

"I will leave Cynewithe."

"Just leavin' won't do no good, Bran," Trygg said without looking up.

"Why not?" Branwen snapped.

"These people are branded with the mark of your friendship. They cannot leave, not all of them."

"What am I to do then? There must be something."

"You must leave Cynewithe for good," Trygg said looking at her now, his face in dead earnest. "You must sell the farm."

"Sell Cynewithe? Who would buy it?"

"I will," Trygg said slowly, leaning back from the table.

"You, Trygg?"

"Oh, I can't buy the whole thing, but my guess is that Ralf

will buy the fields between his house and the west road; and Beorn has always wanted the woods beyond the crossing.''

"But I need you, Trygg, and I can't believe you want to stay here for the rest of your life. Do you?''

"Someone has to stay and look after the old ones. Then there's the baby. Budda's small use to you now and she wants to stay,'' he added.

"Why, Trygg? Why must I sell?''

"We will say that Beorn refused to go on acting as your steward and there was no other to take his place so you had to sell. When you are gone and Cynewithe is no longer yours, it will be easier for those who remain behind, and, in time, the others will forget you, too.''

She went over to the doorway and stared into the darkness outside. She stood there for a long time without speaking. Finally she sighed and turned back to the light of the fire. "Very well,'' she said dully. "See that the contracts are drawn up.''

She left two days later, going up to Maldon with only the child. Trygg had offered to drive the cart and see her safe but she would not let him.

"It's two days to Maldon and back,'' she said. "Who will protect your family while you are gone?'' she asked bitterly.

Trygg did not answer her.

She took nothing from Cynewithe when she left except the chests which she had brought with her and a small, dark, covered basket.

The king returned to Winchester where Thorkell and Emma were waiting for him together with the rest of the court which had stayed behind. It was a time of high holiday and celebration followed celebration. Through it all Knut held oddly aloof, avoiding Thorkell on all but the most formal state occasions. Three days passed so, until the evening when they found themselves momentarily alone together in the center of a crowded room.

"What's wrong, Knut? You might as well tell me.''

"Did you enjoy your sport with the queen while I was away?''

"Don't be a fool. I never touched her.''

"Then why is she so cool to me? It's always you she smiles at, talks to, and in my bed . . . ha!''

"She's very angry with you, you must know that."

"Why? What've I done?"

"She knows about Aelgifu."

"Well, of course she does. I can't keep any secrets. But why should she be angry about that?"

"Why should you be angry at the very thought that I slept with her while you were sleeping with Aelgifu?"

"But that's different."

"She doesn't think so."

"Yeah, well I've got plans for Aelgifu which should make Emma happy."

"Oh?"

"Aelgifu is not doing very well as regent in Denmark."

"Really?" Thorkell asked blandly.

"Yes, really." Knut laughed. "She may not be quite up to it, is that what you're thinking? I'll grant you she's not too bright, and is incredibly tactless besides, but then I'm going to make you co-regent with her. After all, you did such a splendid job here, keeping everything rolling along smoothly. Well, what do you say?"

"It's quite an honor. . . ."

"Damn right," he said, his voice rising. "Just one thing," he added looking at Thorkell over the edge of his goblet, "you're going to marry Aelgifu."

"Go to hell," Thorkell said with a grin, thinking for a moment that it was just a joke.

"That ought to get Emma off my back."

"I won't do it," he said grimly, as he began to realize Knut was serious, that he meant what he said.

"You'll do it all right, damn you." The king's voice was low and his eyes, light blue like glacial ice, burned with the challenge. "This time you'll do what I tell you, Branwen or no Branwen."

"Why, Knut?" Thorkell asked softly, in a voice only the king heard. "Why can't you leave us in peace? What power does she have that she haunts you like this?"

"She snatched the kingdom from my hands once. . . ."

"At Ashington?"

"She won't do it again."

"She wants nothing from you but to be left alone."

"She may make you believe her, Thor, but never me."

"And the only thing which stops you from moving against

her—what would you send? Assassins in the night—is me. Get rid of me and who is left to protect her? Certainly not her brother.''

"Her brother is a fool."

Thorkell laughed.

"I'm not asking any more, Thor. I'm commanding you and this time you have no choice."

"How long?"

"Six months."

In mid-June when the king left Winchester, going down to Southampton to hawk in the marshes where the River Test empties into the Channel, Thorkell sent word to her that he would come to Maldon before going up to East Anglia to see to his holdings there.

Branwen, standing beneath the cloister, now covered with roses in full bloom, was watching Harald in the courtyard beyond. He was playing with a litter of puppies born some weeks before to the mongrel bitch Jack used for hunting. Branwen smiled to herself, remembering how glad Jack and Bridey had been when she came up from Cynewithe.

"It's been quiet here too long, my lady. 'Tis good to have you back once more," Bridey said, wiping her hands on her soiled apron as she stood in the kitchen doorway.

At supper that first night Bridey removed her apron and stood, her hands folded over her ample stomach, watching Branwen and Harald enjoy their dinner. She had prepared *swete chyken* for them that day, killing the fattest hen in the yard and using the last of the summer honey.

"You'll be needing someone to look after the boy," she had said when they finished. "And to take Budda's place. There's two young things orphaned when my brother died last summer. I think they'll do quite nice if ye've a mind."

So Deora and Chadd had come to live with her—to see to her needs, caring for her son, learning to serve at table, seeing her clothes and Harald's were kept clean and mended. They were young and glad for the work, learning quickly what was expected of them. When word came that Thorkell was to arrive, she only needed to find a woman to help Bridey with the extra work in the kitchen.

She smiled, watching the tall Dane ride in, frightening the puppies back into the barn. He wore no armor though the thegns who rode with him did. His hair had grown long and his moustache drooped elegantly. His clothes were of the finest weave, dark blue, intricately tucked and pleated. The scabbard which hung at his hip was thickly crusted with gold and jewels. He was every inch a great prince. Dismounting he picked up his son who ran to him, not shy at all, though it had been three months since they had seen each other. Branwen longed to run to him as well for his coming seemed to put all the world to right, even those parts she had not known were askew. And he knew her heart. Looking across the cobbles at her as she stood there, he smiled, holding her eyes with his own, the child forgotten in his arms. But the yard was full of men and the noise and confusion of horses and dogs, the crying of hawks and the scolding of hens. She waited, knowing her time would come later.

Then, late in the night, in the quiet stillness which followed their love-making, she felt the pain buried in his heart. "What's the matter?" she asked, suddenly frightened.

"Can't I have even a small secret from you?" he asked tenderly, brushing her hair off her face.

"You know you can't, not since you came to my father's house so long ago when your heart first spoke to mine."

"Knut is making me regent of Denmark."

"But," said Branwen, relieved, "that's wonderful! You will be a fine regent. Surely the Danes will be pleased to have you rule in the king's name."

"And you wouldn't mind leaving this land and going to another to live, would you?" he said, holding her close.

"I won't mind," she said. "It will be good for Harald to live in Denmark for a while." And we'll be further from Knut, she thought. He didn't say anything and she felt his anguish grow until at last, when she could stand it no longer, she said, "What is it? Tell me. Please."

"It isn't enough. He wants me to marry Aelgifu."

"Marry Aelgifu?" she echoed, suddenly cold.

"I'm supposed to set my affairs in order here and make ready to leave for Denmark before the autumn storms."

"And if you won't do it?"

"There will be no denying the king this time. He has great power in the land now. There is no hope for anyone who would oppose him."

"Yet you will not wed her," Branwen said softly.

"No, my love," he said. After a moment, he went on, "What time he gives me I will use. In the fall the men who still serve me will take what wealth we can gather and sail with me to Jomsborg. Knut will be many years building strength enough to take that place."

"And me?" she asked.

"You and Harald will come with me."

"You would have done better to have taken another to wife," she said wearily.

"Aye," he said; and he held her very close until at last they both slept.

When she woke at daybreak he was standing at the window watching her. "Some day," she said, "I would like to wake up still in your arms."

He grinned and came over to sit beside her on the bed. There were grey hairs mixed in among the brown. She had not noticed them before. Harald, waking on his cot, got up and came over to them. His mother lifted a corner of the bedding and he climbed in beside her.

Thorkell smiled and said to his son, "You've not been hawking yet, I hear."

Harald, large-eyed with waking, shook his head.

"Well, it's high time you went. After breakfast you shall come out with the men. You can sit in front of me on the great grey. Would you like that?"

Sliding quickly out of bed, Harald began to tug at the buttons on his night shirt.

"Hold on, little bear," Branwen said. "If you rip those buttons Deora will be angry with you." Smiling to herself as she helped him slip off his shirt, she couldn't help thinking how young he was to be spending the morning in the field with the men. She hoped he would at least stay dry and not disgrace himself.

Not until late in the afternoon did she and Thorkell find time to be alone. It had begun to rain, a chill, soaking summer rain that made her grateful for the warmth of the fire which had been lit in the fireplace along one side of the small treasure room. The floor was spread with the thick brown pelt of a giant bear killed in the land of the Rus far to the north. It had been a gift to Thorkell many years earlier from Eric of Norway. She stood holding a golden goblet of wine, watching the flames. On her hands were the jewels of a great chieftain's wife, gold

and amethyst, amber and sapphire. She wore a tunic of traditional Anglo-Saxon design, dark green over a soft moss-
colored shift of finest linen, delicately embroidered in yellow
around the cuffs and neck. The great raven of gold and enamel
which Thorkell had given her when their son was born hung
around her neck. Her hair was caught back with green ribbons
for she wore the matron's white veil only when necessary.

Thorkell had unlocked the cabinet doors, going through the
treasure of gold and silver he had stored within. "We will have
to take all this to Jomsborg," he said. "It will be many years
before we can come back." He turned to look at her. "Perhaps
never, Bran."

"I will see to the packing, my love," she said quietly.

He came over to her. Tilting her chin up, he looked into her
face and said, "Would you pack for me if I were going to
marry Aelgifu?"

"What do you want me to do then?"

Turning away he began to pace up and down the small
room. "I've told them you're going to marry Eilaf," he said at
last. "I've spoken to him and he agrees it's the only way. He's
coming here next month on board his ship. I will send the
Raven's Wing as well. Eilaf will see to it that what's mine is
packed aboard my flagship and what's yours put on the *Song of
the Waves*. No one will suspect that he will take you to
Jomsborg rather than back to his lands along the Severn."

"And you are convinced the king will believe this?"

"Not only the king, but Emma as well, and your brother.
They all believe it's true. And it's not so impossible, is it,
Bran?"

When she didn't answer, he said, "Sometimes I wonder if it
wouldn't be a better way after all."

"Oh Thorkell, it's you I love, not Eilaf."

"Love is a luxury, Branwen, which few can afford."

"Oh no, you're wrong, Thorkell," she said quietly. "Some
people trade love for what they mistakenly treasure more
highly and then when love is gone they find they have nothing
but straw which crumbles away between their fingers."

He laughed warmly, gathering her into his arms. "Whatever
was the world like, little one, when your race ruled the land?"

Suddenly the front door opened and the hallway was filled
with the noise of Thorkell's thegns returning cold and wet from
an afternoon at the horse fair. They had gone to purchase extra

"If you belonged to any other man I would have taken you long before this," he said, turning to face her, his voice harsh. "Even now," he went on, "if you ask, I'll take you with me and the tall Dane be damned."

Branwen looked down.

"Is that what you want, Bran?" he asked gently.

Branwen smiled, there in the darkness. She stood up and went to him. She touched his face with her fingertips and said softly, "Eilaf, would your eyes still laugh if I asked you to betray him?"

He gathered her roughly into his arms and held her without speaking. She clung to him, tasting the bittersweet knowledge that she loved this man no less than he loved her. "If you had asked me to go with you," she said at last, "I would have gone."

"I wonder if Thorkell knew how close he would come to losing you." Eilaf said, setting her down.

She slid her hand into his, feeling the places where sword and axe had hardened his skin. "He knew, Eilaf, or else he wouldn't have given us a choice."

"How could he?" Eilaf said, suddenly angry. "What right had he to test us?"

"Oh Eilaf," she cried, "don't you know how much he loves us both?"

Eilaf turned away. "We'll never talk about this again," he said, his voice thick. "Do you understand? Never." After a moment, he said, "Tomorrow we'll start loading the ships."

Chapter Fifteen

The sun glared off the water so that her face ached with squinting. Eilaf stood in the bow, his back toward her, looking out over the sea. The sun did not seem to bother him. Perhaps he is just used to it, she thought. Watching him, she thought about the distance which had grown up between them, since they had talked that evening, in the cloister in Maldon. I wonder if it can ever be bridged, she thought, remembering how his eyes used to laugh at her—across the table in an inn, across a room, even sometimes when they were alone. It's all gone, isn't it, she asked herself, that laughter, the way we were. Nothing changed, yet everything is so different. Why? she wondered sadly, knowing the answer.

That evening as they sat together with some of the crew around the campfire, Eilaf said, "Well, Grim, after we get the Lady Branwen to Jomsborg, shall we keep going? Up the Dvina and down the Dneiper to Constantinople?"

"Can we get over the mountains this late in the year?"

"We can try. And if we get stuck there, I know a place. . . ."

Grim laughed. "Aye," he said. "But there wouldn't be anything left of us by spring. Worn away, we'd be."

"It'd be a helluva way to go," one of the other men added quietly and they all laughed.

Branwen felt out of place among them, wishing it weren't so dark, wishing there were some place else for her to go. When the laughter died down, she said, "Will you tell me about Byzantium? Have you all been there?"

"Aye, we've been there, all of us, twice we've sailed the rivers to the great inland sea," Grim said.

Then Eilaf looked at her across the fire. It was the first time he had really looked at her in days. "It's a fabulous place, Branwen. The streets are smooth paved, never muddy. There are buildings many times a man's height and all in stone."

"You couldn't believe the wealth there and the way they live, not unless you seen it for yourself," Grim added.

"Tell me about it," she said, "everything."

The night was long and the fire bright. They had sailed there twice, rowing up the rivers of eastern Europe, portaging the longboats across the mountain spine and past the rapids at Kiev into the wide river which flowed southeast toward the great cities along the Black Sea.

"We bring amber and furs," Grim said.

"And slaves, when we have them," Eilaf added. "They trade spices and finely worked metals."

"The finest swords you've ever seen," the third man added. "There ain't nothing like sitting in their great halls, on these thick carpets, all decorated with mosaics . . ."

"And the food—remember the food? The fruits. Remember them red and yellow ones?"

"Pomegranates."

"And the figs? Not them dried up ones we get, but fresh and green and juicy."

"We'd sit in their halls, Bran," Eilaf said, "eating their food. . . ."

"Their women draped all over us," Grim said.

"Listening to songs of Viking bravery," Eilaf went on. "They always want us to stay."

"To serve in the Emperor's guard, no less."

"Have you ever heard of the Varangian Guard, Bran?"

"No," she said.

"It's the finest corps they have," Eilaf said, his eyes staring into the fire now.

"All Norsemen, it is."

"They wanted Eilaf to stay and command the Guard," Grim said, his voice hushed at the enormity of the honor.

"Why didn't you stay?" she asked.

He looked up. "I'm not sure," he said, "lots of reasons, no reason. It really doesn't matter, does it?"

It took them almost a week to sail from Maldon across the

North Sea and then north along the coast, around Hedeby, and east to Jomsborg. The weather held for them and they were often able to set sail and run with a favoring wind. One afternoon, with the sails set, and the lines creaking in the wind, Eilaf asked her to sing for them.

"I'll need my dulcimer. Do you think you could find it?"

"I'll go," someone said.

Several of the men moved closer, to be able to hear her better. While they were waiting, she looked at them and said, "Will you tell me about Jomsborg? What's it like?"

"It's a fortress . . . laid out different, it is," Grim said. "Not much of a place for ladies."

"Almost a hundred years ago, the Byzantine emperor sent engineers to lay out the fort," Eilaf said. "When Harald Bluetooth was still a young king."

"It's the best fortress I've ever seen by far," Grim said.

"It's more than a fortress," Eilaf said. "It's a school where the sons of Viking warriors are sent to be trained. It's a huge place, big enough to maintain and support a standing army. Big enough to give Knut nightmares at the thought of Thorkell controlling it."

The *Song of the Waves* sailed into the harbor beneath the brooding darkness of Jomsborg just at sunset. Branwen shivered as the shadow of those dark walls fell over her and pulled her cloak close. Raised above the land on an artificial mound built of the dredgings of the harbor at its feet, Jomsborg lay hidden behind a massive parapet of hewn timber. The iron-bound gate lay open and a narrow bridge had been lowered over the ring ditch. But not for her. Not for her nor for any of the women who would come, following their men across the North Sea. No woman had ever passed through that shadowy breach in the black walls; had ever gone into the dark stronghold of the legendary Jomsvikings. She and the others would make new homes in the village still hidden from view beyond the curved parapet.

She thought of her son then as she had countless times in the last three months. What will he think of this place? she wondered. His father was only five when he first came here. It's a grim-looking place for one so young.

A cart was waiting for them. "A hall has been prepared for you, Lady Branwen," the driver said as she stepped onto the stone landing. "If you will wait while we unload your things, I will drive you there myself."

The narrow quay had come alive with men, pushing wagons, pulling thick hawsers, shouting, swearing, anxious to get the longboat secured before dark. She looked around for a place to wait, out of the way.

"The lady and I will walk while you load the wagon," Eilaf said, coming up behind her. "No doubt you will catch up with us before we have gone too far."

Her legs felt strange on the firm ground after so many days at sea. She was glad that Eilaf chose the middle of the rough cart path, allowing her the narrow strip of smooth roadway which lay between the deep ruts and the tall weeds along the edge. The shadows were softening into twilight as the sun slipped down below the horizon, but it was still light enough to see the carefully tended farms which lay on the hills beyond the fortress, separated from each other by strips of woodland. What crops had grown close to the road had already been harvested. The fields lay mown and bare. They walked along in silence for a mile or more until they came to the village. The buildings were small; some were thick-thatched but more were roofed with sod. A hundred yards down the street was the onion dome of a small wooden chapel. They climbed up two steps onto a wooden sidewalk which ran around the edges of the village square. There was no one in sight. The houses were closed and shuttered against the night. A dog growled but did not stir himself as they passed. Branwen, cold and very much alone, wanted to slip her hand into Eilaf's, wanted that much warmth and companionship, but the distance between them was too great and they walked alone together, in silence, until the quiet was broken by the rattle of the wagon as it lurched along the ruts behind them. They waited for it to catch up with them for neither of them knew which house was hers. The wagon banged past and stopped in front of a low, long hall just ahead.

"The brothel?" Eilaf said with a grin.

"Is it true?" she asked. "Must I live in a brothel?"

"Oh no, my lady," the nameless Viking driver said. "'Tis no bawdy house now. Them women is all moved out. There was official orders, you see. Oh no, my lady, it's quite all right, you'll see. A bit bare inside but then once we get your cart unpacked . . ." The man was almost pleading with her.

"It will be fine, I'm sure," she said, pitying him.

"Right this way then," Eilaf said, still grinning.

Inside, the room was dark. By the dim light from the open doorway, she could see that it seemed to have been swept clean for her. It looked bare and empty, only the massive benches and long serving tables along the sides loomed in the shadows. A great fire pit ran the length of the room. It's like Thornbury, she thought, like my father's hall.

"Will you light the fire?" she asked Eilaf.

"If you're sure you're ready for this," he said, striking flint to steel.

The fire which had been laid in the hearth was well dried and caught easily, flaring up brightly. Suddenly she could see that all the posts and beams were carved and painted. And then, embarrassed, she did not know where to look, for from every corner, from every post, an obscene figure she knew must be the Norse god, Loki, the trickster, the joker, stared back at her, his phallus at attention,

"Oh, Eilaf," she said.

"It is the finest house in the town." He laughed.

"But what am I to do about all this," she pleaded.

"You'll get used to it, Bran," he said.

She shook her head disbelievingly.

But he was right. By February she had achieved a truce with the mischievous god and no longer noticed him. Now the benches were spread with warm furs. Intricate tapestries hung on the walls blocking the drafts which crept through the cracks. Torches lit the room from sconces high on the pillars. Richly carved and brightly ornamented chests held their clothes and household goods. One end of the great hall was taken up with the cooking fires. Big enough to serve the men who had visited the brothel in other days, it functioned equally well in a more domestic role. Here Thorkell entertained regularly, sitting on the benches among his men, often with his son beside him. Men and women wore rich wools and thick furs, gold and ambers, silver and ivory, and held jeweled goblets filled with honeyed mead. Whole pigs, deer, and sheep roasted over the great hearth. Silent slaves moved among them, dark-haired among the golden Vikings. And through them all Branwen moved easily, filling a goblet, stopping to speak to a friend, soothing a fretful baby with a fingertip dipped in honey or a crust of bread warm from the ovens.

The gracious ambiance had not come easily. In the beginning there had been difficulty over the slaves for she had never had them around her before. Although some families in Wessex had had slaves when she was a young girl, her father had refused to have any at Thornbury. She remembered how he had said they coarsened their owners, often making them less human. But here, where there was a surfeit of slaves taken on raids in the south or east, customs were different. Fifteen slaves had been sent from the traders in Hedeby as Orm ordered in letters sent from East Anglia. They slept, men and women together, in a drafty shed between the great hall and the stables. It promised little warmth in the frozen winter. They wore filthy rags which barely covered their nakedness and their feet were bare though many of their tasks were done in the barnyard and woodlot where frost already covered the ground in the early morning. But those were problems easily dealt with. Branwen sent word to the merchants that she needed boots and thick woolen cloth. They were not slow to provide her, knowing as they did that she was spending the wealth of Thorkell the Tall. And it took three slaves only two days to repair their sleeping quarters, patching the cracks with mortar, thickening the thatch so that when their work was done there would be a warm hearth to sleep beside.

But there were other problems with the slaves which were not so easily dealt with. Soon after they arrived, she had come upon Eilaf kicking a pregnant slave woman who was struggling under a load of firewood he had told her to carry in, for the hearth fires had burned low.

"Stop that," Branwen had said sharply. "The load is too heavy for her. She will lose the child."

"Bleeding pig," Eilaf said lightly. "Any babe of hers were better off not born."

"That may be," Branwen said quietly. "Still, I won't have her treated so in my house."

"Whatever you say." But he grinned.

Branwen knew that her father had been right.

The slave leaned against the wall, supporting her bulging abdomen with her hands as she rested. Branwen waited for her to be able to go on. After a moment she said, "Leave the wood for another. I'm going to need someone to help with my son when he arrives. It will be easier work, I think, at least until you are stronger again."

There was no gratitude on the woman's face, however, only a nod of resignation.

"What's your name?" Branwen asked.

"Thir," the slave replied.

Branwen frowned for it was a word which meant 'drudge' and not a real name at all. "Haven't you got a proper name?" she asked.

"Thir," the slave repeated.

Life settled into a routine not very different from life anywhere else. There were meals to see to, chores to do, and a never ending round of social obligations all the more important because of the smallness and isolation of their community. And Branwen worked hard at it without appearing to make any effort at all. Not once did she fall back on her magic, patiently cultivating trust and friendship among the women, knowing that in time they would forget the stories they had heard about her. She had only to be ordinary enough, smiling at their children, working with them, sharing their talk of recipes and men. And no one knew what it cost her.

Thorkell taught her to ski that first winter, taking her out into the hills and open fields around the fort, showing her how to move easily across the snow on the strange boards he strapped onto her boots. She took to it easily, loving the soft sound of the skis in the stillness, the cold clear air, the light and the wind. Whenever he could get away from his duties in the fort, they would go out, often for hours on end, across lonely miles, with only a single farmhouse smoking in the distance. Later, they taught Harald to ski as well, although his short legs slowed them down and it became more of a game in the snow.

It was snowing again when she woke early one morning. She could hear the snow rattling on the shutters as the wind blew against the wall. Beyond the thick curtains closed around their bed she heard the slaves stomping the fresh snow off their boots as they came into the hall with wood for the fires. Thir was dressing Harald, over his protests, in warm layers of wool and fur.

"But I can't move with all this on," she heard him say in his small shrill voice.

She laughed and burrowed deeper into the down and fur, her back against Thorkell's warmth.

But he was awake and, feeling her stir, he rolled over and said, "I never thought I'd grow old like this, Bran."

"And have you grown so old?" she asked with a smile. "I hadn't noticed."

"You know," he sighed, "I find myself thinking things I heard old men say when I was young—things I could not believe then—like the goodness of a warm bed and a gentle wife when the wind blows cold."

"A gentle wife to warm your bed," she said softly, not wanting her voice to carry beyond the heavy drapes which hung around them. Propping herself up on one elbow she looked down at him and asked, "Is that all you want?" She traced one fingertip slowly along his lip and then, lower, back along his collarbone and down the center to the little hollow below his chest muscles. Leaning down she kissed him softly.

He reached up and pulled her down onto him. His hands roamed over her back and along her legs with knowing ease for there was no awkwardness between them. She fitted herself comfortably into the familiar shapes of his body, smiling at the way his manhood stirred now with a life of its own. They lay thus, unhurrying, knowing the sweet sureness of their pleasure in each other, feeling it build until he turned her under him and she buried herself in his warmth.

And so the winter passed and she was content with his love and called it happiness. In those few moments when it was not enough, when her lost soul cried out in misery, she turned away and would not hear it, pretending to believe it was only a mood such as men say all women are prey to. She would not give in. Once before she had tried and failed. She would not fail this time. She put the magic things out of her mind. Another woman served as herbalist and midwife. She never spoke the ancient language and the wild creatures hid from her as from any other woman.

But she could not bring herself to work at the loom. Weaving was too much a part of her soul, too close to the surface of her folk memory. Her people had always been the sacred weavers and the pain of that craft was too great, aching in the wound left where she had cut away part of her soul. She sat instead, one of the women's group but to the side, teaching Harald and the other children their letters.

One day, when the snow had melted and the early summer primroses were in bloom, she stood on the hilltop overlooking the harbor. Her son and the dog Jack had given him as a puppy stood beside her watching a ship rowed up to the pier beyond the great gate of the fortress. A magnificent dragon's head was carved into the high prow, and the gleam of polished shields lined the sides in a double row. Ulf had come with messages from Knut.

"Do you know Lord Ulf, mother?" the boy asked.

"Yes, Harald. He's Eilaf's brother."

"So they say, but yet Lord Eilaf doesn't seem glad his brother has come. If I had a brother I would be glad to see him."

Branwen smiled down at him, running her hand through the soft brown hair which had replaced his fine golden baby hair. Oh, little bear, she thought, not every man loves his brother.

The waning moon had just risen that night when she heard one of the maids go to the door to let someone in. She got up, drawing her fur robe closely around her for the nights were chill and the fires were banked.

"Thorkell," she said as he came in. "I didn't think you were coming tonight."

"I didn't either," he answered taking her in his arms.

"What is it?" she asked as she felt his anger.

"That son of a bitch . . ."

She waited.

"He sent that fool to tell me I am to come next month to the Isle of Wight."

She slipped out of his arms and went to the table. Filling a goblet with wine, she held it out to him.

"No, no more, my head is thick with it already. He sent no gifts, no offers of peace, no promise to lift the ban of outlawry, nothing. By Odin," he said, fury written on the lines of his face, "he bids me meet him, like a man snaps his fingers for a dog." He paced up and down the length of the room.

She drank the wine herself, waiting for his anger to cool. After a while he stopped in front of her. Putting his hands on her shoulders he said, "I feel like putting every man and boy on the longships. We would fall upon him and then there would be a reddening of spears to sate the eagles."

Branwen said nothing.

"But we can't do it, can we, Bran?" He laughed hollowly. "Is that why you're so quiet?"

"You and the king and the men who stood in the moonlight at Ashington will not fight again, Thorkell," she answered simply.

"What am I to do then?" he asked, sinking into his great seat along the wall.

She went over and knelt on the furs at his feet, laying her head in his lap. He touched her dark hair, braided for sleep, caressing her.

The woman who had opened the door for him stood nearby.

"Go to bed now, Thir. We won't need anything more," Branwen said, not lifting her head from his lap. They remained unmoving for a long while after the thrall left, drawing peace from each other.

"And Eilaf?" he said at last, "what am I going to do about him? His shame at such a brother stings deep."

"Send Ulf away. Don't let him stay here any longer."

"Aye," he said, "I had thought to—at first light."

After a while Branwen asked, "What will Knut do?"

"I don't know. He hasn't built the ships to attack us here. And he'll have trouble raising men and money for such a war." He paused and then added, "Unless we are fools enough to raid this summer."

She looked up, curious to see his face, for she had not heard this spoken of before. But the candle gave little light and his face was in shadow.

"The men are spoiling for a fight, Branwen," the tall Dane said gravely. "They won't stay next year if there is no raiding soon."

He did not spend the night with her, leaving early to return to the barracks where Ulf's men were still feasting. By the time the sun was well up Ulf was gone.

Early the next afternoon Thorkell came into the hall. Eilaf was with him, carrying young Harald on his shoulders. They stood near the doorway, their eyes unaccustomed to the dim light and Thorkell shouted, "Branwen, where are you?"

"Here, my lord," she said, annoyed that he should shout for her while the women were still there.

"Eilaf is off for Byzantium," he said.

There was a stir of excitement among the women who had

stopped to listen to him. The children, playing on the floor, jumped up at the news, clapping their hands, dancing around. At that the dogs began to bark. Eilaf set Harald down in their midst.

"Are you going with him, Thorkell?" she asked, her annoyance forgotten.

"Not this time." He laughed. "There's too much to keep me here."

She looked at Eilaf. Does he know, she wondered, what it must mean to him to be left behind? Poor Thorkell, the old commander, left behind while the young men are off adventuring?

"The merchants have been most generous in their terms," Thorkell was saying. "We just came to an agreement this afternoon." He draped one arm around Eilaf's shoulder; with his free hand he took the mead cup Thir held out to him.

"How long will you be gone, Eilaf?" she asked.

"Until spring," he said casually, without looking at her, "maybe longer. They've need of fresh troops in the Guard. The pay is good."

"Well," she said, forcing a bright smile, "we'll give you a feast worth remembering then."

For two weeks they worked preparing for the celebration which had been set to coincide with the long days of the midsummer holiday. Carpenters built trestle tables and benches along the wooden walkways. Tents were put up for the families who came to say goodbye to sons sailing with Eilaf. Wagonloads of cheese and wine, fruits and ale arrived from the merchants in Hedeby. Coming in with the wagons were music makers, tumblers, acrobats, and prostitutes all ready to contribute their share to the merriment in exchange for a gold coin or a silver penny. Even a priest came. He opened the long-closed chapel and prepared to beg God's blessing for the men before they left.

There won't be many at your service, sir priest, Branwen thought, as the three days of feasting went by and the stack of empty wine butts and ale kegs mounted. By late afternoon on the last day of the feast Branwen had rolled back her sleeves and tied an apron around her waist like a common drudge. It had been a long party and the slaves could scarcely be pushed further. Most of the other women there were losing sons or lovers the next day and could hardly be asked to work this afternoon. So Branwen and the dozen or so wives from the village whose husbands were too old for adventuring and whose sons were too young, pitched in to do the serving and at least what washing up couldn't be put off for another day.

The steam from the cauldron of chicken and leeks she had been stirring had teased Branwen's hair out of its gold netting and it hung in her eyes. Unable to see where she was going as she carried the heavy pot out to the serving table in the square, she set the chicken down with a sigh and pushed her hair away from her face with the back of her hand.

Eilaf, who was leaning against the gable end of her one-time whorehouse, said, "A serving wench? Whatever happened to the young lad I used to meet? He suited you better, Branwen."

"Poor lad," she said with a rueful smile. "He died before we came here."

"I don't think so, Bran. Here, let me take that for you. He's only waiting for you to admit you need him."

"Never, Eilaf."

" 'Never' is a long time."

"I've caused Thorkell enough grief," she said. "No more."

"Don't be a fool, Branwen. What grief have you caused him? He's happier here than he ever was as Jarl of East Anglia. The men would do anything for him, follow him anywhere."

"He would rather be going with you."

"He only thinks that today. This is where he belongs. He has built a world here to his standard, where every man is judged on his deeds and he is but first among equals. He would be miserable in Constantinople."

"Perhaps," she said with a small shrug.

Across the square they saw Thorkell standing with a group of men. They were deep in conversation. Thorkell's hand rested on Harald's shoulder.

"He's so proud of that boy," Branwen said. "He gave him that wooden axe last year when he turned five. He takes him up to the fortress with him every afternoon now, you know."

"I know," Eilaf said, watching her watch her husband and their son.

"I'm glad we're here, away from Knut, where they are both safe."

"Are you?" Eilaf asked.

When they set the cauldron down beside the table, Branwen

turned and would have gone back to the kitchens for the trencher loaves which were needed, but Eilaf said, ''Let someone else go.''

He took her hand and led her away from the crowd.

As they walked, the noise and the shouting died out, and she said, ''He will miss you, Eilaf. You are the lighter side to his despair.''

''My Loki to his Odin, is that it?'' Eilaf answered. There was a bitterness in his tone and she turned to look at him.

''Perhaps,'' she said. ''I have never understood the Viking hopelessness in both of you but I know it's there. He needs you, Eilaf. Don't be gone too long.''

''He has you. What right do either of you have to ask me to return?''

''None, Eilaf,'' she whispered. There were tears glistening in her eyes.

He took her in his arms and held her for a long time and neither of them spoke. At last he loosened his hold. She looked up and he kissed her, tasting the salt of her tears.

''Don't cry,'' he said. ''Don't cry, Bran.''

''Please come back.''

''I'll be back.''

Chapter Sixteen

When Harald turned six in the fall, Thorkell took him up to the fort to begin training with the youngest boys. Branwen stood in the road, shading her eyes with her hands, watching her son walk away beside his father, so proud to go, carrying a bundle of his clothes and bedding, his dog trotting along behind him. And Thorkell, leaning over a little, talking to his son. She knew how much this meant to him, a son to carry on the tradition. She tried to be glad, and she was; it was time for Harald to grow up. He couldn't stay a baby forever. But tears stung her eyes; she brushed them away with the back of her hand.

As the days went by, the hall seemed empty without him and her lessons with the other children were empty, too. He might as well be a hundred miles away.

"Can't you bring him home with you for dinner—just for an hour?" she asked when he had been gone a week.

"Do you want to single him out even more? It's hard enough for the boy," Thorkell said. Then seeing how disappointed she was, he added more gently, "I miss him, too, Bran. But he's where he belongs, with the boys."

"But you see him every day."

"Hardly," he said with a smile. "Training the young boys is not my concern and it's better for him if I'm not around too much." He leaned down and kissed her. "Don't worry, little one, he's fine."

Perhaps it was because Harald was not there; perhaps she

was not paying attention to her lessons with the children the way she had before, because they began to grow restless through the long afternoons. She found herself more and more often scolding them crossly. Once, when she had grown very angry over a little one sliding under the bench to play with the dogs, she felt the silence around her and realized the women were watching her.

"Sorry," she said, embarrassed. "I guess I'm just tired."

That night Thorkell sent word as he had often in the past months that he could not get away. When the hall was quiet, most of the fires banked, the slaves gone off to sleep, only Thir remaining in the hall with her, she took a candle and went over to a small chest partly hidden by the curtains around the bed. She lifted the lid and took out a dark, covered basket. She ran her hands thoughtfully over the rough reeds and laid her face on the cover. After a while she put it back in the chest again. She had not opened it. Thir came and warmed the bed for her with a pan of coals from the fire.

"Don't close the curtains tonight," Branwen said. She lay in bed a long time, watching the shadows move in the firelight.

As the winter snow fell and then deepened, she began to ski, alone in the empty spaces, needing the quiet and the peace, needing the hard physical exercise, to still the growing unrest in her heart. She was often gone for hours on end, not returning until dusk, skiing for miles and miles over the rolling hills, not caring where she went. It was later than usual one evening when she got back. The dusk had deepened to night as she unbuckled her skis and leaned them against the side of the house. Thir was waiting for her, her face pale, her eyes full of fear.

"Oh lady," she said, "I was afraid the wolves had gotten you. Listen to them."

Branwen listened and was surprised to hear wolves howling quite close by. She had never noticed the sound before.

"You mustn't go out alone. Not now. It isn't safe."

It isn't safe. Once she could have gone anywhere, done anything, talked to the wolves. Not now. Not now. She felt trapped. Oh Mother, why does it have to be so hard, she prayed.

But she didn't go out alone again. Thir was right.

Spring came at last. The ice melted on the rivers, the barley fields were pale green with new growth. She had decided to make a new shirt for Harald. His wrists had stuck out of his old one when he came home for the St. Beltane's Day fires. She went out along the edge of the great marsh looking for madder root to dye the fine woolen cloth she had bought. She was tired of the yellow and green of the commoner dye stuffs. The madder root would yield a bright red if only she could find it. She saw it clearly, growing in that oxbow of the Coombe below Nettleden in Wessex, all she could want. It grew in great clumps, too, she remembered, where the Chelmer flows past Beeleigh Abbey, an afternoon's pleasant walk outside of Maldon. But here, where she wanted it, she could not find it. She might have asked the small animals who hid at her footsteps. She might well break the long silence and speak with them. What harm could it do? Who would know? They could tell her where the madder grew. But she did not. That part of her was dead. She would not wake the dragon that slept, leaving her at peace—dull, aching, empty peace.

Suddenly she was aware that a man stood nearby, watching her. The low sun was behind him and she shielded her eyes with her dirty hands, squinting to see who had come out to this lonely place.

"Eilaf?" she asked. "Is it really you?"

"Hello, Bran."

"I'd heard you were back," she said, smiling. "Why didn't you come before?" She walked up the slope toward him. When she drew near enough to see his face clearly, free from the shadows of the setting sun, she stopped. "Oh Eilaf," she said, "what's wrong?"

"Surely you've heard. We brought the fever back with us from the East. The men are dying from it."

"I heard there was fever but . . . I thought Anna . . . I picked meadowsweet . . . I sent it to her."

"They're dying, Bran," he repeated. "Seven dead already among the men. Now in the boy's house as well . . ."

"Harald?" she asked, frightened.

"Not yet. Thorkell's sent him home. He's there waiting for you. You must help."

"I cannot," she groaned.

"Haven't you learned anything?" he asked angrily. "Are you going to wait this time, too, until the graves are filled?"

"Who told you to say such things to me?" she asked desperately. "Did Thorkell send you? Why didn't he come himself?"

"He didn't send me," Eilaf said wearily. "How could he? What right has he to ask you to be what you have denied for his love? But he's not the only one who knows what you are."

"How could you know?" she whispered.

"Hemming told me, just before he died. He was lying on the field at Ashington. He told me then."

Branwen said nothing. Tears rolled down her cheeks but she didn't seem to know it.

"Will you let these men die too?"

"What price this time, Eilaf? What price will I have to pay?"

"Can any price be too great?"

"Too great?" she said bitterly. "Too great? What do you know? I only hope," she added, "when you find out what price must be paid you won't be sorry you asked."

"Then you will come?"

"How can I not?" she groaned.

Her step was heavy and dull as she made her way back to the village. It would all be destroyed. All the life they had built here. The little happinesses, the ordinary warmth. If she woke the sleeping dragon, he would destroy it all as he had destroyed her peace at Cynewithe, as he had destroyed Blaec.

Inside the hall she took the rough basket out of the chest which stood beside her bed.

"What's in it, Mother?" Harald asked.

She looked up at Eilaf as if she expected him to answer the boy.

"What would you do if someone told you that your mother was an evil woman?" Eilaf asked, crouching down so that he looked directly into the boy's eyes.

"I'd kill him," the boy said solemnly.

"And if he were bigger and stronger than you and you could not kill him?" Eilaf persisted with a half smile.

"Then I would tell my father and he would kill him."

Eilaf laughed. "And you will always remember how good your mother is—no matter what lies anyone says, won't you?"

"Yes, Lord Eilaf," the child said, his eyes wide.

She held the basket on her lap for a long time. Harald did not ask again what was in it. He and Eilaf stood quietly, watching her, waiting. Finally she lifted the lid.

"It's only old, dried leaves," Harald said, disappointed.

Branwen smiled at him. "They will cure the fever," she said, "so that no more will die of it."

"Are they magic then?" the boy asked.

"Yes, they are a kind of magic."

"Do you know other magic as well, Mother?" he asked.

She looked up at Eilaf, her eyes full of tears, but this time he didn't say anything.

"Yes, Harald," she said at last.

"Will you show me—please?"

"Not now, Harald," Eilaf said. "Now we must take these herbs up to the fortress. Your mother's going into Jomsborg."

Harald looked up at him, amazed. Women did not go into Jomsborg; it was not permitted. Only old Anna did. The herb lady. But the look on Eilaf's face was so grave, he fell silent. His mother stood up, holding her basket, and they left the hall.

She walked between the man and the boy and the colors around her glowed with new life. The air was filled with voices she had not heard for too long. The birds soaring overhead called to her and she smiled, knowing she was free again, free to join them once more. The decision having been made, she was free. Hopelessness washed over her, freeing her. She had nothing left to lose. All of the walls, the restraints which had grown up around her were crumbling. She felt as if she had been dead for a long time and had suddenly come back to life.

Thorkell met them at the gate. He looked at her and saw the change which had come over her. "I'm glad you've come, Branwen," he said.

She smiled at him. "We tried, didn't we?"

"We tried," he said. "but it wasn't the same, was it?"

"Let's go," Eilaf said.

She went into the looming fortress and no more men died, although it took several weeks before they were all well once more.

And it began to come apart, the tissue of her life, just as she had known it would. It started with a young woman from the village who stopped her on the street. "If you had such power," the woman hissed, "why did you let my baby die? Why didn't you save my baby, the way you saved those men?" The woman had struck her, hard across the face, then crying bitterly, had turned and run away.

There were others, too, not many—a man whose wife had died in childbed, another who had lost three children to the fever the winter before. Not many, but enough.

Communication was slow and unreliable but the news which reached Jomsborg from the west had not been good. Distances were too great for Knut to rule two kingdoms, separated as they were by the stormy North Sea. He needed a regent he could rely on in Denmark, Swein, his first-born son, was not yet ten. Though Aelgifu, the child's mother, had been acting as regent, she was clearly not up to the task. Rebellion simmered just under the surface. Already men had come to Jomsborg to speak with Thorkell, sounding him out should an open revolt break out. Knut would have to act, and soon, if he were to hold on to his northern kingdom.

So few were surprised when a messenger arrived bearing letters from the king to his friend, Thorkell the Tall.

"He's bringing young Harthaknut with him," Thorkell told his wife that evening as he read through the parchment.

"He's young to sail so far from his mother. I'm surprised Emma let him go," Branwen said, not lifting her eyes from her needlework.

"He's not much younger than Harald, Bran. He must be almost seven."

Seven. Seven. The word tolled in her heart like a great bell ringing out the time. Suddenly memory flooded over her and she knew what price she would pay for the fever cure. Seven years, the Mother had told her, seven years to hold her son. Despair, dull deadening despair which could not cry out in protest, flooded through her and her handwork dropped from her lap. He would go back with Knut. He would be fostered to the king. Harthaknut was coming to stay here in his place.

Thorkell felt it wash over her and he went and stood beside her, his hand on her shoulder. "It would have come sooner or later, Branwen," he said gently.

"I will gather his things together," she said, shrugging off his hand, "so he won't be ashamed when he is among the king's men."

"Oh Branwen, if it hurts you so much I won't let him go," he said, reaching out to hold her.

"But you have to," she said pulling free of his embrace.

"There isn't any other way for you to be sure of each other again. You must exchange sons."

"What are you going to do?"

"Do?" she cried. "What can I do? Don't you see it's my fault?"

"It's not your fault," he said incredulously. "Whatever made you think that?"

"Every time I call on the old powers, I have to pay the price," she said.

"Don't be ridiculous, Branwen," he snapped.

"Ridiculous," she screamed. "Is that what you think? Then you are a fool!"

Thorkell looked as if he would strike her. Fury mounted and she closed the doors of her mind, protecting herself from his anger. He stood glaring at her, his hands clenched, until his temper cooled and he said, "It was arranged a long time ago, Branwen. If you weren't so self-centered, you'd remember. We spoke of this day when he was newly born, and again when he was christened."

"It wouldn't have happened. It didn't need to happen. We are far away from Knut here. He didn't have to suddenly remember us. I reminded him. When I woke the power. I reminded him," she said wearily.

"You're wrong, Branwen," he said patiently, "but I can't stay and argue with you now. Later we'll talk about it again."

"Will we?" she asked and then she laughed, a ragged, haunted laugh. "You'd better go now. The king will be waiting for you."

He leaned down and kissed her, coldly, because what she said had cut deeply.

It took the two men a day and a half to agree to exchange their sons and thus end the quarrel between them. It was a great honor for the tall Dane.

It was another full day before Eilaf came to tell her what else had been decided.

"He sent a servant to tell me Harald had been fostered to the king," Branwen said calmly. "What can be so bad that he sends his second-in-command to tell me?"

"He would have come himself, Bran, but . . ."

"Yes, I know, Eilaf," she sighed. "Let me get you some wine."

Eilaf drank deeply from the goblet she offered him. "He's accepted the regency in Denmark," he said at last.

Branwen turned away so that he could not see her face.

"He will replace Aelgifu. There is no talk of marriage this time."

"What's Aelgifu going to do?"

"Apparently, after a period of transition, she will retire to her country home in northern Denmark until Swein is old enough to accept his father's crown and the Danish throne."

"She must hate Thorkell."

"Maybe not." After a moment, he added, as if to reassure her, "He'll be a damn good regent, Bran."

"Yes, I know," she said, "I told him that myself once."

When Eilaf had gone, she stood by the open window looking out into the night sky. What about me? she asked the stars. Can Knut have forgotten he has a wife? Will he let me walk freely among the nobles of Denmark? What is still hidden?

She saw little of Thorkell while the king was in Jomsborg. He was busy, she knew, and he was angry with her. Funny how he accepted her as different from other women, had seemed glad when she had gone into the fort to cure the fever, proud, and yet he did resent her power. Perhaps he is angry that I cannot use it and then put it down, the way he wields his battle axe. I wonder if he will ever accept it as part of me. Probably not, she thought, sadly, almost bitterly.

After a week Knut left. Harthaknut remained behind to live and train with the boys at Jomsborg. Harald sailed with the king. Branwen watched from the hilltop as the king's ship was rowed out of the harbor. Her son's dog whined and licked her hand.

"Whatever will we do without him?" she said to him. Crouching down, she put her arms around his neck and buried her face in his dark fur.

When the longboat had cleared the harbor, the rowers shipped their oars. Free to run before the wind, the brightly striped sail was unfurled, lying slack for an instant until the wind caught it, filling it, pushing the prow up and out onto the white foam of the front-running curl.

Thorkell came up the hill toward her and they watched together until the sail was at last out of sight.

"If there had been any other way, Bran. . . ."

"I'll be all right. If I could have kept him mine, I would not have. To be fostered to the king is a great honor for the boy."

"He's more of a king now than he was three years ago," Thorkell said thoughtfully.

"Do you suppose Emma is satisfied?"

"She has good cause to be proud. She has made her mark upon him."

She turned and looked out over the land for a moment before starting down off the hill. The air was different now, shadowy, thinner. She reached out and took his hand.

"What is it, my love? Are you frightened?" he asked, sensing her feelings. "There is nothing here. Look."

"It's nothing. Just a . . ." she said. There was no way she could tell him what she saw. No way she could make him believe that the king's coming had spoiled the land. That it was no longer simple. That greater powers were loosed. First hers and then his. That they would war here. He would think she was being ridiculous and he would be angry with her again. She wouldn't let him be angry. Not now. Not when there was so little time left to them before the storm broke.

"The boy will be all right," Thorkell said, smoothing her hair with his hand. "Don't worry."

He held her hand in his as they started down the slope toward the village. "He sent the body of Alphege back to Canterbury last April. It's been ten years. Your brother went with him," he said and then he added, "He laid Alfred's crown on the altar."

"He did it for you, Thorkell," she said simply.

"Yes, I know." He stopped to call the dog who had lagged behind.

After they had gone on a little way she asked carefully, "When are we leaving Jomsborg?"

"I . . . have to go alone, Bran." He stopped walking and faced her. "I can't take you with me, not right away."

"But why?" she asked, tears stinging her eyes. Dread rose up in her; she felt the earth grow thin as it had once before so long ago.

"Let me deal with Aelgifu alone, my love. When she is safely away from court, then I will send for you. A month, perhaps two. It will be easier this way."

"No, no," she cried. "You musn't go alone. Take me with you—please."

"Now, Bran," he said firmly, "you know I won't be alone—Eilaf will be with me. But I want you to stay here. It won't be long; two months at the most, I promise."

She clung to him then, weeping silently.

Two women passed by. One said, "Ach now, 'tis hard to lose the little one."

Thorkell held her gently. After a while he tilted Branwen's face up to his own and kissed her.

"Two months at most, my love," he repeated. "I promise."

After Thorkell left Branwen was very much alone. More and more the villagers shunned her. Even the slaves, all except Thir, were sullen, avoiding her whenever possible. She stood it for three days until she could no longer remember why. And then, one crisp, beautiful autumn day, turning her back on the village, she walked off into the hills and did not return.

She went into an upland meadow, carpeted with asters, tiny white stars, and pink bells. She stood in the middle of the open space, shook loose her hair, running her fingers through her tight braids, freeing them. And then she began to call—a calling not heard in centuries—a great, wild calling, to all the animals, to the field mice, badgers, to the shy ermine, the fox, even the wolves sleeping in the pale sun. She called through the skies to the raven first, and then the gulls, the plovers, the hawks, harriers. Even the eagle heard her cry and came swooping down to see who had the power to call him. She didn't know why she was calling them. It was not anything she had planned to do. She called to them out of her loneliness, and she called them all because she was confused and frightened. She told them of her need and they laughed, innocently, amused that a human would come to them, could call them and then ask anything of them. But she had come looking for their friendship and it could not be commanded.

While they were still talking, a murmur rippled through the crowd. Branwen looked up to see what was happening. There, at the edge of the meadow, just under the trees, the unicorn stood, watching her. She smiled and moved toward him. The small animals made room for her, opening a path.

When she had come close, she heard his voice in her heart.

Wait here, he said. *Let the animals heal your heart and make you whole again. She Who Sent Me will come, when you are ready.*

Branwen reached out to touch him but he melted away from her, disappearing into the forest which grew beside the meadow.

She had been there a month, denning with the wolves to keep warm, flying through the sky with the ravens, exulting in the freedom, rediscovering the power that was hers, almost happy, until one day, soaring high over the coast, she saw the *Raven's Wing* inching its way along the coast toward Jomsborg. Thorkell, she breathed, spiraling down to the warm cave where she had left her body among the sleeping wolves. Moments later, she was hurrying north, across the hills, back to the village. She wanted to have time to wash and change her ragged clothes, comb out the tangles from her hair, before she met him.

She met Eilaf before she reached the village. "Oh, Branwen, thank God you're here. They said you'd gone. That you were dead. No one's seen you in a month," he said. "Oh God, Bran, you've got to come. Thank God you're here," he said again.

"What is it?" Branwen said, the color draining from her face. "What's happened?"

"It's Thorkell. Poison, we think."

"Where is he?"

"On the ship. We rowed all night, Bran," he added feebly.

She looked at him then, suddenly understanding what it was he said. "He's dying, isn't he?" she screamed. "That's the price you made me pay. It wasn't Harald at all. It was Thorkell. He's going to die."

"No, Branwen, no," he said hoarsely. "You can save him. Come on, we've got to hurry. Here, take this. I found it in the chest," he said handing her the small, rough-covered basket. "Oh, Bran, you've got to save him."

She went on board the *Raven's Wing* and knelt beside the man whose heart had spoken to hers. She laid her face against his hand which rested pale and still on the coverlet. There, when they touched and the ship was very still, she heard his heart speak to hers once more, pleading this time, asking to be set free.

"No," she cried. "Not yet."

"You're too late," he whispered.

"I love you. If you leave me, there will be nothing left."

He smiled, a smile so small only Branwen noticed. *Don't be ridiculous,* she heard him say in her heart.

"Tell them to do it. They must not wait . . ." he whispered.

"Oh, my love," she said. Her voice choked, her eyes filled with tears so that the figures around her were blurred.

She stood up and said. "There's nothing. . . . Where is his axe? I must . . ."

"Here, my lady," someone answered.

"No, Branwen," Eilaf said, standing beside her. "I'll do it," he groaned.

"Then do it quickly," she said, "for his soul yearns to be off."

It was only a shallow cut he made in the great man's arm, beside the faded white scars of wounds made many years ago. Only a few drops of blood beaded up and spilled onto the cover, but it was enough—the symbolic wound—his passage to the warrior's hall, his passage to Valhalla.

"My love go with you," she said softly, feeling the life go out of his hand.

Eilaf was weeping when she stood up. She stood beside him, looking out over the harbor. "He wouldn't have wanted you to weep, Eilaf," she reminded him gently. "You were his Loki."

Eilaf went over and stood by the rail, his face turned away. Orm, beside her, reached down and touched Thorkell's face tenderly, smoothing back the hair which clung to his fevered forehead. All around her, the men stood still, their faces stony. At last Eilaf turned back to them and said, "Break out the mead barrels. By the gods, as he feasted me before I sailed, so shall we feast him now before he sets sail this last time."

They feasted for three days and Branwen feasted with them for it was proper that a Viking chieftain's wife do so. She wore his jewels and gold, she dressed in his furs, she did him these last honors. She poured mead into Viking cups from a gold pitcher. She gave rich gifts to every man from the treasure of Thorkell the Tall. She did not weep. Not for the three days of feasting, not when they laid him on his flagship, not when they laid his axe and broken sword beside him and his battered helm upon his chest; not when they piled the ship high with branches of resin-rich pine, not when they towed it out to where the current would take it far from land, not even when the torch was set to the pine and, flaming, the boat drifted out onto the sea.